ℰ ℭ

"Belos!" I shout, letting my voice carry my ang

I draw breath to shout again when he appea square, lit by a faint blue glow. My heart gives an anxious thump.

Wind stirs around me, lifting the fine hair framing my face, and I silently beg Logan to wait. I need Belos engaged with me before he and the others jump in.

"So," I call to him. "Is this what you wanted?"

"One of many things."

Unbound

KATHERINE BUEL

THE GRIEVER'S MARK SERIES

The Griever's Mark
Chains of Water and Stone
Unbound

Unbound

ISBN-10: 8553877095
ISBN-13: 979-8553877095

BOOKS BY KATHERINE BUEL

The Griever's Mark series
The Griever's Mark
Chains of Water and Stone
Unbound

Standalone novels
Heart of Snow

CHAPTER 1

The boom wakes us both. Logan shifts beside me, rising to his elbow. I can only make out a few lines of his body in the darkness, but I feel the tension in his leg where it lies under mine. I sit up beside him, but I don't move my leg. If I do, he'll get out of bed.

For the last several days, since the fall of Avydos, the elements have cycled through fury and calm. Sometimes a fit passes on its own. Other times, the Earthmakers have labored to pacify tearing winds, tossing seas, and bucking earth around the city. It has occurred to me that the sanctuary Heborian granted the Earthmaker refugees was not entirely selfless. Without them, Tornelaine would be rubble.

I hold my breath, hoping the earth will still itself. This is the first night Logan has not woken from a nightmare, the first night he has stayed with me so long. I know that exhaustion, not relaxation, is responsible for his sleep, but it's better than nothing.

I tug his arm. "It's just another tremor." Maybe he'll get back to sleep.

He starts to ease down, but when the castle shudders and dust shakes from the ceiling onto our heads, he jerks up and pushes from the bed.

I shape a Drift-light and let it bathe us with its soft blue luminescence. Logan snags his undershorts from a chair. I watch him shamelessly, studying the angles and curves of his naked body. This is so new for me, and it feels fragile, as though if I look away I'll lose it.

The castle trembles again, and the curtains stream inward on a sharp gust of wind. I start wrenching on my own clothes. They still smell like lanolin from the time I spent yesterday helping move sheep in from the hills outside Tornelaine. I did not find it funny when Horik told me that if I ever needed work, I would make an excellent sheepdog. I must have popped in and out of the Drift eighty times to scare those addle-brained things in the right direction.

Logan, dressed now in rumpled clothes, is bent over the wash basin, scrubbing at his face. He straightens, raking wet fingers through his sleep-tousled hair. All the turmoil and uncertainty out there, and all I want to do is look at him. Water slides along his gold-stubbled jaw. He wipes his face with the back of a sleeve. Even in the soft Drift-light, I see his weariness. Dark shadows curve under his pinched eyes. The other Earthmakers can help in and around Tornelaine, but only Logan can venture out farther. Only he can touch the heart of the storm.

Because of that, he has spent much of the last few days away from me. Each time, it's a little harder to pull him back.

I have tried to follow, but I can't penetrate that elemental madness. Whenever I brush near the heart of it, my mind splinters under its force. I spiral out of control. Once, I washed up on a beach ten miles from Tornelaine. When Logan found me, the stark terror on his face was a bit annoying—I *can* take care of myself—but it also filled me with that particular warmth I am coming to know with him.

I pull my hair over my shoulder to braid it. Logan watches me. He wants to say something. I'm afraid I know what it is.

"Please, Astarti. Promise me."

I drop my eyes to the hollow of his throat, and he sees the evasion. He steps near. He covers my hands with his, stilling me. The three ropes of hair stream from our fingers. He takes the sections from me and continues the braid. I shiver at the gentle tug as he works, at the way his fingers brush my arm and breast. I dig in my pocket for a tie, and he secures the end of my braid.

His eyes lift to mine. Even in the soft blue light, I can see the gold swirling through them.

"*Please*, Astarti."

Another boom shakes the walls, making the pitcher dance across the wash table. As the pitcher falls, I slip a tendril of Drift-energy under it and lift it to the bed.

I touch Logan's arm, urging him toward the door. The muscles strain and twist under my hand, but I can't set him at ease. I won't make that promise.

We jog down the dimly lit hallway. A door opens ahead of us, and Aron emerges, looking as rumpled as we do. He glances down the hall, then does a double-take. His eyes harden.

My face heats. Avydos may have fallen, but apparently a Drifter is still not acceptable for an Earthmaker. Of course, Aron doesn't know that Logan is no more an Earthmaker than I am. We're both half. But where my other half is Drifter, Logan's is…something else.

Aron motions us to walk with him. "This one felt closer."

Logan grunts acknowledgement.

I remind them, "They've not yet attacked Tornelaine directly. And, Logan, you said you've never sensed the one Belos…has." I don't want to say "Leashed," but the snap of tension through Logan's body tells me he heard it anyway.

Aron mutters, "I still can't make sense of that."

I shrug. "The Old One is powerful. Belos may not have control of him yet."

Aron shakes his head. "I mean I can't understand why the Old One doesn't break from him. Is the Unnamed that strong?"

The question is directed at me, but it's Logan who answers. "The Ancorites were that strong. You think it impossible that Belos could be?" His voice is harsh, lashing through the word "Ancorites."

Aron and I both tense. This is the first time I've heard Logan mention them. I know he thinks of them. I know they shape many of his dreams. But he doesn't speak of them. In fact, he doesn't speak of anything that happened to him. Not of his imprisonment and torture, not of Belos's possession of his mind and body, and certainly not of the Ancorites.

I hook a finger through Logan's belt at his back. He may not let me into his thoughts, but he always accepts my touch. Though he doesn't look at me, his body loosens.

Running footsteps make us all turn. Bran jogs to catch up with us. His eyes go to my hand on Logan's belt. He gives me an unreadable look. Humor? Surprise? It's not disapproval, like I get from Aron, but even so I let my hand drop. All my life I've controlled and hidden my thoughts. I have been a liar and manipulator, creating deliberate impressions, subtly directing those around me to think as I want them to think. When I am with Logan, all of that falls away. I am bare, exposed, my feelings so obvious. Maybe I shouldn't touch him so much.

Yet, my hand feels cold and useless when I take it away. I shove my fists into my jacket pockets.

We find Heborian and his Drifters up on the wind-swept battlements facing the sea. Blue Drift-light glows in torch brackets. No flame could withstand the wind whipping across us. Heborian's fur-trimmed cloak snaps, and his dark hair streams back from his face. He's more fully dressed than anyone else, as though he never went to bed. It's almost dawn. Does the man never sleep?

The wind eases around us, and my braid settles against my back. I look over my shoulder to see Bran's relaxed but focused expression.

"Thank you, Primo Branos," rumbles Heborian's deep voice.

At Heborian's side, Horik rubs dirt from his watering eyes.

Light flares in the distance. Mount Hypatia has belched flame periodically over the last few days. I shudder at the memory of the mountaintop exploding with liquid fire, at the image of a woman's gigantic, fiery form rearing from the top. The light vanishes, leaving the horizon dark once more.

Beyond our bubble of calm, the wind continues to rage, and the sea batters the cliffs. The earth trembles, vibrating through stone all the way into my bones.

There's little that Drifters can do against this onslaught. As Polemarc Clitus arrives with his Wardens, the Earthmakers work to extend Bran's protective shell. Even so, wind rips through from time to time. The fact that the Earthmakers can affect the elements at all indicates the storm is not directed at us. If it were, Tornelaine would look like Avydos, a blackened husk.

Horik and I step into the Drift and begin a circuit of the castle grounds. We are within Heborian's barrier and cannot move beyond it from the Drift, but we can still see beyond. There's no sign of Belos or the Seven.

As we sweep back to the battlements where the Drifters and Earthmakers stand, I pick out Logan's lighted form. His energy whips and lashes through him. It's different from when Belos lodged a sliver of his own energy in Logan. Then, Logan's energy clenched around his heart, twisting inward. Now his energy surges against the boundaries of his form, as though seeking escape.

When I step from the Drift beside him, his still face and body give little indication of the turmoil I saw. His fingers tighten on the stone-toothed crenellations and he shifts restlessly, but no one would ever guess at the degree of his agitation. It's unfair, in a way, to see what he's hiding. But it's a reminder that just because he seems all right doesn't mean he is.

I want to ask what he's thinking, but I know he won't tell me. Instead I say, "The Drift looks clear."

I hear Horik making a similar report to Heborian.

Logan nods, but I detect no relief. Apparently, it's not fear of Belos that's gnawing at him.

The earth trembles so violently I careen into Logan. The sound of breaking stone comes from a distant section of the castle grounds. Several of Heborian's Drifters vanish, seeing to the damage. The earth settles at our location, but wind keens across the open ocean.

"I'm going," Logan says.

My heart gives an anxious thump. He will try to draw them away. He is drawn to them, as they are to him. That is why he can lead them away from Tornelaine. But what if they get a hold of him and he can't get back? We don't know what they want. We don't know whom they serve.

A more selfish fear rattles inside me: what if he chooses to not come back?

"Please, Astarti, promise me."

"I promise to do no more than I deem necessary."

He growls, "That is not what I meant."

I look away from him, focusing on the distant ocean, where predawn light bleeds the world to gray. "Don't ask me for promises you know I won't keep."

He exhales sharply, annoyed. "We'll discuss this later."

While it irritates me that he seems to think he can tell me what to do, my heart lifts to hear him speak of returning. I don't know why I'm so afraid he'll leave me, but I am.

The castle shakes again, and a sharp lash of wind cuts through the calming influence of the Earthmakers.

"Logan!" Heborian shouts from farther down the wall.

Logan calls back, "On my way!"

He leans down. When his lips press mine, I clutch at his neck. His hands find my waist. He breaks away first, but his eyes stay locked with mine as he begins to dissolve. A cool finger of wind brushes my cheek, then he's gone.

℘ ℭ

By mid-morning, the worst of the tremors have stopped, but Logan has not returned. With Heborian and his Drifters, I make my way to the bridge connecting Heborian's castle to the city, then we travel the Drift to the harbor. Though the waters are quiet now, several docks have broken from the port road. A sailing vessel floats on its side, its mast lying brokenly across the smashed deck of another ship.

Using Drift-energy, we help drag the fallen ship upright and gather the worst of the debris to the port road. The sailors and ship-masters set in on the rubble, seeing what can be salvaged.

The wind carries a chanting sound to me, and I turn to squint at the rocky bluff across the harbor. A small crowd has gathered there. The bleating of a sheep sounds faintly.

"Runians," Horik says, pausing beside me. "They beseech the gods to take pity on them."

The bleating cuts off abruptly.

I turn away. "I don't think the gods are listening."

When I slide into the Drift, intending to return to the battlements to wait for Logan, I spot a lone figure far out in the water. Someone has been swept out to sea.

As I streak toward the figure, I realize it's not a person, but a fish, though it blazes with too much energy for one. It's swimming away from Tornelaine.

I draw closer. No, not a person, but not a fish either. The upper body is shaped as a woman, but from the waist down pumps a powerful tail.

I know only one woman who can take such a form, though I don't why she would be swimming away from Tornelaine.

I follow Gaiana into the sea.

Chapter 2

LOGAN

We chase one another, tumbling through wind and water. I whip the sea's surface, shooting spray high into the air, where it sparkles with the sun's light in a rainbow of color.

One of the Old Ones laughs, and the sound is high and light. She shapes water into a human face, peeking above the surface like a naiad from the old stories. She vanishes.

I dive into the water behind her, and now I am fluid, slower and more languid. The light fades as I move deeper, but it doesn't matter. My senses become those of the ocean: vibrations, subtle shifts in temperature, little currents, the slide and undulation of sea creatures.

Schools of fish dart past me, thin slivers of light gleaming on their bright scales. They are finer, more beautiful than gold.

A gurgling, trilling sound pulses through the water. It starts low and rises high. It sounds playful, like a question, like a mystery.

Closer to me, I hear an unmistakable giggle. It beckons me to follow. We chase through the deeps until far above us glides the massive form of a whale. Light limns its paddle-like fins. The tail sweeps up and down. For all its size, I have never seen such grace.

My companion giggles again and dives deeper. The light is gone now, a thing only of the world above, and I am darkness, a rich, mysterious darkness.

Bluish light blooms, enveloping me, and the sea floor stretches to infinity, an otherworldly landscape of caverns and cliffs. We dive into one, slipping through nooks and crannies, brushing past branching coral and soft, rippling fronds that might be plant or animal, or perhaps a little of both. Thin-legged crabs skitter away. A creeping octopus shrinks back into a cave with a pop and slide of his suckers.

My companion laughs at him and shoots upward. I follow, laughing as she does. We pick up speed as the light grows. Fish, some small and darting, some large and menacing, streak away from us. We explode through the surface like the spray from a whale's spout, only a hundred—a thousand—times more powerful.

We dash across the surface, blending water and air. Others dance around us, laughing. Some leap through the water like dolphins. Maybe they are dolphins. The difference doesn't matter.

My companion dives low again, but I don't follow this time. I am too light, moving too fast.

When a boom sounds from below, it is deep and resonant. The sound shudders through my being, and I nearly burst with the power of it. I feel the tremors coming, and I laugh when the waves rise and toss. They swell and swirl, a mountain in one moment and a valley in another. I skim along one rise then ride the top as it surges.

Something in the distance catches my eye, a shape too regular and straight to be natural. Curious I streak toward it. My companion bursts from the waters, a streaming nude form. She laughs and follows me.

As I draw near the shape, my joy falters. A feeling gnaws at me. I try to ignore it, to lose myself again in simple, uncaring joy. But the creaking of wood, the ripping of cloth, and the frightened shouts of men weigh me down until the joy is gone, and horror slides into its place.

CHAPTER 3

The Drift shivers with diffused energy. I sense the push and pull of water, the whipping air, the trembling earth, the bite of the sun. They bleed through, too forceful to be contained within the physical world. Or perhaps the source of it all is here and is bleeding outward. Five elements, my mother believed, all interwoven.

Most of the fish and other sea creatures have fled. We are reaching the heart of the storm.

Ahead, Gaiana swims through the swells. She struggles more now, her tail beating against the currents, but she is pushing on, trying to reach them.

I follow her far into the ocean before I see lighted forms gathered, contained within the shape of a tossing ship. The ship rises on a swell before plunging into a trough. I cringe, expecting it to smash, but the wave eases just enough for the ship to rise again.

12

I hate to leave Gaiana. If she needs help and I'm not here to give it, how could Logan forgive me? But she is making her choice. The men on that ship have none.

I streak toward it.

I slide from the Drift onto the ship's pitching deck. I try to brace, but the heaving waves are too strong. I roll and scrape across the wet deck until I snag a rope and anchor myself to the gunwale.

Men shout with fear as the ship rises again, though their voices are all but lost in the roar of water. They are past trying to fight. They cling to the ship as to life, but they have given themselves over to fate.

At least, all have but one.

A man, white-haired and weathered, is bound with ropes to the mast. His head is tilted, face lifted to the shifting sky. I see no fear in him, only focus. Despite the madness around him, he is calm.

An Earthmaker.

The ship plunges again. He works the waves to slow our fall, but he is not enough. The descent is too steep.

I work an eye over the side as we plunge. My stomach soars into my throat at the sight of a mountain of water and the unforgiving trench into which we are racing. I draw hard on my energies, frantically shaping a blast, a shield, a battering ram.

I send the blow to the ship's prow and let it barrel into the water ahead of us. Water divides and sprays as the ship strikes the trough. My blow cuts a path, keeping the ship from tipping, letting us ride up and through the next wave.

Men scream as the ship sweeps to the top once more. We climb nearly vertical, and my legs hang in the air. The ropes, wrapped around my arms, strain against flesh, and my shoulder sockets threaten to give. A scream fades as someone tumbles down the deck and into the deadly waters.

I thud to the deck as we crest and plunge again. I blast another path as the Earthmaker slows us as best he can. I brace for impact, for the cold rush of water, but once more it's only spray as we whip through the trough.

Again and again, we rise to the top of the world then fall into its depths. My body is distant, a strain and thud, something not quite real. I am only this eternal, unstoppable motion.

Eventually, sensation fades. Darkness edges into my vision. I reach further into myself for the Drift, but the energy is a sluggish pulse, and my next blast cuts no more than a shallow trench before us. Water slams the prow of the ship and streams over us like a waterfall. The ropes tighten around my arms until pain flares through my numbness. I wait for the ship to crash, to shatter its huge, fragile body like a glass hammer on the iron surface of the ocean.

Slowly, the deck eases toward the horizontal. The torrent diminishes, water streaming away until only a trickle slides along the deck, then nothing. The ship settles in eerie calm.

We are no longer moving.

Above is only sky.

I peer over the side. At the sight below, I clutch the ropes in renewed terror. We are floating in the air, hovering above a rearing mountain of water. Under the ship's belly water whips and swirls, a whirlpool in the mountain's hollowed crest.

A gust of wind blows across the deck, and I know that sensation. I tear my eyes from the mad sight below to the splintered and soaking deck as Logan shapes himself from the wind.

His eyes find mine at once.

My mouth works uselessly. I don't know what I'm trying to say.

He looks angry.

And yet, he also looks like he's not quite here.

He strides toward me, his body shimmering and dissolving as he moves.

He says, "The hull is breached. Can you hold it together with Drift-work?"

I swallow and find my voice. "For a time."

"Be ready. Once I drive them off, I will set the ship down."

I nod.

"If the ship crashes, if I fail, you will take yourself into the Drift at once. Promise me, Astarti."

"I promise."

He looks for the truth in my eyes before he turns away.

"Logan." He shifts back to me. "Your mother. She's here somewhere, in the waters."

Surprise flashes across his face, but he nods.

CHAPTER 4

LOGAN

I have never been good at splitting my focus, but now I must. One part of me must remain with the ship, holding it above the murderous waters. I will do everything I can to save the men, but above all I don't trust Astarti to protect herself. It's not that her promise was a lie, but she will stay a moment too long, try a little too hard, and that moment could kill her. Fear slides through me at the thought, and it's an effort to keep moving away from her.

While I leave a bit of myself behind, I must also drive off the Old Ones. My fury is compounded by my guilt. Like them, I lost myself in selfish enjoyment, and look what has happened.

I tear through wind and water, seeking them, letting my anger seep into the elements. My companion comes to me, unafraid but confused. Her face shapes itself from wind and water. She looks to the ship, then to me. Anger hardens her expression. Though she looks young, her eyes of water and wind are ancient and filled with bitterness and pain.

She dashes toward the ship. Water fans around her and a rooster tail of spray leaps behind. I chase after her, horrified to see her form darken as she grows into the shape and bulk of a whale with a head like a battering ram. The huge tail drives her to a speed no whale could achieve. In her wake, others are coming, drawn by her energy and her anger.

I strain for speed, but I cannot catch her.

I shape water and air into a net, hardening it with the impenetrable will of the earth, and hurl it before her. She screams as her massive whale's body slams into it.

Fins become hands. Her tail splits into flailing legs. She screams with rage and terror as the net snares her.

I sweep to the other side, blocking her path to the ship.

I touch her hand, trying to tell her to calm down, that she is not trapped.

She stills and eases her hands from the net.

Her eyes meet mine, and I see her hurt, her feeling of betrayal. Behind her, others hover, uncertain.

Biting her watery lip, she turns and streaks away across the ocean. The others follow her.

Loss echoes through me, and I am tempted. For half a second, I am tempted. With the ship a fragile life behind me, with Astarti behind me, that impulse, the way I rock toward them as they flee, makes me feel worse than anything.

Even with the Old Ones gone, the waves leap and toss. I blend with them and try to ease them to stillness, but I have little calm to impart.

I plunge deeper, seeking enough pressure and darkness to fill my mind. The mountains of water finally begin to sink toward the ocean's bed, quieting. Far above, the ship settles to the rocking surface.

When something swims toward me, I float to meet it. Drawing closer, I recognize the blend of movement: part human, part ocean creature. It calls me back to my childhood.

I let my shape become familiar, though she clearly knew me without it. My mother laughs and dances around me.

She takes me in her arms, and I am a child. My hands are small and soft as they tangle in her hair. She kisses my cheek.

Time flows like water around me, and I move through this moment as through a dream, not knowing if it's real.

"Bright Fish," my mother laughs.

I laugh with her, and a rocky, chuckling voice sounds from the deeps.

He rises slowly, and when my mother turns to look at him, her eyes dance with delight.

"Kronos," she calls.

He emerges from the dark heart of the ocean, his face like the coarse, strong bones of the earth. When he smiles at me, the sun seems to blaze from the ocean's dark and secret depths.

I reach for him, laughing, but the vision fades. The brightness is gone. My hand is extended—a man's hand—reaching for nothing. My mother floats nearby, watching me with worry, perhaps even fear.

Doubt settles like a stone. What was that? A dream? A memory? But that never happened. And that name, Kronos. I've never heard it before.

The drifting ship draws a shadow over me, and I force my thoughts to the present. I take my mother's hand and draw her toward the ship.

We skim under it, where a faint glow of Drift-energy spans the gaping hole. When we break the surface beside the ship, I shape my mother and myself into the wind and take us to the deck.

I let our energies settle into their usual forms. My mother is nude, and I shift before her, shielding her from the view of strangers. I tug off my sodden tunic and wring it out. Water splatters the already-soaked deck. I shake out the tunic, and my mother takes it with a wry quirk of her mouth. She has never been modest. She struggles with the wet cloth for a moment. With an aggravated look, she suffuses it with heat and air. When she pulls it on, the damp hem reaches to mid-thigh.

I spin to meet Astarti, whose quick footsteps tap across the deck. I grab her into my arms. Her clothes are soaked, her braid heavy with water. I pull back enough to see her face, and her pale blue eyes cut right to my heart. How can it be that anything in the Old Ones drew me away when she is right here?

"You're all right," I say, needing to speak aloud what I see.

"And you?" Her hands tighten on my waist. There is uncertainty in her tone. Don't I look all right? I try to still myself further, to close down my mind. So much skitters along the edges of my thoughts.

"What are you doing here?" Unable to fully banish my lingering fear, I shake her a little. "You could have been killed."

She frowns, drawing away from me, annoyed with my tone, or my shaking her, or my evasion. I take three deep breaths. I have to restrain myself better with her. She, above all things, does not want to be controlled. I understand that all too well. I don't want to control her. I love her freedom. But she scares me. When she takes these risks, she scares me to death.

"I followed your mother, then I saw the ship."

My mother comes to my side. "You followed me? I never saw you."

"I was in the Drift. I was worried." Her tone is apologetic, as though my mother will be angry, but my mother offers her a small smile.

My mother's smile fades, however, as she looks around the deck. "I will see to the wounded."

Men lie twisted in ropes or slumped over barrels, groaning, stunned and exhausted, some injured. A few bodies are completely still. Only one man is upright, and he is pulling against the ropes binding him to the mast.

I cross the deck toward him. Astarti's footsteps follow. Amidships, she sucks in a breath, and the man at the mast freezes. I look over my shoulder to see what the problem is. I follow Astarti's gaze down my body and jolt.

My form shimmers and fades, and I realize I have not been hearing my own footsteps. I will my body to solidify. The returning aches in my bad knee and shoulder mark my success. I didn't feel them before, and I have a terrible suspicion that this is the first moment I have been fully within my body.

Astarti's lips thin. Normally she would touch me, but she holds back, as though afraid I won't be there.

I force myself onward and find blue, Earthmaker eyes trained on me. The man's face is weathered and grim. He is the oldest-looking Earthmaker I have ever seen. Gray eyebrows draw low as I approach. His look is a challenge and a warning. I stop.

"I only want to untie you."

He gives a short nod. I edge around behind him and work at the knots, but the wet rope holds fast.

"Astarti? Do you have a knife?"

"I always have a knife, Logan," she says with a hint of amusement, and her humor—no, simply her voice—helps me sink into the calm I need.

I move away as she shapes her spear. It glows silvery-blue. It is menacing and beautiful, like her. She slashes through the ropes, and the Earthmaker collapses to the wooden planks.

"I have to go below deck. I feel my patch weakening."

I nod, but Astarti hovers beside me. Her fingers brush my arm, leaving a trail of goosebumps.

"Get us in quickly, all right?"

I want to touch her, but I'm afraid I wouldn't be able to let go, so I just nod again, and Astarti is gone.

I turn back to the Earthmaker. His eyes focus on mine briefly, widening a little. I try to still myself, to force my eyes to hold blue, but I'm too unsettled. I can't see them, of course, but I know. The Earthmaker's gaze drops to my bare chest, skimming over my scars. I think of those on my exposed back, which I am showing to everyone. I force the thought away.

Though the Earthmaker's wet clothes cling to his wiry frame, I see he wears the loose linen trousers and billowing shirt typical of a sailor. Even so, I ask, "Are you a prisoner?"

His eyebrows slash downward. "I told them to tie me as soon as we saw the storm coming."

I glance around the ship, noting for the first time the huge dark blood stains, the crossbow-like contraptions mounted along the gunwales, and the brick stove for boiling blubber down to oil.

I look at the Earthmaker again. "This is a Valdaran whaling ship."

"Yes."

"And you an Earthmaker." If he is not a prisoner, there is only one explanation for his presence here. Stricken. Long ago, I suspect.

"So are you." His eyes narrow. "Kind of."

I ignore that. "Are you the captain?"

He snorts and jerks his chin to where my mother is crouched beside a man with a face white from pain and a forearm bent at a sickening angle.

As I make my way to the captain, impatience gnaws at me. I must get this ship moving.

21

When my footsteps fade, I have to stop and concentrate on forcing myself back into my skin. I hate the extra delay, but I can't help these people if I can't control myself. Measured breathing doesn't work, so I imagine a whip lashing across my back. I let memory bring me the pure, mind-clearing flash of pain. I let it anchor me in my body. I let it settle into my bones with familiar weight.

Centered now, I open my eyes.

"Logan," my mother calls from across the deck, "help me straighten his arm."

Impatience seethes, but I go to them. I need the captain's help.

I crouch beside him. I grip the man's elbow, pressing it to my knee to keep it stable.

"Ready?" my mother asks, and I feel the captain tense. He nods, and my mother, gripping his hand, pulls the arm out and straight. The captain howls with pain, and I don't blame him. I hold his arm steady while my mother lays her hands on the rapidly swelling flesh.

The captain clearly had no idea what to expect because when the pain vanishes, he jerks away. His face is full of wonder. He says something in the guttural tongue of Valdar. I know enough of the language to understand his, "thank you," but what he adds after is lost on me. It doesn't seem to be lost on my mother because she laughs, blushing a little.

I say in crude Valdaran, "Sail, up." I point to the helm with its huge wheel. "You, steer. Kelda."

The captain shakes his head and says something I can't follow, though I think he says something about Ibris. I look to my mother for translation, but the strange Earthmaker speaks behind me. "He says we are headed for Dalamas, in Ibris."

"Tell him he won't make it to Ibris with a hole in his ship the size of a whale's head."

Before an argument can ensue, I stride across the deck. Most of the deck has been washed bare, but I step around the occasional groaning sailor or mass of tangled rope. I pass the broad brick oven, where even the torrents of water haven't cleared away the lingering stink of oil. Behind me, the captain shouts orders.

We are on our way more quickly than I dared hope. I drive the ship across the waters, filling tattered sails with wind. A split in one lengthens with the sound of ripping canvas, but I don't give the shouting sailors time to take it back in. I stir the waters to push us even faster. Astarti looked exhausted. I don't know how long she can keep the ship together.

I try to hold my body to the ship, to let only a fragment of myself enter the elements.

I don't make it more than a mile.

I glide through wind and water, reveling in the freedom, driving the ship with rolling waves and relentless wind.

The hull groans a warning. Another sail rips.

I try to ease the push, to find a balance between freedom and control. I let a sliver of wind slip through the cracks in the ship to touch Astarti, and the answering hum of her energies settles me.

I sense the rise of the ocean's floor as we near Tornelaine, then the rocky bluffs jut from the water. I itch to drive the wind and water against the cliffs, to feel the impact of the elements.

I slow myself. I don't want to smash the ship.

Of course not.

As we draw near Tornelaine's harbor, the waves rush ahead to knock broken ships against one another. When I try to draw the waters back, I only manage to bring a wave against the prow. Men shout as spray explodes across the deck. The Earthmaker onboard tries to calm the waves. He's not powerful enough to counterbalance me, however, and we come wobbling into the harbor, spraying water over the port road as the captain steers us alongside.

Chapter 5

The panicked shouts from above deck, audible even over the roar of wind and water, warn me to brace for impact. I grab onto a support beam and widen my stance. Even so, the slamming of the boat into what I assume is the port road jerks me away from the beam and throws into one of the barrels.

I lie across the barrel for a moment, letting the pain in my hip settle. Then I hear pouring water. I flood more energy into my patch and renew the Drift-light I've kept floating above me. I don't want to be in the dark down here. The smells of blood and meat and oil turn my stomach, and I'd rather see the weapons fully than catch glimpses of their blades when light filters from above. The harpoons are two and three times the length of my spear, and they hook back with wicked barbs to anchor in the flesh of whales. Thick ropes trail from the blunt ends to coil on the wet, stained floor.

"Astarti?" inquires Horik's rumbling voice from the top of the stairs.

"Down here."

Horik and another Drifter, Jarl, tromp down the steps into the hold.

"Gods," Jarl mutters, dragging his tunic over his nose.

Men start filing into the hold behind the Drifters. They shout to each other in what sounds like Valdaran and start wrestling the barrels toward the stairs.

"The captain wants to save his cargo," Horik explains. "It might take them a while to clear the hold. You want some help?" He eyes the gaping hole in the stern, where the murky water of the harbor sloshes against my faintly glowing patch.

I nod Horik closer. "It's a lot of pressure."

When Jarl and Horik have built a shield that lines mine, I let mine dissolve. Some of the energy dissipates; some seeps back into me. I sag with weariness and relief.

I wait until the sailors, grunting and cursing, have heaved another barrel onto the deck before I trudge up the steps. The sudden light makes me wince.

Logan and Heborian are talking near the rail. Logan's arms are crossed. He looks jittery, like he's trying to get away from Heborian. Seeming to sense me, he spins around. He leaves Heborian in the middle of a sentence and strides across the deck to me.

His eyes swirl blue and green. His hands skim over my hair, then my shoulders.

"I'm fine," I assure him.

"When the ship hit, I—"

"I'm *fine*, Logan."

A muscle feathers in his jaw, and I know what's coming before he says it. "You scared me today. Don't do that again."

My temper flares. "I did what was needful, as you did. Don't tell me not to take risks when you take them."

An argument swirls through his eyes. He closes them and takes a calming breath. His body is rigid, as though he's forcing himself to remain solid. I shiver at the memory of him dissolving—he didn't even realize it was happening. My fingers itch to trace the lines of his body, to feel that he is really here. He turns at the sound of Heborian's approach.

"As I was saying, Logan." Heborian sounds annoyed. "You felt nothing of the one Belos has Leashed?"

Logan's body tightens further at that last word. "No."

"Can you communicate with them at all? Can you ask them—"

"They've never spoken to me with words."

Heborian's eyes narrow. "But they speak to you some other way?"

Logan shifts uncomfortably. "It's more of a feeling. They are..." Logan frowns, hunting for an explanation. He shakes it off, abandoning whatever he was going to say. "They weren't attacking Tornelaine. The city just got caught in the ripple."

Heborian raises a dark eyebrow. "That was a ripple?"

Logan jerks his chin toward the ocean, where the Floating Lands, ominously still, continue smoking. "Yes, that was a ripple."

Once the hold has been emptied and the ship allowed to sink to the bottom of the harbor, the day fills with slow work in the city. Heborian's Drifters and soldiers check buildings and look out for any conflicts among the city's inhabitants. Logan and I join the Earthmaker Wardens as they scout the refugee camps for the same.

We enter the market square, where waxed canvas tents form neat rows. The crowding is less severe than it was initially. Many of the refugees have moved outside the city gates. I don't know whether pride or fear motivated them, but given the danger of falling buildings within the city, they may be safer out there.

Gaiana disappeared before Logan and I left the harbor, vanishing with Logan's shirt. I certainly don't mind the view, but the muscles move tightly under Logan's skin. He doesn't like for people to see his back.

Aron catches sight of us from across the square. His step falters when he draws near. He shrugs off his overtunic and hands it to Logan. I'm not sure whether that was for Logan's benefit or for Aron's. Aron doesn't like to see Logan's scarred back any more than Logan likes for it to be seen.

We follow Aron to the edge of the encampment, where a neat row of tents dissolves into a mess of broken tent stakes, trampled canvas, and scattered goods.

"Keldans?" I inquire.

"They're frightened. And they don't want us here."

"Anyone hurt?"

"Not badly. Feluvas and Korinna have seen to the injured." Aron anticipates my next question. "On both sides."

"Good."

Aron sniffs disagreement. He looks across me to Logan. Questions show in Aron's eyes, so I hold up a staying hand.

Logan notices nothing. His eyes are fixed on the paving stones ahead. He has not dissolved again, but the effort to stay in his skin is obvious. I want to get him back to the castle. I need to talk to him, to know he's all right.

We help restore the damaged tents. The Earthmakers can do it themselves, but it's important that everyone see cooperation.

Apparently Heborian is of a similar mindset. Rood steps from the Drift, startling me as I shake dust from a blanket.

He grins. "I've been wanting to do that."

"And I've been wanting to see how a prince folds a blanket." I hand him the other end.

He frowns but helps me fold. It feels odd doing something so ordinary with him.

"Impressive," I say as he raises his end to join mine.

He rolls his eyes.

I check on Logan, as I have been doing every few minutes. He's setting up a cooking tripod for a mother with four children. There is no man in sight, and I wonder if the father is dead. Given the somber faces, I would guess that he is.

Logan strikes fire into the dry tinder. The movement of his hands takes me back to the time I spent with him in that abandoned hut in the Floating Lands. In these simple tasks, he is comfortable. Some days, I long for that quiet stretch of beach and the ramshackle hut. It feels like another lifetime. I wonder if the hut is even still standing, whether that tiny, removed island has survived the desolation. I decide to imagine it has.

Rood eyes Logan with suspicion. "He draws them away. Why do they follow him?" When I don't answer, Rood prompts, "He's a lot like them."

"It's none of your concern."

Few know that Logan is a son of the Old Ones. If he wants people to know, he can tell them. I won't.

Rood slides a sideways glance at me. "I think it's everyone's concern."

"Ask your father, if you think he'll tell you."

Rood looks hurt, and I wonder if he has already asked Heborian and been denied an answer. Though I will never take Rood's political position, I begin to understand why he feels threatened. He is jealous of the time Heborian spends with me, little as it is. He envies my involvement. Before Logan, I couldn't have understood that. I never had anything I was afraid of losing, no one's attention that meant so much to me. Now, having seen Logan with the Old Ones, remembering how he touched the hand of one, fear clenches my guts. How quickly we can lose what we love. How easily it turns from us.

80 03

It's late in the afternoon before Logan and I get back to the castle. Two trays of food await us in the sitting room. I know it's just the way of things here, but I hate how people come and go from our rooms while we're gone, sometimes even while we're sleeping.

I sandwich a chunk of roast beef between slices of bread and sit on a footstool. I silence my groan as the juices hit my tongue. Almost, I can forgive whoever intruded to bring this food.

Logan eats quickly, obviously hungry. He drains a glass of water and refills it. Even though he is solid and real and right beside me, he is so far away. I touch his knee and watch him gather himself back to me.

"What happened today?"

He frowns. I give him a minute to sort out an answer, but he doesn't give it. I bite back my frustration and focus my next question away from him. "What do they want?"

His frown deepens. "Nothing. And everything."

He meets my eyes at last. His are a riot of color, green streaking through the blue, gold firing along the edges. His stillness, his containment, is a lie.

I wonder how long it will last.

"I don't know what that means." Frustration slips into my voice.

Logan scratches his gold-stubbled jaw and hunts for better words. "They are like children. Playful. Easily distracted." His eyes harden. "And just as careless."

"But you like them." I meant it to be a question, but it comes out as a statement, maybe even an accusation.

His lips thin. "They are dangerous."

"But…"

He is silent for a long time. "They tempt me into things I don't want."

I wonder if he hears the contradiction—how can he be tempted by something he doesn't want? I let that pass, but there are other things I want to know, deeper fears that were stirred today. I pick at my sandwich, trying to bury them. I can't.

"What happened on the ship? With you? I've never seen you struggle to keep your body."

There. The words are out. My heart hammers as they hang in the air between us. Logan is frozen on the edge of his footstool, trying, perhaps, to not hear that. But he does. Tremors start working through his body. He tries to suppress them, but they travel along his limbs until his hands are shaking.

Guilt worms through me. I wish I knew what to say, that I were better with words. I can use them to lie and manipulate, to harm. Belos taught me those skills even as I learned to speak. But I never learned how to use words to help someone.

I try to touch Logan's hand, to take back my question. His hand closes in a fist, a silent refusal. I tuck my hand into my lap.

His body stills as he pulls it all back in. He takes several measured breaths. When he speaks, his voice is almost normal.

"There's hot water in the bathing chamber. Why don't you clean up first?"

I have to look away. It's almost worse to watch him exert such unnatural control over himself. I know what I'd see if I stepped into the Drift; this control is only skin deep. Even so, he makes it happen, giving me only this thin outer shell. Whatever is going on with him, he doesn't want me to see it. He trusts me with his body, but not, apparently, with his mind. My fingers tighten, smashing through the bread of my sandwich into the warm meat.

"No, you go first."

"Astarti…"

"You go," I repeat, more sharply this time.

He hesitates then pushes to his feet.

31

I can look at him now that his back is to me. As he walks to the bathing chamber, he tries to hide the soreness of his damaged knee, but I see the hitch in his gait.

I chastise myself. It's only been a few days since he broke free of Belos, only a few weeks since he was tortured by him. Add to that all that's happened with the Old Ones and the Ancorites, all we've learned? He's not ready to talk about anything that touches on those subjects. He has no answers yet. I thump my forehead against my knee. I know, I know. I have to be more patient.

When the bathing chamber door closes, I dutifully finish my sandwich, though I barely taste it. I take the empty trays to the door. I set them in the hall so no one will have to come inside for them.

When Logan emerges from the bathing chamber, I slip inside. He's barely used the water, leaving it warm for me. I sigh in relief as the itchy salt washes from my hair. I soak in the tub until the water cools.

By the time I finish my bath, I am more relaxed, ready to compromise. If Logan is not comfortable with words, I will not use them. I will speak to him in the way he is able.

I find him in the bedroom, standing by the window and looking out into the darkening garden. He still has the bathing towel cinched around his waist. He must not hear me come in because he starts when I touch his back.

I skim my fingers along the edge of the towel, enjoying the warm solidity of his body. He sucks in a breath as I trace the cut of muscle at his hip, following it below the towel. When I brush his aroused flesh, his stomach muscles tighten. He turns to me and leans down. His lips brush along my jaw to my ear. I shiver.

I tug the towel away so I can see all of him, and it is a beautiful sight. His hands find the edge of my towel, but he pauses.

"What is it?" I whisper. His fingers barely touch me.

His voice comes out rough. "I'm not…under control."

Doesn't he understand? That is the point of this, to let go. I brush my fingers down his torso to his body's most intimate places, and he groans.

He pulls my towel free. His hands skim my breasts, my waist, my hips. He is trembling with desire, his need answering my own. He lifts me and carries me to the bed, his body gliding against mine. I cling to him, amazed that my weight is nothing in his arms. His physical strength is exhilarating. When he lays me down, he hesitates again, trying to stop himself, so I hook my legs around him. His resistance crumbles.

He is more restrained in his movements than usual, not relaxed, not comfortable. He wants this, even needs it, but he doesn't trust himself with it.

We both find some release, but it leaves neither of us content, and in the end I am left wanting something beyond what my body found. As I lie in Logan's arms, I feel his tension behind me, the way he is unhappy with himself. His face presses into my hair, and he breathes deeply, forcefully. He's trying to fight off what's coming. I strain to stay awake because I, too, know what is coming.

But the day was too long, and I am too tired, and, in the end, I fail.

₮ ℥

I wake during the night to find Logan gone. My guts twist. For all the time I spent under Belos's control, I have never felt so powerless, so utterly helpless. Strange that love would teach that to me better than fear ever could.

I slide into the Drift and move through the castle, searching. My brief, foolish hope that he might simply have gone for a walk vanishes. I hover, tempted to search the city. I know what he's doing, and I know he wants to be alone in it. Should I respect that? Is it my place to stop him, to tell him he can't do as he chooses? Am I supposed to tell him what is and isn't good for him?

When I spot Heborian in his tower room, I decide to let that distract me from these questions I cannot answer.

I step out of the Drift at the foot of the stairs. Heborian has taught me too well, and I easily undo his locks.

I pass into the tower's outer room, where the cot's rumpled bedding indicates interrupted sleep. Heborian has been spending most of his nights here.

A bluish Drift-light glows from the workroom, and I let my bare feet slap across the boards to announce my approach. Despite this, I find Heborian hunched over the broad table, engrossed in his notes. Papers and tools are spread around him in an arc. Dark hair curtains his face as he studies the notes, tossing one paper aside to scrutinize another. Bold but messy handwriting covers the page, though I can't read any of it from here. His wrinkled shirt is unlaced, the cuffs rolled to his elbows to expose muscled forearms. A Runish tattoo curls around his right wrist and down his hand.

When I clear my throat, Heborian leaps to his feet. A Drift-sword flashes into his hand, then vanishes when he sees me. He glares. The blue tattoo hooking his right eye looks black and angry in the Drift-light.

"Couldn't sleep?" I inquire.

Heborian thumps back onto his stool. "Apparently this castle is full of insomniacs. I assume Logan is...out?"

I keep my face still, but I grimace inwardly. Logan has done this enough to catch Heborian's notice. But then, little escapes Heborian's notice.

"What are you working on?"

Heborian eyes me, letting me know he's noticed I won't answer. "Plans. Ideas."

I take a few steps into the room, scanning the notes and tools. Oddly, a harpoon launcher, salvaged from the whaling ship, is propped in a corner.

"Something I can help you with, Astarti?"

I shrug and rest a hip against the table. I'm only wearing a long tunic, which feels weird around my father, but I won't let my discomfort show.

Heborian tidies his papers, pulling a few of them away from me. "Several of the whaling crew reported that a giant whale tried to attack their ship. They claimed the whale turned into a woman. Did you see the same thing?" Heborian looks at me over the stack of notes he's squaring.

I saw her. I saw Logan stop her, and I also saw him touch her hand.

Heborian nods at my unspoken confirmation. "You didn't think that was worth telling me?"

"I had other things on my mind."

"We have one purpose right now, Astarti, and that is to understand our danger and prepare for it. Belos will come at us, we know this. It's the gods I can't anticipate. You must not withhold information. You must not put Logan ahead of the greater good."

I let his words slide away from me, though they leave a cold, icy trail in their wake.

I say, "They're not really gods, you know. I think, in this one thing, the Earthmakers are right. They're the Old Ones, the first ones."

Heborian huffs. "They made the world and they made us. What is a god if not the maker of life?"

I cock an eyebrow. "Is every father a god then?"

Heborian grunts. "If they are not gods, there is no such thing."

"The Ibrisians seem to think there's something more. The Divine Light."

"Don't you think they're talking about the light of the Drift, whether they know it or not?"

"Maybe. But something made the Old Ones. They didn't make themselves."

"And how do you know that, Astarti? And if there is something greater even than the Old Ones, what is it? Why have we never seen it? The Old Ones—the gods—make more sense."

"I don't think you can put 'god' and 'sense' into the same sentence. The Old Ones are beyond us, yes, and I don't claim to understand them, but I don't like the term 'god' and don't think it fits. It makes them sound untouchable, and they're not. We've seen that."

"Aren't you just the little theologian today?"

"Don't be an ass."

Heborian sighs. He's silent for a while, frowning at his notes. I feel a flash of pride—he's thinking about what I said.

Suddenly, he asks, "Do you think Logan will try to join them? The Old Ones, if that's what you want to call them."

To hear Heborian state so bluntly what I fear makes my stomach flip. I say, forcing myself to believe it, "No." Unfortunately, I can't help adding, "Why do you ask that?"

Heborian leans an elbow on the table, more comfortable now that I am not. "His control is as thin as spring ice on a pond."

"That's not true, and what does that have to do with it anyway?"

Heborian, of course, doesn't answer. If he answered, I could argue. If he says nothing, I'll have to chew on his words. Bastard.

To get back at him, I snatch one of his papers from the stack. He grabs it back so fast it leaves a paper cut on my palm.

"What are you working on up here so secretively?"

Heborian sets the papers beyond my reach. "I have plans to create further bone weapons."

His frankness surprises me. "Oh?"

"I need more bones. Now that Belos and his lot are out of the Dry Land, I can get to the Broken City."

"And you want me to come? I can't see why else you would have told me."

"I wouldn't say no."

"Would it kill you to say you want my help?"

"Another Drifter would be useful, but it's up to you. I can understand if you don't want to go back there."

I search his face for signs he's using this to prod me, but I find instead a softening in his dark eyes. I look away. I would have preferred a prod.

"I'll go."

I read surprise in the stillness of Heborian's body, which I see from the corner of my eye. He doesn't ask for my reason, but I give it anyway.

"I want to see that fortress in rubble. I barely glimpsed it when Logan, Horik, and I fled the Dry Land. In my mind, it's still standing. I want to change that."

I feel Heborian studying me, and it makes heat creep up my neck. "What?"

"Sometimes I can scarcely believe you never knew your mother. You're so much like her."

I push away from the table. I don't want to engage in this particular conversation. "When do you go?"

"In the morning."

I turn for the door.

"And, Astarti? You are like her."

I say gruffly, "Goodnight, Heborian."

"Goodnight."

I return to my and Logan's rooms to find him still gone. I should sleep, store up my energy for tomorrow, but I can't. I lie awake, listening for the door.

It opens at last, and Logan moves quietly through the room. When he lies down beside me, I catch the scent of all the angry back alleys of Tornelaine. I lie there stiffly, trying to decide whether to confront him. I know it won't help, and, despite how tempting it may be at this moment, it won't actually make me feel any better.

I roll over to him. His skin is overly warm and a little sticky. I smell the alcohol and sweat and blood. Even though it's dark, I close my eyes as though I can shut it out.

Logan is tense, expecting me to say something. When I don't, he lets out a slow, relieved breath. At the end of that breath, he passes out.

I lie against him for what seems hours. What he's done to himself offers him only temporary relief, but it's more powerful, apparently, than anything I can give him, and that bothers me. On a selfish level, it stings that I'm not enough. Silly, maybe, but there it is. What's worse, what eats at my heart, is that he has to hurt himself to find peace.

If peace is even what this is.

CHAPTER 6

LOGAN

I wake alone.

I deserve it.

Morning light bleeds through the curtains to lie softly where Astarti's body should be. I scrub a hand down my face, surprised by the sting and ache around my eye as my fingers pass over warm, swollen flesh. I hope it was still dark when she left.

I groan as I slide from the bed. Since I'm alone, I allow myself to clutch at my sore ribs. I explore them with my fingers. Nothing feels broken.

I know I shouldn't do this. It's stupid and pathetic. But I have to get back inside my skin, and this is the only way I know to do it. I have to force that fist to tighten inside me, to lock everything up.

If I don't...

If I *don't*...

I force the thought away.

I wash the stink of Tornelaine from my body. There's a fist-sized bruise on my stomach. I can hide that from everyone's eyes but Astarti's, but the black eye will be harder. I don't want anyone to say anything about it. I just want to quietly go back to being myself.

I dress quickly and go to find Bran. When he's not in his rooms, I head for the library.

Light pours through the high, east-facing windows to fall in stripes across the maze of shelves. At my approach, the thin, pale librarian stands from his desk. He folds one hand over the other. One of the Ancorites used to use that deceptively quiet gesture. My skin is crawling by the time I reach him.

"May I help you?"

His voice is deep and very human. Some of the tension leaves my shoulders. He sounds nothing like the Ancorites.

He does, however, eye my bruised face.

"Is Branos here?"

"In the scroll room."

Like I know where that is.

The librarian reads my annoyance. "I'll take you."

He leads me through the maze. We pass a mess of toppled shelves where frowning scholars carefully sort through the scattered books. One makes a sound of physical pain, and I spin to see what's happened. The scholar shows his companion a book whose cover has been torn away, and they both shake their heads sadly. I picture the captain's broken arm that my mother Healed. Better a book than an arm. Better an arm than a neck. Three men were killed on that ship yesterday. That no one was killed in the city is all but a miracle.

I follow my guide to the back of the library and a series of doors. One stands open, and the librarian gestures toward it.

I watch him walk away, one hand folded over the other in that nauseating way. My stomach heaves a little, and I taste the acidity of bile in the back of my throat.

"Is that you, Logan?" Bran calls from inside the room.

I swallow the horrible taste and go to the door. The room is dark, lit only by Bran's glass-faced lantern.

"What's with this room?" I grumble, letting out my agitation. "It's like a tomb."

Bran looks up from the scroll he's been studying. The corners are weighted down with small felt bags filled with dry beans.

"Sunlight damages old scrolls." He squints at me, then his mouth tightens. "By the Old Ones, Logan."

"I need a favor."

He groans.

I walk to Bran's table. I know he'll do this for me. "What's the big deal? I just need you to go get Korinna."

"It's not fair to do this to her, you know. You're asking her to hide something from Mother."

I sit in the chair across from Bran. "Our mother doesn't want to know. Do you want her to know?"

It's the very reason I can't go find Korinna myself; I don't want to run into my mother. I can handle Bran's irritation, but I don't want to see my mother's worry. I've worried her enough for a lifetime. Though I guess she got me back a little yesterday. When I looked for her to ask what she had been doing in the ocean, she was nowhere to be found.

Bran closes his eyes and exhales slowly. When he opens them, he studies me. "When are you going to stop this?"

I don't answer.

"Do you know what this does to Astarti?"

I wince. The deadness I worked so hard to achieve last night fades like the lie it is. I fist my shaking hands in my lap so Bran won't see.

With uncharacteristic ruthlessness, he plows on, "She came to see me this morning. Do you want to know what she asked me?"

Yes.

No.

I'm too conflicted to answer.

"She didn't mention this"—he waves a finger to indicate my face—"but she asked me whether I thought you trusted her."

My eyebrows contract. "Why would she ask that? Of course I trust her."

"I don't think she meant that kind of trust." He eyes me. "Have you talked to her?"

"About what?" I growl, daring him.

He dares. "It's only been a few days, Logan, and you're trying to pretend you're fine. You're obviously not. I can see that, and so can Astarti."

I make my voice a threat. "Drop it, Bran."

"What did he do to you?"

"Just go get Korinna."

"*Logan*—"

"*Bran.*"

"Logan. You have to find a better way to deal with this. You're hurting yourself *and* her."

Does this hurt her? She seems angry, but does it hurt her? I am only hurting myself, and I need it. Bran's words fill me with doubt.

"She cares about you, Logan. She loves you. That's why this hurts her. And it does hurt her, whether you see it or not, whether she admits it or not."

I don't want to hurt Astarti. By the earth and the sea and the wind and the sun, that is the last thing I want. My lungs seize. I can't breathe.

Bran is beside me, though I didn't see him get up. He lays his hand on the back of my neck like he used to do when I was a child. He gently pushes me down until my head is between my knees.

Three deep breaths. The first two are hard, but my lungs loosen on the last one.

"Again," he says.

I do as he tells me, and then I'm better.

I am fine.

Bran takes his hand away, but I don't sit up.

"I'll go get Korinna," he says but remains at my side. He waits for me to nod, to show him I'm through it, then he leaves. I let my head rest on the edge of the table.

By the time Bran returns with Korinna, I've managed to sit up.

I shift in my chair to take in Korinna's appearance. She still has her tight blonde braid and still wears her green tunic and leather breeches, but the Warden's vest is gone, as are her bracers. Bit by bit, they're peeling away what she wanted to be and making her a Healer.

I see her gift. I've felt it. But it still bothers me to see her remade by someone else's design.

"I'm sorry, Korinna," I mutter, embarrassed now that she's here.

"I don't mind."

Bran sits on the edge of the table while Korinna kneels by my chair.

"May I?" She raises her hands a little.

I don't know if she's just polite or if she's afraid of me.

I lean forward, and she places her cool hands on my face. My skin warms as the bruise Heals.

"I'm sorry," I say again as I sit back. "I know it's a waste of your skills and energy." I only want it gone so no one asks me about it.

Bran says grimly, "Let's see the rest of it."

"There's nothing more," I lie.

I can't bring myself to further abuse Korinna's gift, even if it means Astarti will scowl every time I take my shirt off. I can handle that, but I cannot handle everyone staring at me all day with questions in their eyes.

The tension in Bran's body tells me he knows I'm lying, so I change the subject, albeit awkwardly. "How is it going in the infirmary? Is Feluvas still butting heads with the king's physician?"

Bran huffs annoyance, but Korinna grins, and for a moment I see her resemblance to Astarti, her cousin. A light version of Astarti's dark.

"You should have heard them this morning. Did you know it's possible to have a twenty-minute debate about the properties of willow bark?"

I snort.

"The Prima smoothed it all over."

"My mother, the peacekeeper."

Korinna shrugs. "Someone has to be."

"I don't know. If Feluvas would just set the man's pants on fire and teach him a lesson, that would probably solve it well enough."

Korinna snickers at this mental image. "I'd better get back. They'll wonder where I am."

"Thanks. For this."

She says seriously, "My service is my life, and I give it freely."

She means well, but the use of those traditional words, meant to signify a Warden's dedication, fills me with shame. This is not a service I should have asked of her. Even so, I make myself nod. I won't throw her dedication back in her face.

As she reaches the door, I call out, "Korinna?"

She pauses.

"You won't…"

"I won't tell anyone."

When she's gone, Bran settles into his chair once more. He clearly thinks I'll leave without another word, and I normally would. When I don't, he looks up.

I don't want to voice the question rattling around inside me, so instead I ask, "What are you reading?"

"Early accounts of the Old Ones. They're not firsthand. This one was written perhaps four hundred years after the binding."

"Why are you reading that?"

"I want to understand them, Logan. I want to know what we have forgotten or ignored. Aron sees this as a battle like any other. Heborian is more interested in my research, but he only wants to know their weaknesses. I don't think this will be that kind of battle. We need to learn all we can." He pauses. "There are things I would like to ask you."

He leaves this open, inviting but not pushing, but I can't walk into it. I spent a long night disentangling myself from the Old Ones.

The momentary thinning of Bran's lips reveals his frustration. "And this one"—he thumps a more modern book with his forefinger—"is about Belos's war." He notices my eyes lingering on the scroll. "But you're more interested in this, aren't you?"

I want to say, "no." I need that fist to stay closed; I need to move on. Why am I still sitting here?

My question slips through my guard like a finger of wind. "Are there…names in that?"

"Names?"

My heart hammers a warning, but I persist. "Of the Old Ones."

"No. Why?"

Relief wars with disappointment. "No reason." I push up roughly from my chair, annoyed with myself.

"Logan?"

I can see he wants to say something, and I silently beg him not to. He sighs.

"Astarti is in Heborian's study."

When I reach the study, the guards open the double doors before I say anything. I'm not sure I like that they were expecting me.

The room is full of Drifters. The energy washes at me. I catch hints of every person's energy, like a scent coming from a person's clothes when they move. With Drifters, the effect is magnified, and right now it feels like I'm walking into a smoky room. Most of my adult life I've been able to shut this out, but ever since I started using my power again, it's been coming at me more strongly, and I don't like. The only one I don't mind feeling is Astarti; I like sensing her near me. My eyes find her now, where she stands beside Horik's huge form, and her pale blue eyes anchor me in this mess.

Heborian clears his throat to get my attention. I meet his impassive gaze.

"We're planning a venture. We leave soon for the Dry Land and the Broken City to collect bones."

A shiver passes through me at the mention of the Dry Land. I feel a phantom impression of scorching heat and blinding sun. I feel the black ooze of Belos's will violating my mind and body.

Because everyone is watching me, I clench all of this deep inside.

I lower my voice to steady it. "What do you want them for?"

"That's my business. I will get them with or without you, but Astarti is going."

I snarl, "You can't make her."

Astarti comes to my side. "He's not making me."

"Why would you want to set foot in that evil place?"

Heborian interrupts, "Logan, will you come?"

I can tell Astarti wants to protest, but she doesn't embarrass me by doing it in front of everyone.

I don't want to go back there. Icy water pools in my gut at the thought of it. But I'm not letting Astarti go to that place without me.

I glare at Heborian. "Yes."

Astarti can't hold back her protest any longer. "Are you sure that's a good idea?"

"If you're going, I'm going."

Her eyes harden. She definitely has something to say, and I doubt I'll like it.

Heborian clears the room with a sharp, "In the courtyard, one hour."

As soon as Astarti and I are back in our rooms, she snaps, "Why do you think you can tell me when to come or go when I'm not supposed to tell you that?"

My temper flares. "This is completely different. What you did yesterday was dangerous, getting on that ship. I had no idea you were there. You could have been killed!"

"Lots of people are getting killed, Logan. This is a war."

Her calm acceptance of that riles me further. "That doesn't mean you should seek out danger!"

"I was trying to protect your mother!"

I growl because she has me on that one. All I can say is, "You worry me. You scare me to death. I don't like it."

"Do you think I like worrying about you?" She stalks toward me, but everything in her body language changes when she reaches for my face, fingers lightly touching where the bruise was. "Logan," she says with an edge of desperation, "Logan."

I try to take her hand, but she pulls it away. She lays it lightly against the bruise on my stomach. She knows exactly where it is. She closes her eyes, and I see that Bran is right. I am hurting her.

"I'm sorry," I whisper.

"I know you are, Logan. But I'd rather hear you say you'll never do this again."

I want to say that. I open my mouth to try to make that promise, but nothing comes out.

Instead, I wrap my arms around her, begging her to accept this, as she has accepted so many ugly things about me. She is stiff at first, but then she clings to me, and I let her presence fill my mind and push out everything else. I don't want to think about last night.

This is all I want.

Part of me knows I will do it again. There will come a moment—tomorrow, next month, sometime—when there is something I can't bring her into. I have to do this. I have to. I will shield her from it as best I can, but that is all I can promise. Bran says it hurts me, but the hurt is only physical. I wish he understood—I wish Astarti understood—that it helps, that it's the reason I can stand here so calmly right now.

It's twisted and upside down, but it's true.

A cruel voice whispers, *She will leave you.*

I tremble at the thought. She has every right to leave me. I pray that she won't.

Astarti draws back, looking up into my face with pain that I put there. Fresh guilt slides through me.

She says, "I don't think you're ready for this. The Dry Land. I wish you would stay here."

"Not a chance." She watches my eyes, which I'm sure reveal even more than my voice. She sighs.

"Will you let me take you through the Drift? If you prefer, you could meet us there instead."

I stiffen at the thought of entering the Drift. The energy is too much. Everything is too exposed. *I* am too exposed. Yet, riding the wind is slower, and I would get there after them. What if there was trouble and I arrived too late?

With a grimace, I say, "Take me through the Drift."

CHAPTER 7

I let the others get ahead of me and Logan in the Drift. He doesn't need them to see this.

His energy rolls, coiling and winding through him. It's nothing like Belos's, whose energy is comprised of all the souls he's Taken. Belos's energy fights itself, one form strangling another, one will struggling for brief dominance. Logan's energy is like a building storm, wild and dangerous, but with its own internal rhythm.

I have the feeling that if he lost control here, he would be like the Hounding, the ripping wind that once haunted the Drift. The Ancorites told me the Hounding was a filament of the Old Ones as they strained for freedom. You could feel the madness of it. In retrospect, I wonder if it wasn't really madness but only a mind and will beyond my ability to comprehend. Either way, that's what Logan comes from, and it scares me to bring him here. If he lost himself in this, would I ever find him again?

I strain to make sound. "*Focus.*"

His energy shivers, but he gains a little control. I take his hand and pull him along to catch up.

We reach the Dry Land, and Belos's barrier glows in the distance. I know now that the threads are souls, torn apart, stretched, and rewoven to prevent passage through them. Heborian has the same around his castle grounds. I shudder at the sight. Heborian calls it a necessary evil, and I still can't decide if he's right.

Within the barrier, a single form glows. It's not bright enough to be Belos or any of the Seven, so it has to be one of the human servants. Heborian sees it. He angles toward the twisting threads.

We step from the Drift just outside the barrier. I wince at the glaring brightness of the sun. Beside me, Logan brushes himself off like he might have gotten dirty in the Drift.

The narrow slope leading from the dusty flats to the top of the plateau forces us to walk single file. Though danger is unlikely, Horik takes the lead, keeping Heborian behind him. Logan and I bring up the rear.

I'm unaffected by this place until we reach a section of torn ground. This is where Horik was trapped by Belos when he and I came to rescue Logan. It makes me remember how Logan walked up this slope, stepped over Horik, and emerged into the torchlight. For one second, I see his eyes in my memory— black, cold, reflecting a will not his own. I resist the urge to look over my shoulder and see his face. His mind is his own now. I know that. But sometimes I still dream he's possessed by Belos. I'm sure he dreams that, too.

We reach the rubble-strewn courtyard. No longer able to resist, I turn to study Logan. His face is still and controlled, much like when I first met him on a day that seems a lifetime ago. I know what it means now; he's shutting everything out.

No. That's not right. He's shutting everything in.

His eyes give him away. They turn blue for a second as he gets control, then green whips through them. I wonder what it's doing to him to be here again. I wish he would just tell me.

At the edge of the courtyard lies only a scattering of broken stone, but the rubble mounts higher and higher to the shattered fortress. One jagged wall is still standing. When Logan caused this destruction, we had to escape and I never got a good look at the mess. I take this new image into myself and let it stand for the end of something.

Bizarrely, I feel a slight wrench. I lived so much of my life here. I hated it, yes, but it was all I knew. I think of what lies buried, my thoughts catching on the ugly little doll I made from rags. She had no face because I had no paint, and she was filthy because there was no water to spare for washing a toy, but I used to sleep with her under my pillow. I can't remember her name. Maybe I never gave her one.

Logan shifts beside me and asks quietly, "Are you all right? Astarti?"

I touch his warm, strong hand. I love to touch him.

"I'm fine. You?"

His face looked worried when he spoke to me, but as I turn the question back at him, that mask slides into place. He dips his chin. That's all the answer I'm going to get.

At the sound of a shout, my head whips in the direction of the rubble. A figure moves at the top, in the shade of the jagged wall. From the corner of my eye, I see Horik and Jarl raise their hands. Any faint glow of Drift-work is lost in the harsh light, but a ragged figure comes tumbling down the rubble pile. I wince as the man is bounced over stones. He lands in a groaning heap before Heborian.

I push my way through the gathering as Heborian rolls the man over with a booted toe.

"You know him?" Heborian asks.

I study the dirty face. The man's skin and lips are cracked and peeling. He must have found some water or he'd be dead, but he's in bad shape. His thin chest jerks sharply with each breath.

"His name's Fordan. One of Belos's. Obviously."

"One of his what?"

I shrug. "Servants? Hangers-on? He attracts all sorts. Those who make deals want something for themselves, but some just want to serve him. He wouldn't know anything."

Fordan is gasping out a word, and I crouch down. Skeletal fingers with broken, filthy nails reach for my face. Someone knocks Fordan's hand aside. I squint up into Logan's furious face.

"He wasn't going to hurt me."

A muscle bunches in Logan's jaw, but he moves back a pace, visibly trying to calm himself.

I turn back to Fordan, but he's passed out. I don't like his kind, the ones desperate for a scrap of attention from Belos. Belos Leashes them and puts them to work, and they are thrilled to be "chosen." Despite the disgust I feel, pity flickers inside me. Men like Fordan believe they are nothing, and they feel worth only when someone like Belos deigns to look their way. He's not the only one like this, but he does seem to be the only one who survived the collapse of the fortress.

"Why don't we just kill him?"

I turn at Rood's question. He looks genuinely confused.

I explain, "He's Leashed to Belos. Killing him only gives Belos another bit of power."

Rood frowns. "There can't be enough power in him to make any difference."

Heborian says, "We'll take him back to Tornelaine."

I look at him in surprise. I expected him to agree with Rood.

Rood asks, "So you'll cut his Leash, then kill him?"

"If that's the best use I can make of him."

I squint at Heborian, trying to catch a hint of his meaning, but his face gives nothing away.

With the unconscious Fordan bound and dragged with ropes of Drift-energy, we make our way beyond the barrier. I take Logan back into the Drift, where he can't hide his agitation behind a forced expression. When I catch Heborian's eyes on him, I grow suspicious. I was surprised Heborian wanted Logan to come. At first I thought Heborian knew it would be an argument and had decided it wasn't worth the effort to push the matter. Now I suspect Heborian wanted Logan in the Drift on purpose—to see him, to judge his control.

When we reach the Broken City and step again into the heat and light, I glare at Heborian as he watches Logan. Logan stills behind me, aware of Heborian's attention. Heborian turns away.

Leaving our prisoner bound and tethered with Drift-energy, we head into the ruins. Spires of stone jut from the earth like enormous fingers. There's some rubble, but most of it has been worn away to nothing, leaving only the stony fingers. Perhaps someday they, too, will wear away to nothing. Bran says this was the first home of the Old Ones, that it was once a lush and beautiful place. I wonder if it's true that they destroyed their own creation in their lust for change and movement. *They just cannot stop*, Bran said.

Our group spreads out. I don't know how Heborian hopes to find the bones, but my stomach turns at the thought. When I first held Heborian's bone knife, I regarded it as nothing more than a tool. Now I see more clearly that it was once part of a body. The Shackles are the same. When the Old Ones were still trapped, the Hounding was drawn to those tools within the Drift. They sense them, recognize them. I wonder if what we are doing would make them angry.

Logan is a step ahead of me. I watch the way he walks, the way he moves his arms. His movements are confined, tightly controlled. I take his hand, which is stiff and unresponsive, and draw him into the shadow of one of the spires.

"Logan."

His eyes meet mine. His are mostly blue now, but when I slide my fingers inside his belt, green and gold swirl through his irises. He sucks in a breath. I work my fingers under the hem of his shirt and brush upward over the notched muscles of his stomach. I graze his tightened nipples. He leans against me, pressing my back to the rough stone.

He is more himself today, more what I'm used to. I hate that he hurt himself to do it. I hate that touching him works now when it didn't last night. But I can't stop myself. It feels wonderful to have him unwind under my hands, to feel suppleness and desire sweep away his rigidity.

My hands travel around his back. His muscles loosen at the touch. His hips press against me. His arousal matches my own, and I want nothing more than to leave this place and be alone with him.

When I lick the sweat from the hollow of his throat, he moans. His mouth finds mine, and his tongue sweeps inside. I want to tear at his clothes and pull him harder against me, but I force my hands to gentle. I stroke his back, slow my kiss.

He breaks the kiss and presses his lips to my temple. He breathes in the scent of my hair before drawing away.

I give his shirttail a tug. "You might want to tuck that back in."

He flashes me a crooked grin, and my breath stops for a second, like it always does when he smiles.

As we walk back into the sun, I touch his back from time to time, afraid he'll stiffen again, but his movements stay fairly relaxed.

We wander among the spires, not really looking for anything. That, I figure, is Heborian's job. Logan is half a step ahead of me, leading the way to nowhere.

He stops.

His expression is distant. I want to ask him what's on his mind, but he'll either tell me or he won't.

He says neutrally, "While I was bound to Belos, he brought me here a few times. I don't know why. Maybe he was drawn to this place. Maybe I was. In my memory, I can't really distinguish his thoughts from mine."

I try to stay relaxed, but this is the first time he's offered to speak of this, and I desperately want him to go on.

He squints into the sun. "One time, I had a...vision? I guess that's what it was. I saw a green valley here. Water, trees. And towering stone structures. These, I suppose. A man rose up from the ground. Or out of the ground maybe? In one moment, he was the size of a man; in another he was a colossal figure. He looked out across the sky."

Logan stares into the sky, seeking something.

I hazard a question. "What do you think that vision was?"

"I don't know. I had forgotten it until just now. All that time is muddled." He makes a dismissive gesture with his hand, as though tossing something behind him. I know the past cannot be so easily cast off, but it helps sometimes to pretend.

Logan and I walk on, and I let him continue leading the way.

He stays relaxed for a while, then he tenses and turns to look behind. "Your father is following us."

I look around but see only flat land and spires of stone.

Logan clarifies, "He's in the Drift."

I've known for some time that Logan can sense something of the Drift even from outside it. I understand this better now. As my mother believed, the Drift is the fifth element, the element of spirit. The Old Ones were masters of all, making no

56

distinction between them as Earthmakers and Drifters like to do. Logan can use them all as well, including the Drift. He doesn't quite know how and he certainly doesn't want to, but the ability is there. I have a similar ability to access all five elements because of my mixed blood. My power isn't as strong as Logan's, and I'm glad of that. Mine is learned and therefore controlled by my thoughts. Logan's is so instinctive that his thoughts seem to dissolve within those greater forces.

I've learned my lesson about doubting Logan's instincts, so I slide into the Drift. Heborian freezes, surprised to have been caught. I jerk my thumb to tell him to get out. When we both step from the Drift, I fix him with a stare.

"How long have you been spying on us?"

He takes a deep breath, raising his chin. He's not going to answer, which means it's been a while. I feel my neck heat at the thought that he probably saw me and Logan behind the spire.

Logan demands, "*Why* have you been following us?"

Heborian crosses his arms comfortably. "I was only following you."

"And why were you following me?"

"I had a hunch. We'll see if I was right." He lets out an earsplitting whistle.

"What is this?" I snap.

"Don't get excited." Heborian brushes past me to stand beside Logan. "You were looking at this spot. In fact, you've been moving this direction for fifteen minutes."

Logan says tightly, "Your point?"

Heborian claps him on the shoulder. "I think this is good place to start digging."

CHAPTER 8

LOGAN

Astarti and I stand aside while Heborian and his Drifters blast at the flat, hard earth. The sun bleaches the blue flares of Drift-light, but the occasional tremor through the ground tells me how much force they're exerting. Still, they're not making much progress. Astarti grins at me. I feel myself smirk in response. It *is* rather amusing.

Horik straightens, digging his fists into his back and stretching. He calls, "Are you two going to help or not?"

Astarti laughs. "Oh, no, it looks like you're doing just fine on your own." —

"Piss off."

Astarti chuckles.

Heborian stalks over to us. "Are you going to make me ask?"

"It's good for you." Her expression is playful, but I know she won't yield.

So does Heborian. He sighs. "A little help?"

That, apparently, counts as "asking" to him.

Astarti sniffs and takes her time. She looks a question at me.

I shrug. "If you think they've embarrassed themselves enough."

She's suddenly hesitant, uncertain. "I don't know if I can do it."

My heart thumps. If she can't, I'll have to. But I say, "Just relax. Don't pressure yourself."

She nods. Her skills are improving. She's sensing the elements more easily, learning to blend herself with them. I'm not much help in teaching her. I can't explain what I do. Actually, some of her explanations have helped *me* better understand. She's smart like that. She figures things out, puts them into words.

Astarti says the key for her is finding a balance between her own will and that of the elements, finding a way to work together. It's not that I don't believe her; it's just that I don't feel that. She enters the elements and remains herself.

I do not.

I try, I really do try, to hold onto my thoughts. I keep them for a moment, then I'm just gone. And it feels so good. Even now I itch for it.

That's the problem: I *want* to let it take me.

I've spent my whole life denying myself that release. Now that I've started using my power again, letting it take me over, I don't know if I can stop, and that scares me.

All my effort last night to pummel that deep inside myself, and it's already rising up.

I take three deep breaths, calming myself with the exercise I've used all my life. Heborian, the bastard, watches me do it.

Astarti stands a little ahead of me, her head bowed in concentration. She starts to vanish then solidifies. She tries several times before shaking her head in defeat.

She returns to me and Heborian looking frustrated. "I can't get to it."

She shouldn't be so hard on herself. "It's more difficult here than anywhere else. The earth is less responsive."

"Logan?" prompts Heborian.

I scrub a hand through my hair. Already, the two halves of me are splitting: the one that wants this and the one that doesn't. I'm trembling with anticipation, and yet, there's a cold pit in my stomach. The more often I do this, the more I let out, the harder it is to draw everything back and put it in its box again. I didn't expect to do this today. I just got back to being myself.

I could refuse. I *should* refuse. But I say, "Clear out."

The Drifters have moved back several paces, and Heborian strides away from me.

I laugh humorlessly. "You're going to want to stand a *lot* farther back."

Heborian warns, "Don't destroy the bones."

I keep my back to him. "I can't promise anything."

When I have a half mile radius, I try to relax my mind as I told Astarti to do, but that just lets everything creep in. I don't like when I do things I don't understand. I want to scoff at the idea that something drew me to this spot. I want to say I don't expect to find anything. I wasn't thinking about the bones, wasn't choosing a path. I shudder at the possibility that my mind is not in control even when I think it is.

I exhale slowly, letting that go. I'll think about that later, when I don't have people watching me.

I feel for the deep, sleeping power of the earth. It's not a conscious thought but more an extending of my senses, of my very self. I try to do it with restraint, to tease out a thread of power from the clenched fist inside me.

Nothing.

No, not nothing. Something dark creeps along the edges of my mind. I ignore it and try again to open that fist, but it's clenched tight, resisting.

I pry at it, annoyed and impatient. Then memory slips over me like a cold shadow.

This place.

I've been here.

With *him*.

I thought I could keep those memories at a distance. They like to slither into my dreams, but I can usually hold them off when I'm awake.

It's this place.

This is where he raped my mind. Again and again, he forced himself on me. He made me nothing.

His voice echoes: *Submit yourself!*

I shake my head to clear it.

Your will is mine!

And just that easily, memory makes me powerless, a thing in his hands, less even than an animal.

I bend over my knees, dry-heaving.

I close my eyes, praying Astarti is too far away to see me. I take three deep breaths and swallow the bile sliding up my throat. Belos isn't here. No one is forcing me. I make myself straighten.

I wipe sweaty palms on my leather pants, willing the tremble to go away.

I stare into the blinding sun and let it burn away all thought. I can't hover in this space between my two halves. I can lock everything away, or I can let go, but nothing is more dangerous than the space between.

I choose.

I let the sun fill me. Soon, I can't see anything but brightness, neither before my eyes nor within my mind. I am clean and empty of thought. I am earth and air, water and fire. I am not a man at all.

I am more.

I am power.

The fist holding everything inside me springs open. All the energies of the world are there to answer me: the faint, anemic sighs of the wind; the distant, angry sun; the deep, buried power of the earth with slender fingers of water sliding between its bones. They call to me from their dim dreams. They want me, and they promise me release.

I plunge into the sleeping mass, and it awakens at my touch. This land wants to be more again. Its craving answers my own. I tear through it, stirring it to life. I draw the waters up until they are exploding around me. The release is so powerful that I feel my mind splinter and dissolve in it. I shout with joy, and my voice is a rocky grumble, a stream of water.

My elemental senses brush something. I feel another power, something sleeping. Many somethings. They are scattered around me like jewels in a mountain, sparkling as light filters into the dark. They are earth, yes, but they are all the other elements as well, even that strange, tingling element that is the Drift.

But they are death also, which the elements cannot be. Loss echoes from them.

Bones.

Awareness creeps through me, weighing down my freedom. I'm supposed to be doing something.

I sweep around the bones, wondering whose they were, wondering at the power echoing within them all these ages later.

I hear a voice from a great distance. I hear a name, and it takes me a moment to recognize it as my own.

I charge on, churning through earth and water, skimming over the bones.

I hear my name again, shouted in fear, and I can't ignore her voice.

With more will than I thought I possessed, I disentangle myself from the elements and force myself to become nothing but a man again. I draw away and tighten that fist inside myself once more.

I stagger, oppressed by sudden heat, dizzied by harsh light and shadow. Hands touch me.

I blink to clear my vision and look down into Astarti's worried face.

She glances at our feet, and that's when I feel the water. We're standing in a narrow crevice, a roughly cut trench of stone. Clear, cool water washes over our toes, seeping through the leather of my boots.

With one hand still on my leg like she's afraid to lose contact with me, Astarti bends down to scoop up a handful of water. She splashes it over her face.

That fist is threatening to spring open inside me again, teasing me with whispers of power and freedom, so I sink down on one of the tumbled stones and put my head in my hands. I take three deep breaths. I do it again.

Astarti's hands are in my hair. Her fingers trace the tendons of my neck. Arousal fires through me, but I breathe it out. Her fingers dig into the tension in my shoulders, and I lean against the stony wall with a sigh, letting some of the tension go. Not all of it, because I need some, but a little.

"Look what you did," she says. For a second I think it's an accusation, but then I see her smile. "You found water. In the *Dry* Land."

"There's more. It's just deep down." My voice comes out rough.

She scoops some up and splashes me. The coolness hits my hot face. I sigh comfortably. "Do that again."

She splashes me, grinning.

I love that grin.

Looking at her, I am centered. The fist closes, and I am myself, back in my skin. I know that skin is fragile. I feel that sickening need to punish it, to get control of it, but I can't right now. Focusing on Astarti works just as well, but it lasts only so long as I don't take my eyes from her. That's the problem. I can't rely on that. I have to control myself on my own. But since I can't do that right now, I let Astarti help me, whether she knows she's helping or not.

She scoops up more water to wash her face. The combination of yellow-gray dust and water has turned her clothes into a muddy mess. I glance down at my own and find them equally filthy.

I scoot off my rock to crouch in the water. My left knee, the bad one, cracks loudly.

I scrub my own face with the cool, clear water. When I stand, Astarti is looking down the length of the crevice. There's a bend ahead, so we can't see anything, but I hear the sound of voices.

I follow Astarti through the water, catching her when she stumbles. The earth is a rocky mess, the stones slippery. When we round the bend, the crevice opens onto a basin. Heborian and his Drifters splash through hip-deep water, gathering floating pieces of white bone. Though they are fragments, they're clearly too large to be human. The men toss the largest pieces up onto the ledge of the basin and leave the splinters floating.

They have no right to disturb these bones, to mine a power not their own.

Heborian hurls a long, heavy bone up to the dry ground. He catches his breath and says, "Good work."

I close my hands into fists. "You shouldn't take these."

He gives me a measuring look. "No one needs them. Except me."

I bite out, "And what will you do with them?"

"I thought I made that clear. These will be weapons to defeat our enemy. Isn't that what you want?"

Astarti touches my wet sleeve. "Logan. You've seen the power of the knife. We need everything we can use against Belos."

Logically, I know she's right, that Heborian is right. But in my gut, this feels wrong, wrong, wrong.

80 03

We travel the Drift back to Tornelaine with the bones and our half-dead prisoner in tow. As always, I hate being here.

Energy swirls around us. Astarti, beautiful in her energy form, looks at me with worry, as though I am doing this. I don't think I am. I try to bury all the energies threatening to escape my control. Maybe something is getting out.

Energy whispers over us. The Drifters speed up, and Astarti pulls me along faster. I know I should be able to move myself through the Drift, but to do that I would have to release some of my energy, to use it.

I don't want to do that. It would be like trying to pump a cupful of water from the ground and accidently bursting a dam. I let Astarti pull me along instead.

As we draw closer to the bright glow of Tornelaine, the energy around us grows increasingly agitated. It passes over all of us, lingering on me, swirling around the gleaming white energy of the bones.

When we reach Heborian's barrier, I brace myself for the squeeze, then gasp in relief as I am thrown into the physical world.

As the guards swing open the heavy gates to let us into the courtyard, the hair rises on the back of my neck. The air crackles with energy, much as the Drift did. Clouds roll in with unnatural speed, and thunder booms overhead.

Everyone goes still.

We aren't alone.

Lightning splits the sky, then the rain starts. Light at first, then it comes in heavy, angry drops.

A figure appears in the rain, and I recognize the Old One who tried to sink the ship. She is both part of the rain and not. She floats to the pile of bones, which someone dropped. She traces a tender, ghostly hand over them.

Drift-light glows around all the Drifters as they prepare for attack. She ignores them.

She turns to me, moving in and through the rain. Her rainy hand touches my face. In that brief touch, I feel a power like my own, elemental and wild.

But I picture the ship, full of lives that meant nothing to her. Astarti was aboard that ship.

I harden myself, clenching the fist that holds me together. Because it's not enough, and those fingers are too weak, I look to the one person who can save me from myself.

The Old One follows my eyes to Astarti, who stands a few feet away, drenched in rain and unmoving. Astarti watches me with sad, accepting eyes. She believes I will leave her.

I close my own eyes to shut that out before it drives a knife into me. When I open my eyes again, there is nothing but the rain.

CHAPTER 9

Sitting propped against the headboard, I keep my Drift-light faintly glowing. My foot is pressed to Logan's hip, waiting. I yawn at my book, and the lines of text blur. I blink a few times to clear my vision. I reread a paragraph. The book is a collection of Runish tales. It's a translation, so I don't know how much has been altered from the original, but I'm finding it difficult to make sense of these stories. In the one that keeps going blurry, the gods walk backward along a river, growing younger around each bend.

Logan twitches, and I am suddenly wide awake. He mumbles something in his sleep, then relaxes. The sheet is pulled up to his chest, hiding the bruising, but I can picture it well enough. I will not let him do that again.

He sleeps quietly for a while, and I go back to my book. One of the gods trips on a stone and complains, "That wasn't here before." Another laughs, "Did you imagine the river would be the same? Walk it again tomorrow, or yesterday, and it will be changed once more."

Logan twitches again. His arm jerks, and I lay my fingers on his shoulder. He settles only briefly before the shudders start through his body. I drop the book and shake him gently. His muscles are knotted tight, his torso and neck straining and slick with sudden sweat. He makes a choking sound, and I shout his name, shaking him harder.

He lurches up. His hand shoots out, fingers spread as though clenched around someone's throat. He is snarling, furious.

I lay my fingers on his rigid arm. I say his name a few times before he gasps. His arm drops. His stomach jerks with his harsh breathing.

When he starts to throw the sheet aside, I spread my hand low on his belly, pinning the sheet. "No."

He is frozen, undecided. He won't look at me.

"Come here. *Logan.*"

He pulls away and swings his legs out of the bed. He props his elbows on his knees. My Drift-light paints cool blue over his sweat-slick, scarred back.

I slide out of bed and grab the waiting cup from the washstand. I hurry around the foot of the bed before he can get up. I crouch before him, but he still doesn't look at me. His fingers are laced together, twisting.

"Please don't leave," I beg him.

He takes a shuddering breath. He hasn't said a word. I lay my hand on his thigh. He's shaking like he's cold, but his skin is too warm. I tighten my fingers, asking him to look at me, but he doesn't.

I press the cup at his hands. His fingers twitch away from it. "Please," I implore. "Don't leave."

Slowly, his hands unclench, and he takes the cup. I hold my breath when he hesitates with it halfway to his mouth. He puts it to his lips and drinks.

I let him sit there for a few minutes, but the fast-working sedative soon makes him sway. I nudge him until he lies down. Right before the drug takes him, his eyes meet mine. His eyes beg me for something, but I don't know what. His pain dissolves into oblivion.

℘ ℜ

I wake with a start, then ease back to my pillow when I feel Logan beside me. Morning light paints his face gold and gleams in the waves of his hair. I brush my knuckles along his stubble-roughened cheek, but he doesn't stir.

He never shifted positions during the night, and he lies so still that I sit up, worried. I press my fingers to his throat, right under his jaw. His pulse beats a regular, steady rhythm.

I slip from the bed and tug on my clothes, watching Logan all the while. If I hurry, maybe I can make it back before he wakes.

As I cross through the sitting room, I hear someone moving about in the adjoining suite. Though that suite was meant to be mine, I haven't done more than gather clothes from it since Logan and I returned to Tornelaine. I go to the door between the suites. I'm sure it's nothing, but suspicion is a deeply ingrained habit.

When I catch a few notes of Clara's humming, I quietly back away from the door. A floorboard creaks, and I freeze. Clara's humming cuts off. Her light footsteps approach the door. She knocks. I curse silently and debate whether or not to answer.

"Astarti?" she calls quietly through the door.

I sigh and open it.

Clara sucks in a disapproving breath when she sees me. Her soft brown hair is pulled into an elegant knot at the nape of her neck, and her gown of green and white silk sweeps along the

69

feminine curves of her body. Her fingers twitch as she eyes my hair, and I resist the urge to scrape the loose pieces away from my face.

"Not today," I say quietly. "I have things to do."

Disappointment pinches the skin around her eyes. "I could just—"

"Nope. Sorry. No time."

Frustration gets the better of her. "But you're really quite lovely, underneath it all. You never do anything to show it."

I stare at her in disbelief. "You do realize we're in the middle of a war?" Fear moves through her eyes, so I soften my tone. "What does my hair matter, at a time like this?"

She knots her fingers. "It's my job. I don't have anything else to do."

I want to say it's a not a very important job, but Clara doesn't deserve my meanness. Even so, I can't delay any longer simply to make her feel better. "Another time."

"Really?"

Oh, dear. Have I just made a promise? "On the right occasion. Not today." Hopefully that's vague enough.

Her lips tug up in a smile. "It's a deal."

Fingers walk up my spine at the word. Of all the deals I've brokered, surely this one is the most harmless. "Deal," I echo, letting the word mean nothing more than it really does.

I walk down several hallways, moving steadily toward the infirmary. With any luck, the Healers won't be there yet and I can get a good supply of sedative from Heborian's physician, Renald. It's not that the Healers wouldn't give it to me, but they would ask questions. I don't want to lie to Logan's mother, but Logan should choose what he tells her.

The quickest route takes me past the yawning double doors of the throne room. The hum of voices from within makes me pause. I lean against one of the ornately carved and gilded doors, which stretches to a sharp peak some twenty feet above me.

I've never been inside the throne room, nor have I known Heborian to use it. He is perhaps a little too Runish to make use of such an imperious space. The huge, rectangular room with its vaulted ceiling is lined with columns. Morning light, bright from yesterday's rain, filters through the high, stained-glass windows, casting amber, blue, and yellow light over the gathered Earthmaker Council. Several dozen Earthmakers sit on long benches set in a semicircle, taking up less than a quarter of the room's space. Behind them, a dais rises several feet to elevate an ornate, gold-leaf throne.

Heborian has granted permission for the Council to use this room for its sessions. Such sessions, I'm told, are public by Earthmaker law. However, their definition of "public" is that other Earthmakers may attend, though they are not to speak unless addressed by a Council member. Heborian insisted that, in his castle, public would mean anyone could listen, and I spot Heborian and his advisor, Wulfstan, on one of the benches.

Of course, Heborian allotted the Council this particular room for a reason. Even though he sits on the benches with everyone else, the throne oversees the discussion, reminding the Earthmakers who really holds power here.

I'm told the Council room in the House of the Arcon is circular and has stone benches that rise level by level to overlook a round speaking floor. No doubt that would lend the whole enterprise a bit more grandeur than can be managed here with the mismatched benches and everyone craning their necks to see the speaker of the moment.

I don't recognize the man in the center of the semicircle. He turns as he speaks, addressing everyone. He wears a typical Earthmaker under-tunic and loose cross-body robes gathered at one shoulder.

"We need information," he proclaims. "How can we make decisions, how can we guide our Wardens to proper action when we know nothing of what the Unnamed plans?"

Aron speaks from a bench. "And how should we discover his plans, Counselor Argos? The Wood has burned. We cannot reach Avydos, not in secret, not even openly."

Polemarc Clitus stands from beside Aron. "I will say it again: we must put ourselves under King Heborian's command."

Those around Heborian stiffen, and Counselor Argos argues, "No disrespect, Polemarc, but are you so eager to abandon your authority? No disrespect to Heborian either"—he notably leaves off Heborian's title—"but we are allies, not subordinates."

"You are missing the point, Counselor," insists Clitus. "We have not the luxury—"

Someone behind me says, "Eighty-five years since I've see this, and nothing has changed."

I spin to find the Earthmaker from the whaling ship standing with his arms crossed, scowling over my shoulder at the gathering. He is dressed like a sailor in salt-stained sandals, loose linen trousers and a billowing shirt, but there's no mistaking those eyes or that particular stillness of the face that even being Stricken cannot change. At least, Logan says that must have been the man's fate.

The Earthmaker backs out of my space and looks me over. "You are Astarti, the king's daughter. You saved our ship. I did not thank you."

"Logan brought us in, not me."

"He is your lover?"

Heat blooms in my face at the blunt words.

The Earthmaker makes no note of my discomfort, only says bitterly, "Let us hope that some things, at least, have changed in that Council room."

"Is that why you were…?"

"Stricken," he says sharply. "You can say it, girl; it's just a word."

He seems very alone, and I can't help wondering what became of the one for whom he gave up so much. The question must be written on my face because the Earthmaker's eyes soften a little, and he says, "I gave her all I could, but long life was not in my power."

"I'm sorry."

His lips thin. "Your man. What is he? I'm told he's the Prima's son, but he looks nothing like I remember Arathos. Oh, don't look so angry. I don't care if he's a bastard. I'm only curious. Those creatures—he moves like them."

"Creatures? Did you abandon your gods along with your people?"

Anger flashes through his eyes. "I abandoned nothing."

Benches scrape inside the throne room. Voices mix, growing conversational, and footsteps ring across the marble floor.

The Earthmaker edges away even as I do. "Good day to you, Astarti."

I grit my teeth as he turns away. He knows my name, but I didn't ask his. I don't like feeling at a disadvantage. But the Earthmaker disappears around a corner, so I head on my own way.

My heart sinks when I peer into the infirmary. Feluvas hovers over a worktable, sniffing one steaming bowl, then another. She adds a pinch of gray powder to one, a few drops of something to the other. Korinna and Gaiana sit on one of beds lining the wall, speaking with a heavily pregnant woman. Gaiana hands the woman a packet and offers instruction on the dosage of the herbs within.

Renald isn't here. I start to edge away.

"Astarti," Gaiana calls and beckons me inside.

73

Caught, I force a smile.

Gaiana and Korinna help the woman to her feet and lead her to the door. We all watch the poor woman waddle down the hall.

Gaiana comments, "As if bearing a child isn't stressful enough, she must do it during this awful time. She is not the only one. Life was in the middle of happening for us all."

I make a sound of agreement.

Gaiana adds in a low voice, "It's something I've been wanting to talk to you about. Korinna? If you would help Feluvas?"

I shift uncomfortably as Korinna hurries away. Gaiana motions me into the room. The only escape would be through horrible rudeness, and I can't quite make myself do it. Gaiana has been kind to me from the beginning.

She sits on one of the beds. I perch stiffly on the edge of the one across from her. Our knees almost touch. Mine are enclosed in tight woolen breeches, hers draped with a filmy robe.

She gets right to it. "Astarti, have you been taking precautions?"

"Precautions?"

"To see that you don't become pregnant."

My cheeks flame.

"There's nothing to be embarrassed about, child. But you should be wise. This is a dangerous time."

"I, um…I don't have regular courses. I haven't had one for months." Not since the time I spent in Belos's dungeon before I even met Logan, long before we lay together. My palms break out with sweat. I have never discussed this sort of thing with anyone, and she is Logan's mother, of all people.

A line wedges between her brows. "That happens sometimes. Stress, malnourishment, many things. I can give you something for it."

My face is absolutely on fire. "No, it's fine. Honestly, it's a blessing right now."

She nods understanding but says, "All the same, that is very hard on your body. You may want children someday, and you must take care of yourself."

I give a jittery laugh, though nothing is funny.

Gaiana gives me a small, warm smile. "I'm sorry. I tend to forget that you've spent precious little time with other women. It must have been difficult for you, when your courses first came."

My ears are surely about to burst into flames. Difficult is one word for it, mortifying might be another. I thought I was dying. Gods, how Belos and the Seven laughed at me.

Gaiana doesn't push, but she does insist, "It would be best for you to take a contraceptive anyway if you do not wish to find yourself with child unexpectedly. If you want, discuss it with Logan first."

Oh, gods. We really are talking about this.

A thought rises through my discomfort. She knows I am sleeping with her son. She knows what that could mean for him, yet she doesn't seem upset. I recall the words she once whispered to me. *Take care of him.* As though she knew this would happen, as though she accepts it. I have to ask, "You're not…worried about him?"

Emotion shimmers in her eyes: tears, maybe, or simple fear. "I am deeply worried about him, but not because of you."

"But your Council. Your laws."

"Nothing will be the same again, Astarti. Avydos will never be the same, nor will its people."

I think of the Council session I just witnessed, and I'm not so sure. I tell her this, but she shakes her head.

"Even if nothing changed among our people, I would feel the same. Even if you were not as much Earthmaker as he is, I would feel this way. I've had no hope for him for a long time. You've given it back to me, and I thank you for that. He is better, so much better, with you."

I gnaw on my lip. I can't believe that. He turns away from me. He hurts himself. I haven't helped him at all. And what I am seeking now is a flimsy bandage for a gaping wound. I push sedatives at him because I don't know what else to do. How, then, is that better?

"You don't believe me," Gaiana says, "but I see the truth. You will, too, in time."

Now the confession spills from me. "He cannot sleep unless I drug him. He will not speak to me about any of it. I don't know what to do."

Gaiana lays a cool hand over my clenched fist. "Bones that have not set right must be rebroken before they can be Healed. But I'm a coward, and I always make Feluvas do that. She has a strong stomach, like you do."

I frown. Rebroken?

Footsteps in the doorway cause me and Gaiana to look up. Bran says, "Ah, good. Farston said you were headed this way, Astarti. Heborian has called a meeting. He's requested you come to his study at once."

"I can't," I tell him. "I have to check on Logan."

"Logan is already there."

I jump to my feet. "He was dead asleep not twenty minutes ago."

"Heborian woke him, apparently."

I lurch forward, fuming, as Gaiana rises smoothly. She catches my arm. "Think about what I've said. If you want the herbs, I have them."

"Thank you."

I find myself pulling ahead of Bran as we pass through hallway after hallway. I force myself to slow down. "You have no idea what this is about?"

"It's an odd gathering. You and I, Logan, Heborian, Wulfstan, and Farston? I can't begin to guess."

"Who's Farston?"

"The Earthmaker from the whaling ship."

I frown. It is an odd group. Neither Aron nor Clitus have been called, so whatever is to be discussed won't involve a collective decision. Not that Heborian makes many of those. And yet, few Drifters will be there, and that worries me even more. If action is to be taken following this meeting—and Heborian isn't one to talk and do nothing—it's not hard to guess who will be called on.

℘ ℘

When the guards open the double doors to Heborian's study, my eyes fly straight to where Logan sits in one of the armchairs. His head leans against the chair back. His eyes are half closed, his lips slightly parted. I had also meant to ask Renald for something to dispel grogginess.

While Bran enters the room, I wait impatiently for Heborian to finish his instructions to the guards. Apparently, we're not to be disturbed. Before the guards can close us inside, I snag Heborian's elbow and pull him into the foyer.

He lifts an eyebrow.

"Don't ever go into our rooms without knocking."

"I did knock. No one answered."

"So you just sauntered in when you thought we were out? It's bad enough having the servants do that."

"I knew he was in there and you weren't. I needed him here. What's your problem? You didn't want me to see you've been drugging him? I already knew that."

I glare because there's nothing else *to* do.

Heborian presses on. "Was that the amount Renald recommended? Because he was way out. He's still pretty out of it."

"You should have asked me to wake him. Next time, see that you do."

"Oh, settle down. And, no, you can't shoot arrows from your eyes to kill me, so stop trying. Now, can we begin?"

I glare at Heborian's back as I follow him into the room, but habit prevails and I turn my attention to the room's other occupants. The old Earthmaker, Farston, stands by the empty fireplace. His crossed arms and scowling expression make clear he doesn't want to be here. Farston. It's not an Earthmaker name. Did he take a new one, perhaps, when his people struck his from memory?

Wulfstan also holds himself apart from the gathering. He stands behind the chairs, his hip leaning against a table covered in maps. Bran sits with comfortable patience, though his eyes are on his brother.

Logan rouses when I near his chair. He rubs a hand across his face and inhales deeply, trying to wake himself up. His rumpled tunic is unlaced, exposing his collarbone and the upper edge of the shiny scar that arcs across his left pectoral. His eyes are flat blue, a little dull. Maybe I did give him too much last night. He meets my gaze and blinks slowly. By the time I've settled into the chair beside him, he's slumping again.

Guilt makes me glance in Bran's direction. His eyes travel from Logan to me and back to Logan.

"I'm sure you all want to know what this is about," Heborian begins, "but I will only say that it's about questions."

Those, of course, will be Heborian's questions and no one else's. We all seem to know this, and we are silent, bound by curiosity and by his commanding presence.

"Farston," Heborian says, and all eyes jump to the Earthmaker standing so stiffly before the fireplace. "You tell me you remember Belos as a child." Surprise makes my eyebrows jump, both at the connection between Farston and Belos, and to think of Belos ever having been a child at all. "You said he was curious about the Ancorites, that he asked for books about them."

Logan's head comes up at the mention of the Ancorites.

"Yes," Farston confirms, "but as I explained, there are no books about them. I was curator for the Arcon's library, and I traveled far and wide to build the collection of Prima Gaiana's father, who was Arcon at the time. But I never found anything directly about the Ancorites. I told Belos this."

"And how did he respond?"

"He was frustrated. He began to ask questions about the Drift, and he told me—years later—that he believed the Ancorites made use of the Drift."

I saw this for myself, when the Ancorites tried to bind Logan as they had the Old Ones. Belos, it seems, was way ahead of me. As usual.

Heborian demands, "But *why* was Belos interested? Did he suspect, even then, that the Ancorites had trapped the gods?"

I glance at Logan. A little of the fog has cleared from his expression, but his eyes are still flat blue. I'm almost glad he's too groggy to absorb all this. Heborian should know better than to throw Logan into such discussions.

Farston protests, "I don't know. He gave me no indication of that. But." Farston pauses, remembering. "He did find an interesting passage in an old volume that the Arcon later burned. I can't remember every detail, but Belos kept saying that the Ancorites had bound time. He was obsessed with that book."

Heborian's brow furrows. "What does that mean? They 'bound time'?"

Farston shrugs. "The book was the ravings of a madman. It was terribly disjointed, out of order and full of tangents. The author went on and on about time. He said it was fluid, whatever that meant. The one line I recall clearly is this: 'Time makes children of us all.' Belos would mutter that under his breath as he read. He was a strange child, but he had a sharp, curious mind."

"Thank you, Farston, that is all." Everyone startles at the abrupt dismissal, but Farston strides stiffly from the room without comment.

"What is this about?" I demand.

Heborian waits for the door to shut. "Doesn't it make you wary that Belos hasn't attacked us? None of the Seven have even been seen. What does he really want? Why did he Leash the Old One? He didn't need to. Avydos would have burned regardless." Heborian's eyes flick to Bran. "Primo Branos, are you familiar with the book Farston described? Is there another copy perhaps?"

"I've never heard of that book."

"But the ideas are familiar?"

"Not exactly. Though…" Bran frowns, looking thoughtful. "I did find one particularly puzzling line in an old manuscript. It said: 'time lies within all the elements.' I have no idea what the writer meant by that, but something about it stuck with me."

Wulfstan interjects, "Creation is destruction, life and death the same."

I look up in surprise. Sunhild, Heborian's mother and Wulfstan's sister, used those same words. She told us that the Runians hold that truth dear. "What does that mean?"

Wulfstan explains, "It means many things, but one is that our future and past lie within the present. We carry our birth and death with us always. This is fate, immutable, inescapable."

Puzzling over that, I don't notice Heborian dismissing Bran until the door opens and closes.

Heborian says grimly, "Astarti, I've given him all the time I can. More than I should have. I need to know."

My nape prickles with warning. "What, exactly, do you need to know?"

"You wouldn't push him, so I must."

CHAPTER 10

LOGAN

I swim up from my foggy pit when Astarti's voice rises. "Push him to what?"

"Don't argue with me, girl, or I will continue this without you."

I roll my head in Astarti's direction. She teeters on the edge of her chair, undecided about something.

Heborian calls my name, and I focus on him with difficulty. What is wrong with my head? It feels like there's a blanket wrapped around it, muffling everything. Heborian waits for some sign from me, which I must give because he says, "Belos was very interested in the nature of your power. Did he suspect, from the beginning, what you are?"

The words skitter along the edges of my mind, not reaching all the way through the fog. "I don't know."

"You were possessed by him. You must have experienced some portion of his thoughts."

That makes something quicken inside me, something I don't like. I don't answer.

"Did he intend, all along, to Leash the Old One?"

Kronos, I want to say, but my mouth doesn't work. My thoughts seep away like water into sand. I let my eyes close.

"For the love of the gods, Astarti, what did you *give* him?"

"Renald gave it to me."

I hear shifting bottles, then Heborian crosses the room toward me. My eyes open as he crouches before my chair. Memory shudders through me. Astarti, crouched like that, smiling coldly, delighted by my revulsion. But it wasn't her. It was Belos, toying with me. I growl, at the memory, at Heborian.

He pulls the stopper from a small glass bottle and wafts it under my nose. My consciousness explodes. Morning light streaming through the window slashes into my awareness. The room and people around me solidify, like a dream sharpening to reality.

I push up from my chair, shaking my head. Heborian shifts out of my way, stoppering the smelling salts. I stride past Wulfstan, who edges away from me. I lean on the windowsill. The ocean lies in the distance. Avydos is a black, unmoving spot.

How long have I been like this?

Astarti's boots sound a cautious approach. She stops beside me, not touching.

"Don't ever give me that shit again." My temper must surprise her because she jolts a little, but I need her to understand that I *must* be in control of myself—my mind, my body. "I'd rather—"

"Let's not talk about this here."

My scalp prickles as I sense the energies of Heborian and Wulfstan. I rake my hair back and take a deep breath, clearing the last of the fog from my mind. What has been happening here? Snatches of the conversation float up through my memory. Belos. The Old Ones. Something about time? I turn to face Heborian across the room.

He nods when he sees my attention. "Logan, we need to understand how Belos intends to use the one he's Leashed. You agree?"

I do, but I hate this little game of let's-all-be-reasonable. I grunt.

"If we can't determine that from what we already know, we'll need fresh information. You are the only one who can give us that information, either from your memory or from reconnaissance."

"It will have to be fresh information because I don't know what he intends."

"When he possessed you—"

I shudder involuntarily as the memory of Belos's possession slides through me. I feel it in my blood, my bones, in the deepest parts of myself.

Heborian must know me pretty well by now because he doesn't waste time pursuing what I won't give him; he changes course.

"The Ancorites. Some of them may yet live. We need to know where they will stand in this."

"Where do you think? They will stand where they always have."

"And where is that?"

"They will want the Old Ones bound again."

Heborian falls silent, and I don't like it. What is he thinking? The thought closes behind his expression. "And you? Will they want you bound as well?"

This time I'm prepared, and when the memories threaten to crowd in on me, I force them back. "Of course."

"Can they do it?"

"I have no idea. Why? Do you want them to?"

"I need to know that you can get past them."

Astarti says in a warning tone, "Heborian…"

Heborian nods to me. "He wants to do it. I can see it in his face."

I try to still myself, but anticipation hums through me. "When do I go?"

"If you're going to do this, I need you focused. There will be specific goals. If you can't stay focused, this will be pointless, and you'll only get yourself captured or killed."

Astarti snarls, "You are *not* sending him to Avydos."

"He's the only one who could possibly go, and we must know what's happening there. No matter the cost."

℘ ℭ

I skim through wind and water, whipping toward the black hulk of Avydos. I force myself to slow before I reach the arms of the horseshoe bay. As I slide through the rocky gateway, I see at once that Avydos is not quite as desolate as it looked from Tornelaine. The Wood is destroyed, certainly, a black plain rising to the blackened slope of Mount Hypatia. But a sharp line lies behind the city, a towering rough wall that halted the flow of liquid fire. The city's white buildings still stand, though they are gray with smoke and ash.

I drift through the empty streets, wending my way to the House of the Arcon.

The air is heavy with energy. It weighs me down, clouds my mind. He's here, the Old One. In the air, in the water, in the earth.

Overlaying it all is the taint of Belos and the Seven. Their energies slide over his like oil over water.

I float through the paved courtyard of the Arcon's house, but the doors ahead are closed. I drift around the side of the house to the open balustrade. It takes every ounce of my will to hold myself to the slow, thoughtless pace of a breeze. The need to *move* builds inside me like a thunderstorm.

I pass between the columns of the balustrade and into the long entry hall. Though everything outside is dull with ash, the Arcon's House has been scrubbed clean. The white and gray patterned floor gleams in the afternoon light.

The bitter and seething energies of some of Belos's Seven are gathered in the dining hall. I can't pinpoint Belos himself. Deeper in the house, in the kitchens, I feel the trembling energies of five or six people. I drift that direction.

Two women tending the bread ovens look up when I breeze into the dim, warm room. I draw myself into a smaller knot, force myself to slow, to be nothing. After a moment, they turn their attention to the ovens again. Another woman and a man hunch over a broad worktable, their wooden spoons whipping around their bowls. A girl of about thirteen crouches before the open fire, stirring the steaming soup in a cast-iron pot hung over the flames. The girl sniffs loudly from time to time, wiping her nose on the back of her sleeve.

"Dela, will you *stop* that sniveling," chides one of the women as she shuts the door to the bread oven.

"I can't help it! It's almost dinner time. I will have to go in!" Dela bursts into tears. "None of you understand!"

The woman's shoulders droop. She shuffles over to the girl and kneels beside her. "Come here, child," she says gently, holding out her arms. Dela throws herself into them, sobbing.

Angry currents spool away from me. What have they done to this girl?

Pots rattle on their ceiling hooks. The flames dance under the soup pot. The woman and girl scramble away from the fire.

"It's him!" Dela cries, frantically grabbing at the woman. Everyone in the room cringes, ducking instinctively.

I forcefully gather my energies back to myself and slide from the room. The girl's cries follow me down the hallway.

I pause in a quiet corner. If I cannot control myself, I might as well leave. I'm here to listen, to gather information. I force my body to take shape because my body, I can control. I lean against the cool stone wall, breathing calm through myself.

Heborian knows as well as I do that I'm not suited to this task. Unfortunately, no one else can listen in. The Drifters could conceal themselves within the Drift, but all they would be able to do is spot the locations of Belos and his men. They would not be able to hear anything.

I take measured breaths until I am calm. I want nothing more than to go back to the kitchens and get everyone out. It's hard to remember the larger goal when something else so important lies right before me.

After, I promise myself. After I find out what Belos plans, I will come back for them. I let myself dissolve into the air.

As I float into the dining hall, I recoil at the wash of tainted energies. They all have a touch of his oiliness.

The dining hall is a rectangular room with a long table running down the center. One side of the room is partially open. The wall comes to about three feet, then columns rise to support the roof. The view was once of the Wood, but now there is nothing to see but a charred slope and the blackened remains of trees.

Four of the Seven lounge on the long benches at the far end of the table. I float near, and they shiver.

"I hate this place," mutters one, rubbing his arms. Devos, I think he's called.

"Quit whining," chides another. Ludos maybe? "It's better than the Dry Land."

"Not by much," says Devos stubbornly. "*This* is not what we were promised."

"Well, *this*"—Ludos gestures around—"is not the end of it. Stop complaining, before he notices."

Devos sighs and rests his head on his arms, which are crossed on the table. Ludos and the other two—Theron and Maxos—slump on the benches. They look exhausted, and I don't know what to make of that. There have been no attacks on Tornelaine. As far as we know, they haven't been doing anything. Why, then, are they so tired?

Suddenly, they all raise their heads and look at each other.

One says, "He's coming. He found it."

The others nod agreement.

They climb to their feet, backs straight.

Only then do I feel him, sliding near through the Drift. How did they know before I did?

Belos, flanked by Koricus and Straton, steps from the Drift. The three of them are soaking wet. Belos's blond hair is slicked back, his leather vest hanging soddenly. He raises his hand to show off the gleaming Shackle in his grip. I recoil, sweeping through the open wall. Belos scowls over his shoulder, as though unsurprised by the sudden draft. He seats himself at the table and drops the Shackle onto it.

"He tried to stop me from getting it. He continues to be difficult."

"We need more energy," says Straton, taking a seat beside Belos. "Why not hit some of the smaller towns, Take a few humans? Or go to Rune. There are still Drifters there."

Belos sneers, "None of you comprehend him. You feel an edge of his power, but you don't really know. Kronos is a hurricane, and you want to hold him in a teacup."

I swirl with agitation. Kronos. That *is* his name. Where did that knowledge come from? Where, for that matter, did that vision of him and me and my mother come from? It felt like a dream, but there was truth in it.

Ludos glances over his shoulder. "Is that him?"

Belos frowns. "It must be, though I thought him deeper. After we found the Shackle in whatever that place was—the ocean, the Drift?—he was…displeased. He's pouting."

Belos rubs his face, then rests his chin on his fist. He looks wearier even than the others. Dark circles hang under his eyes. He's thinner than I remember. Fat and muscle have worn away to expose a body of sharp angles. But the eyes are the same. Too bright a blue, too keen, too cruel. I shudder at the memory of his mind within mine. He found all the things I had hidden so deep and brought them out. I still haven't been able to put them back.

Koricus gestures at Belos's chest. "Bleeding again."

Belos grunts annoyance. The wound Astarti dealt him in the battle for Tornelaine looks less healed rather than more. Belos takes a white napkin and presses it to the wound. Blood quickly soaks through.

Suddenly, one of the Seven—Rhode, I think—cries out. He grips the edge of the table, white-knuckled.

Straton looks from Rhode to Belos with resentment burning in his eyes. "We need one of the Drifters. Heborian, Astarti, any of Heborian's Drifters. Or, better yet, Gaiana's son."

"What a fine idea." Belos's words drip with sarcasm.

Fresh anger slides through me. He will *never* Leash Astarti again. And I will die before I let him touch me.

Heborian warned me I would hear these things. I told him I could handle it.

I was wrong.

I slide near Belos, hovering over his shoulder. Wouldn't his death serve us better than information? Isn't that the ultimate goal?

KATHERINE BUEL

The instant I curl fingers of air around his throat, he vanishes into the Drift. My hands close on nothing.

Belos reappears across the room. "Be on your guard," he commands, but the Seven are already on their feet, Drift-weapons in hand.

My unspent anger swirls within me, seeping out. Tapestries flutter on the walls. Straton's black cloak flaps.

"The Ancorites?" asks Devos uneasily.

"I don't know," Belos snaps. "Something touched me."

"Not Kronos?"

"I don't think so."

"An Ancorite, then," says Rhode. "If we catch him, let's Shackle him."

Belos snarls, "If you can find a wrist to put the Shackle on."

"You got Kronos, didn't you?"

"Do you forget, Rhode, that Kronos was weakened and unprepared? Do you think the Ancorites will be?"

Light footsteps approach from the hall. The girl, Dela, halts in the doorway, a tray in her hands. The teapot rattles loudly.

"Her!" shouts Koricus. "Leash her!"

He vanishes into the Drift and reappears beside Dela, who screams and drops the tray. The teapot shatters, and Koricus leaps back from the gush of hot tea.

"You fool!" Belos shouts. "You think *she* will make one bit of difference? Focus! It's stirring! It's the Old Ones!"

But it's not. It's me. I try to reel it back in, to hide myself, to make this nothing. Maybe I can salvage something of this. Be calm, listen. That's all I'm here to do.

Then I feel them. The Ancorites.

They drift into the room like a dry wind. They swirl around me, whispering. Fingers like bare bones slide through my energies. I shudder—with revulsion, with fear, with rage.

Bind him, they whisper. *Bind him.*

Something snaps inside me. Even without my body, the sensation is physical. I yell, and it is a wind howling down a mountainside. I claw and scrape at the Ancorites, mindless with rage, but they float through my grasp like smoke.

"Logan!" shouts Belos. "Is that you?"

I wheel. Belos!

I streak toward him, half wind, half myself. I want to feel his body break in my hands. The Ancorites are clawing at me, scraping their bony fingers through my energies.

I barrel into Belos, driving him into the wall. My hands solidify around his throat. His face purples, and I revel in the power I have over him.

Glowing bands of Drift-energy loop around my wrists, jerking me away from Belos. I explode through the binding, a gust of wind. But the freedom is short-lived. The Ancorites are clawing, tearing, scrabbling for a hold on my energies. I whirl, flinging them off me.

I need more power. I need something stronger than air. I plunge into the stony floor and the earth below, electrified by the crack and boom as the floor breaks.

I tear through the rocky bones of the earth, letting them explode, letting all that strength and power *do* something.

A deep and ponderous energy stirs. I call his name through stone—*Kronos!*—and it is a rocky grumble, the sound primordial and awesome.

We burst through the floor, and his face, ancient and craggy, shapes itself briefly. His rocky hand reaches for me with curiosity and gentleness. Then he cries out with the most terrible sound I have ever heard. It is the earth breaking; it is unending pain.

I wheel on Belos. He stands on the splintered table, his face tight with concentration. Kronos moans.

Furious, I slam my fist into the shattered floor. The boom ripples through the earth, and the walls shudder. Columns crack and crumble. I will bring down this whole house just to bury Belos in it.

A high-pitched scream pierces my fury. A girl's scream.

Horror slides through me like cold water. I wrench free of the earth and whip through the air to where Dela lies crying, her leg pinned under a fallen column. She whimpers at my approach. I throw the column aside with a gust of wind. She scrambles away from me, dragging her broken leg. I latch onto her. She screams.

The Ancorites tear at me again. Dela howls, and the Ancorites tear at her. Belos shouts. Kronos rises from the floor, a rocky giant. His eyes are empty, belonging to someone else. He lunges for me.

I shape Dela into the wind and blast through the open wall.

CHAPTER 11

I stand on the battlements with Heborian, waiting, as the sun sinks toward the sea. A boom sounds from distant Avydos, and the shock travels the ocean floor to reverberate through the stones under my feet. Below, the ocean tosses in response.

My heart skitters.

"Astarti," Heborian says warningly, drawing out the syllables of my name.

I start to rise up, dissolving, feeling my way between the currents. Heborian persuaded me to let Logan go alone, that I would only give us away. But something is happening, and the time for subtlety is over. Heborian's voice grows distant.

When a gust hits me, the power is unreal, shattering. I scramble for purchase, for control, but I go tumbling away like fluff on the wind. Then he surrounds me and eases me back to my body. For that moment, I am not the master of myself; I am mere matter to be shaped. Even though it's Logan, I don't like the feeling.

We emerge from the wind to the sound of crying. A young girl tears away from Logan, sobbing with terror. She crawls away, dragging a bloody, broken leg. She runs up against Heborian and throws her arms around his knees.

Logan is rigid beside me. I glance up to find his face like stone, though his eyes swirl with green and blue. A muscle is etched in his jaw.

He doesn't respond when I say his name.

"Astarti?" calls Heborian. "A little help?"

I reluctantly leave Logan standing like a statue and kneel beside the girl. She grabs my hands, wringing them so hard the bones grind.

"Hush," I say, "hush. You're safe."

She sobs into my shoulder.

I hear Logan approach. So does the girl. She glances up, and her crying intensifies. Logan backs away.

In all the time it takes to get the girl down to the infirmary and into the Healers' hands, Logan doesn't say a word. Even as he, Heborian, and I walk to Heborian's study, Logan is silent. By the time we get to the study, my shoulders are hunched with tension.

As soon as the door clicks shut, I wheel on him. "What happened?"

"What do you think? I hurt her." His eyes are wild and dangerous, but his body is unnaturally still, as though he hardly trusts himself to breathe.

Heborian says calmly, "Start from the beginning."

Logan's report comes out in fragments and bursts, drawn from him by Heborian's questions. He stiffens further every time I approach, clearly not wanting to be touched.

When Heborian says, "That's enough. Go get yourself cleaned up," Logan turns mechanically for the door.

"Wait!" I jog after him.

Logan pauses with his hand on the latch. His head is bowed. "Astarti, I can't." They are the first words he's said directly to me, and I don't even know what they mean.

"Logan—"

"I'm sorry," he says. "I can't."

He fumbles with the latch, wrenching the door open. I rock forward as he storms out.

"Astarti," Heborian calls from behind. "Let him go."

I glance over my shoulder. "You said that to me once before. I didn't listen then. I don't intend to now."

"I need you here. It's more important. You can find him later, when he's ready to be found."

I exhale an angry breath. Logan disappears around a corner. He doesn't want me—that's clear enough—and I doubt I can stop him from what he's about to do. Should I try, even when it's pointless? Or should I give myself over to larger problems?

"Astarti, you know this matters more."

I grit my teeth as I close the door, hating that Heborian can convince me.

"So," he begins. "What should we expect?"

Chapter 12

LOGAN

The girl's screams echo in my head. I empty my glass and push it back to the barkeep. He gets out the bottle of spirits but pauses with it over my glass, wanting to see my money. I dig some coins from my pocket and toss them on the bar. He fills the glass and slides it back to me.

Maybe it's the way my hand tightens on the glass. Maybe it's something about the way I sit on the stool. Maybe he recognizes me. He says, "You should check out the north end of the port road. They'll be starting soon."

"Starting what?"

He shrugs. "Something that might interest you."

I tip back my head and let the spirits burn their way down my throat.

I do what he says. Because I'm curious. Because I think I know what he means. I find what I expect, and it's exactly what I need.

The ring of torches casts flickering light over the gathered crowd. I spot velvet doublets and tattered leather jackets, rich and poor drawn to the same spectacle. You would think that with war looming, people wouldn't want this, but it makes a certain sense. Here is conflict confined to a circle. Predictable, a game, something to bet on. Win or lose, everyone will go home afterward. Smiling or grumbling, they will go home and life will go on.

The crowd shouts encouragement to the two men in the center as they circle one another, throwing fists. The torchlight gleams over their bare, sweat-sheened backs.

I make my way to where a man in a red coat watches dispassionately. "I want in," I tell him.

He doesn't take his eyes from the fight. "Winner gets half profit, loser gets nothing."

"I don't care about the money."

He looks at me, weighing something. "You looking to hit or be hit?"

"I just want in."

His eyes widen as he gets a good look at mine. "You one of them earthmovers?"

"I want someone better than either of them." I jerk my head toward the ring, where one of the men is already down.

"You can fight dirty, but no earthmoving. You got that?"

"That's what I want."

"Markan," the ringmaster calls over his shoulder. "I've got one for you."

Markan, who is almost as tall as Horik, sizes me up as we step, shirtless, into the ring. The buzz of voices—speculation, bets being placed—fades into the background. Markan rolls his huge shoulders and jerks his head to one side then the other, cracking his neck.

The anticipation clears my mind. I start pulling everything in, bracing. I put up my fists.

Markan lunges for me with enough power to crush brick, but he's slow. I dodge the blow and bring my own fist up, driving it into his exposed armpit. He grunts and shuffles back. When he comes at me again, he delivers a series of quicker punches. I could slip away, get around behind him, but that's not the point. I dodge some blows, but a few catch me in the ribs. I land punches of my own, but Markan takes them like they're nothing, even though they would lay most men out.

Frustration kicks in, and I swing a right hook that takes Markan hard in the jaw. His head snaps around, and he staggers. I could finish it while he's dazed, but I need more out of this first.

Markan recovers enough to charge, but I dodge away. I know better than to let him get me on the ground. I kick the back of his knee as he surges past me. His knee buckles, but as he goes down he spins, swinging. Bright pain slashes across my chest. I stagger back, stunned. Blood wells along a cut that goes from my ribs to my sternum.

Markan climbs to his feet, grinning, a knife in his hand. The crowd shouts, but more with annoyance than surprise. The ringmaster did say we could fight dirty.

Markan lunges, the knife flashing in the torchlight. Instead of leaping back I dive toward him, skimming past the knife to get inside his guard. I cock my arm and whip my elbow up, ramming it into the underside of his jaw. It staggers him but not enough, and now I'm within his grasp. He hooks an arm around my chest, lifting me bodily, and slams me to the ground. My head cracks against the paving stones, stunning me with pain as lights dance in my vision. I have just enough awareness to shift away as Markan's fist comes down. He pummels my shoulder instead of my face.

Markan is hunched over and off balance, trying to finish me quickly, but that's a mistake. He thinks me weakened by the pain, but it's not even close to enough to deaden me. I spin and knock his legs out from under him. Like all big men, he goes down hard. I leap on top of him and let my fists rain down onto his face and neck. He tries to protect his face, but he's dazed, not used to this. When his head lolls, I shove to my feet. He's had more than enough.

But I haven't. I'm hot with anger, looking for more, for another safe place to give and take what I need. This kind of rage is good: it's clean, purely physical, and it will wear itself out.

The crowd is silent, unhappy. I'm sure I just cost a lot of people their bets. Then the ringmaster shouts, "Let's see how he does with two on one!" and everyone cheers.

CHAPTER 13

I shudder as Logan's dazed opponent is dragged from the ring by three men. Logan held himself back, I could see that, but there's still so much burning inside him. Even in these few moments between fights, he's struggling to control it.

I like to spar. The skill it takes, the release of energy. I understand that. But this, what Logan is doing, is something much darker. This isn't about skill. It's neither practice nor a fight against a legitimate enemy. There's a release of energy, yes, but it's ugly, something that revels in the hurt.

Beside me, Horik comments, "He's good."

I mutter, "I don't know how much more of this I can watch."

Horik shrugs, unsympathetic. "You wanted to see what he does. This is what he does."

"It's horrible."

The ringmaster gives Logan a moment to catch his breath, then two more men enter the ring. Everyone here is watching the dodging bodies, the swinging fists. I'm watching Logan's face, trying to understand. I see the way he focuses, the way he becomes nothing but his body. Is that what he wants?

One of Logan's opponents gets a hold of his right wrist, wrenching his arm, while the other one pounds Logan in the face. Nausea rolls through me. I have to look away.

"Astarti?" Horik sounds worried.

"I can't take this."

I stare at Horik's shoulder, trying to shut out the sounds of the crowd and the fight.

"It's almost over. Look. He's got them."

But I don't look. Only when the crowd groans with finality do I lift my eyes. Logan is swaying in the ring, both men unconscious at his feet.

As the men are dragged away, the ringmaster approaches Logan. I don't hear what the man says, but Logan nods. Surely not. But the ringmaster is calling to someone in the crowd.

Suddenly, I am furious. This has been more than enough. I lurch forward, shoving through the crowd. "Hey!" someone complains as I elbow past to enter the ring.

Logan freezes, staring at me through blood and sweat.

"I'll go next," I shout to the ringmaster. Logan flinches at my voice, so I snarl at him, "Is this what you want? Is this what I don't give you?"

The crowd shifts uncertainly, whispering.

"Stop," Logan slurs.

The horror in his face makes my anger burn more hotly. I shape my Drift-spear and point it at him. The crowd emits a collective gasp.

"You have no business telling me to stop something when you are doing this." Horik calls my name from the edge of the ring, but I ignore him. I beckon Logan toward me. "If this is really what you want, let me see it."

He spins away and shoves through the ring of spectators.

I let my spear vanish, and the crowd moans disappointment. I stalk after Logan, bracing to shoulder through the crowd, but everyone scrambles away from me.

I catch up with Logan halfway down the dock road, well beyond the noise and torchlight. I grab his arm, and he grunts. In the moonlight, I see how his arm hangs wrong, the shoulder out of joint. It only makes me angrier.

"Why do you do this?"

He says tightly, "I didn't want you to see that."

"You think I didn't know what you've been doing?"

"I just didn't want you to see it."

For a second, I don't know what to say. Logan shifts, grit crunching under his boots. He says, "I'm sorry."

"Don't tell me you're sorry. I'm too angry with you."

"Astarti." His voice is low, almost a whisper. "I almost killed that girl today."

"So this is what, punishment?"

He makes a frustrated sound and turns away. In the moonlight, I see his head is bowed. He shakes it, then says quietly, "I need this. I have to do it." I say nothing, so he tries, haltingly, to explain, "It…helps me. I *have* to get in control. You've seen what I do! I—"

"This is *not* control, Logan. It's—"

"It's the best I can do!"

"I don't believe that."

He shakes his head, frustrated. "I could have killed that girl. Not because I wanted to. I wouldn't have even known I did it until after."

"And you think getting yourself beaten half to death will change that?"

He ignores that. Then, "Every time I use my power, it's a little harder to come back." The words are barely audible, like that will make them less terrifying.

"Logan," I say, not knowing how I'll go on.

He tenses and steps around me, putting me at his back. "What is it?"

Heborian steps from the Drift. "Come with me."

I edge around Logan. "This is *not* a good time."

"I need you to look at a body."

That gets my attention. "A body?"

"Come with me."

℘ ℭ

Heborian's Drift-light hovers near the cell's low ceiling, casting a blue gleam over the sweating stone walls. A sagging cot stretches along one wall. A reeking bucket of waste sits in a corner. I crouch beside the thin, crumpled body. Even with his face down, I recognize Fordan's tattered clothes, the thinning hair, the skeletal hands.

"Is this how you keep your prisoners?"

Heborian grunts. "I have only so many men. Any that can be spared have been sent to warn the towns and villages. Would you prefer I use my men to tend to the likes of that"—he gestures to the body—"rather than protecting my people?"

I breathe out an irritated sigh.

"A king cannot afford idealism, Astarti."

"If you really believe that, then tell me why Rood isn't here, learning that lesson."

He growls, "Will you focus, please?"

"You don't want him to be like you, do you? That's why you leave him out of the worst of it."

He meets my scrutiny with his dark gaze. Something burns in his eyes, something rawer and more honest than I have seen in him before. "I will finish this war before I die so that Rood doesn't *have* to be like me."

103

Jealousy flickers inside me and, with it, loss. A reality that could never have been mine, to be shielded like that.

Heborian must see something of it in my face because he says, "Do you hate him for that?"

"It's not his fault."

"That's not what I asked."

"No, I don't hate him." I add, trying to diffuse the tension, "But you have spoiled him, you know."

Heborian's mouth quirks. "Maybe."

I spoke the truth. I don't hate Rood. But I do hate Heborian, just a little. For making me respect him. For making me wish he could be more to me.

I turn my attention to Fordan's body. I lift his shoulder to roll him over. Heborian helps me. The dead, unseeing eyes stare into nothing. His mouth is open, exposing rotten teeth. There is a look of faint surprise about him.

"Well?" Heborian prompts.

"Why did you leave him Leashed? You could have cut him free."

"He made his choice. I had a use for him."

"What use?"

"You know I have weapons to test. Must we discuss this?"

I shudder inwardly and lower my eyes to study Fordan's face again. "I think it's likely Belos Took his soul, but I can't be certain, not having seen it happen. There were no guards present?"

"None that witnessed it. The guard on duty said he heard nothing. The body is still slightly warm, so it happened quite recently. You can't say for sure?"

"No."

Heborian stands. "Then we must assume he was Taken, and we must assume Belos did it for a reason. I had hoped for more time. My weapons aren't ready. Regardless, we must attack before Belos does."

"What *are* you making anyway?"

Heborian pauses on his way to the cell door. "I couldn't spare you from Belos, but there are still some things I think you shouldn't know."

Dark foreboding creeps over my skin. I almost push him for an explanation, but I don't think he would give it to me. Besides, I'm not sure I really want to know.

Is that wrong?

Am I allowing Heborian to dirty his hands just to stay clean—clean*er*—myself? And if I do that knowingly, does it really keep me clean?

I don't like the thought, so I push it away.

I follow Heborian from the dungeon and through the maze of the castle until we reach hallways familiar to me. I sense an all-night planning session looming, and I want to find Logan first. He came back to the castle with us, silent and wary, and headed toward our rooms. I don't know what I want to say to him, but I don't like how we left things. I'm about to tell Heborian I'll come to his study shortly when he flags down a pageboy.

"Find Prima Gaiana, and tell her that Logan needs her."

The boy nods sharply, full of awe to be given a direct order by the king, and hustles away.

I narrow my eyes at Heborian. "Why did you do that?"

"I need him, Astarti, and he doesn't do me a lot of good in that condition."

"Can't you leave him out of this? He was just in Avydos this afternoon. You can't keep asking him——"

"I will ask him for whatever I need from him. He can refuse, if he chooses. I certainly can't force him."

I grab Heborian's arm, then snatch my hand back. I have never touched him before. He, too, is aware of this, and he goes very still.

I say in a low voice, "He can't keep using his earthmagic. It's tearing him apart."

"I can see that, and I'm sorry. Don't scoff; I am. But my first concern is Tornelaine, Kelda beyond, even the world beyond Kelda. I cannot afford mercy. I cannot spare one man."

"Well, I am not a king, so I can put one man above all else."

Heborian looks at me with something close to sympathy. "Don't lie to yourself, Astarti. You're too much like me for that to be true."

"I'm not as much like you as you think."

"Perhaps. And I hope you never have to learn whether you are right in that belief."

Heborian turns and strides away, leaving me with a chill in my heart.

℘ ℭ

I find Logan in our bedroom, trying to pull on a clean shirt. He's washed away most of the grime, but the knife slash still drips blood down his stomach, and the bruises are darkening. His shoulder hangs wrong, and he can't move it enough to get his arm in the sleeve. He freezes when he sees me in the doorway. His hands drop to his sides, the shirt strangled in one clenched fist.

My heart pounds with uncertainty. Now that my anger has cooled, I don't know what to say.

When the outer door opens and Gaiana comes hurrying through the sitting room, Logan looks an accusation at me.

"Heborian," I tell him.

Logan's mouth tightens.

I shift out of Gaiana's way as she passes through the doorway in a stream of filmy robes.

"I'm fine," Logan says, catching her hands before she can touch his bruised face. "I don't need anything."

"What happened?" she cries, looking over her shoulder at me when Logan doesn't answer.

I start to edge away. I don't want to get caught between the two of them.

Just when I expect Gaiana to demand answers from Logan, she sighs and says, "Sit down."

I stare at her. That's it? She's just going to let it go?

Logan sits on the edge of the bed. Gaiana lifts his right arm, pulls a little, and slides the joint back into place. Logan's face whitens, but he doesn't make a sound. He's dislocated that shoulder so many times it's no longer as difficult to move the joint in and out of place. Gaiana Heals the bruises and cuts on his face and torso. When she is finished, Logan tugs on his shirt and stands. Gaiana takes his hand and squeezes, but I don't see his fingers return the pressure. She quietly leaves the room, not meeting my incredulous gaze.

Something about Gaiana's softness, her gentleness, makes it hard to be angry with her while I'm looking at her, but as soon as she's out of sight, my temper boils. I cannot believe she didn't confront him. She is his *mother*, and she just let that go.

Grim understanding sinks in. "She's never tried to help you, has she?"

"She just did."

"You know that's not what I mean."

"I don't need help, Astarti. I just need to be allowed to handle things my own way. She may not like it, but she understands that. I wish you did too."

"Because your way works so well?"

His nostrils flare. He's angry. "There is no solution for this. Please, stay out of it. Just accept it."

"No," I say simply.

A muscle feathers in his jaw. "If you cannot accept it, maybe it's best if we just—"

"No. Unless you don't want to be with me. Is that what you're saying?"

Color whips through his eyes. "*No.*"

My heartrate slows its frantic race, but I keep my face impassive, not letting him see my lingering fear or my cautious relief. The only thing I want him to know right now is that I am immovable on this. I know his stubbornness well enough to realize this is the most progress we will make right now.

With an effort, I make myself drop the matter. "Belos is calling in his markers. You remember the prisoner we acquired in the Dry Land? He's dead."

"Taken?"

"Most likely."

Logan follows me through the sitting room to the hallway. I watch him from the corner of my eye. Healed and wearing clean clothes and, of course, that steady, unemotional mask, it seems impossible that only an hour ago I watched him beat three men unconscious.

We arrive at Heborian's study to find all his Drifters gathered. Even Rood is here, as are Polemarc Clitus and Aron. Gooseflesh rises on my arms. There is a finality to this gathering. Heborian is finished with small missions, with collecting information.

The next several hours are quite illuminating. Both Heborian and Aron have been even busier than I realized. Heborian brings out a map of Avydos, and everyone gathers around the broad table to view it. The paper is fresh, the lines recently drawn. Clitus marks a spot on the map, not in the main city but in one of the smaller villages, where he says a tree stands damaged but alive. Apparently, his Wardens have been scouting.

Heborian lays out a plan with decisive strokes of his finger across the map. From time to time, Clitus shakes his head. Discussion ensues, and Heborian draws new lines with his finger. We work on time estimates: how long it will take the Wardens to get through the Current to the tree, how long for them to get to the city. We weigh that against Logan's speed and that of the Drifters. So many minutes needed here, so many there. We make projections about Belos's response and discuss contingencies.

When Rood demands to know why he's not included in this plan, Heborian says, "You are here only to learn. This is not for you to do."

"But Astarti—"

"Is not my heir."

The unspoken part of that statement hangs in the silence. I am expendable, like everyone else at this table other than Rood.

Rood says quietly, "I fought in the battle for Tornelaine. How is this different?"

I answer for Heborian. "Because then you were defending your kingdom. It was a final hope for Tornelaine, with the enemy at the gates. This? Some of us will die, some will come back. If Belos is defeated, that will be the end of it. If he is not, you will have your chance to fight again. But not until it is the last resort. That is why your father is not going, nor is Wulfstan, nor the Arcon. The leaders don't get thrown away until there's no one else *left* to throw away."

Silence follows. The only one for whom this truth is new is Rood. Understanding filters into his eyes. He doesn't like it, but he nods.

Heborian clears his throat and points at the map again. "The Wardens will take position here while Horik—"

109

Raised voices in the foyer make us all look up. Someone knocks, loud and impatient, and Heborian shouts for them to come in.

The doors swing open, and Inverre, captain of Heborian's castle guard, advances into the room. A young man, hat crumpled in his hands, follows behind. His eyes are wide and frightened. I'd guess him to be a farmer by his plain clothing and tanned face. Heborian meets the men in the middle of the room.

Captain Inverre gestures to the young man. "Philippe brings news from the village of Dorelle, forty miles northwest."

Philippe makes a choked sound, unable to get his words out.

"Take a breath, son," Heborian advises.

Philippe chokes in some air. "He—he—came into the village square. Out of thin air! He grabbed Frederic and put a white chain on him. They vanished together. When he came back, Frederic was gone. He said there was nothing to fear, but everyone ran, screaming. There was nowhere to hide. He knew where we were! I was in the tavern, hiding under the bar with the others. He appeared in the room in a blue flash. He grabbed Marise from under a table, put the chain on her and vanished. Jean-Marc told me to get away, take a horse and ride for the city. I'm quiet and fast, see? But the floor creaked when I snuck toward the door. I thought he saw me. I ran. I rode as fast I could. My horse died four miles from the city, but I ran for the gates. Please! *Please!* You must—"

"Thank you, Philippe. Captain Inverre?"

The captain dips his chin and tugs Philippe toward the door. Philippe shouts, "Please, please!" all the way to the foyer. The doors click shut, and his frantic cries fade into the distance.

"So," Logan says tightly, "he's decided that human souls are better than nothing."

Heborian frowns. "Perhaps."

Horik prompts, "You think there's more to it?"

I say, "Why a village so close? He could have gone farther away, where it would have been impossible for word to reach us in time."

"Exactly," mutters Heborian. "He wants us to know. But why?"

I say, "To draw us into the open, get us away from the city and your barrier."

Jarl adds, "But to expose himself and the Shackle like that is a terrible risk. Especially if he's alone."

Horik comments, "But the others could have been anywhere. The villagers wouldn't have known."

"It's obviously a trap," says Wulfstan.

Horik argues, "But a dangerous one for him to set."

"The boy mentioned nothing of Kronos, nothing of wind or earth," Heborian says. "Why is that?"

Logan argues, "That doesn't necessarily mean anything. When I was in Avydos, Kronos was not visible until…well, a human wouldn't have known he was there."

"True," concedes Heborian.

Wulfstan says, "We know that Belos needs more power. We know he wants a Drifter. He is trying to draw us out, thinking we will be moved either by pity for this village or by eagerness to apprehend him. Let us *appear* to be falling into that trap while we set one of our own."

"Go on," urges Heborian.

Wulfstan looks at me. "Astarti, if you went after him on your own, would he believe it?"

Logan makes a sound of protest, but I say, "Yes, I think so. I've done it before."

Heborian folds his arms, thinking through a plan. "The others would have to hide. Logan, Horik, Jarl."

Logan snarls, "You would put her in that danger?

Polemarc Clitus cuts in, "Logan, if she doesn't present herself as a tempting target, Belos won't take the chance on it."

Logan's hands clench on the edge of the table. "I will go with her."

Heborian shakes his head. "He won't take on the two of you together. He'll slip away, try again, wait for a better opportunity. Astarti, you'll have to be convincing. Make yourself look hotheaded, as though you've come after him on your own, against my orders."

"I can do that."

"*No*," Logan grits out. "It's too dangerous."

Heborian lets out a silent, humorless laugh. "And this is why he'll be convinced. He'll never believe Logan would allow it."

"Because I *won't*."

I see Logan's whitened knuckles from the corner of my eye, but I don't look at him directly. "This is an opportunity. We should snatch it before it vanishes. But. I need that knife to free Kronos."

Heborian's jaw clenches unhappily, but he knows I'm right. "Do not let him take it from you. I've tested it. It does work like I thought. He must not have it."

"You tested it?" I can't keep the horror from my voice. Heborian suspected that the knife could kill from within the Drift. There is only way he could have confirmed that. "Who did you test it on?"

"Martel."

Martel. The one who struck a deal with Belos and brought his army in siege against Tornelaine, the start of this mess.

Heborian shrugs. "We caught him fleeing the battle. It would have been a waste to simply hang him. At least his death served some purpose."

"None of that matters," Logan cuts in. "Astarti cannot do this. It's too dangerous."

I argue, "No more so that what we were planning twenty minutes ago."

"I disagree. You will be exposed, alone—"

"We're wasting time," snaps Wulfstan. "We need a decision."

"It's already been made," I say. "Logan, would you prefer I actually slip away and do this on my own? That is the only alternative."

He growls but keeps his mouth shut as we lay out the details of our plan.

Chapter 14

I skim through the Drift toward the village of Dorelle, letting my anger burn brightly. The only part of this that's a lie is that I'm alone. Though I said it to forestall Logan's arguments, it was true: I would have come anyway. Belos thinks he can take and take and take, as though everything is free to him if he just stretches out his hand for it. The more he takes, the more powerful he becomes, and the better able to take even more.

I don't let myself think about Horik and Jarl, their energies hidden somewhere behind. I don't let myself search for Logan, his energies so diffused in the elements as to be equally invisible. Belos must not suspect they are with me.

When I reach the village, I find what I expect: people scattered, hiding, terrified. Belos, unsurprisingly, is nowhere to be seen. I will have to make myself vulnerable before he will attack.

I slide from the Drift in the village center. I am briefly blind in the darkness, then my eyes begin to adjust, picking out the shape of the village well, the dark squares of houses. The only sound is of my boots scuffing the hard packed earth as I turn, hunting for any sign of Belos. I press my arm against the knife, reassuring myself that it's there.

I shape my spear. It flows into my hand with familiar weight and smoothness. The blade gleams a faint blue.

"Belos!"

A faint snorting sound comes from the side of one building. I spin toward it, startling a pig into squealing flight.

I let out a slow breath, and my pulse begins to ease.

"Belos! Come out, you coward!"

I wait a few more minutes, prowling around the well, alert for any sound or hum of energy. I must not be where Belos wants me. I stalk toward one of the buildings where I saw people hiding. I creep up the steps and pause. Still nothing. I kick open the door. People scream. They are muttering, whimpering, frightened. I let a Drift-light form above me as I walk in.

My light paints cool blue over the fallen benches before the bar and the tables scattered through the room. The tavern.

When nothing happens, I call out, "I've come from Tornelaine to help you. Your man, Philippe, reached us with word of your plight."

Voices whisper behind the bar, but I don't go over there. Better that they choose to come out. A middle-aged, portly man lifts his head above the bar to eye me. Dirt smudges his checks and nose, and his gray hair is pushed into a messy peak on one side.

"What's your name?"

"Jean-Marc. Philippe is safe?"

"Yes. Tell me what happened after he left."

"That…man. Was it…?"

"What did he do?" No good will come of speaking Belos's name. It will only terrify these people further.

"After Philippe escaped, he…Be…" Jean-Marc trails off. "He left this building. I thought he went after Philippe. We did not see him again."

"He didn't vanish with any more people?"

"Not from here." Jean-Marc adds hopefully, "Maybe he went on to the next village."

"Maybe," I say, but I doubt that's what happened. Belos wanted someone here, someone with enough power to be worth his while. I can't believe this is not a trap; it is the only thing that makes sense.

I stalk out of the tavern, returning to the open space of the village square.

"Belos!" I shout, letting my voice carry my anger.

I draw breath to shout again when he appears at the other end of the square, lit by a faint blue glow. My heart gives an anxious thump.

Wind stirs around me, lifting the fine hair framing my face, and I silently beg Logan to wait. I need Belos engaged with me before he and the others jump in.

"So," I call to him. "Is this what you wanted?"

"One of many things."

I approach slowly. The moon is near to setting, offering little illumination. My Drift-light diffuses in the open air, falling on him only faintly. He is gaunt, as Logan said, his cheekbones sharp enough to cast shadows down his face. I can't see his eyes.

He surprises me by shaping his Drift-sword. I did not expect him to willingly engage. The Seven must be nearby, waiting for the same opportunity for which Logan, Horik, and Jarl are waiting.

He points the sword at me. "I could see the knife from within the Drift. Thank you for bringing it."

I ignore that. He surely realizes the knife cuts Leashes, but I have to hope he knows nothing else about it. I won't be fooled into giving anything away.

I itch to slip into the Drift and cut his Leash to Kronos, but I have to be patient. The Seven could be right beside me within the Drift, waiting for me to do just that so they can grab me.

I adjust my grip on my spear and charge.

Belos sweeps his sword up to knock my spear aside. It sets me into a spin, and I use the momentum to whip the butt around and crack it into the side of his knee. He grunts as the knee buckles. I am too close now to use my spear. I skip away, but he brings his sword across in an angry slash. It catches in my jacket, but I don't feel any pain.

I dance back, bringing my spear around. Belos passes his sword from his right hand to his left and back again. That teases something in my memory, something not right. I am still distracted by that when Belos leaps forward, jerking his sword in another uppercut. I manage a clumsy block, but my spear shudders in my hand, rattling my bones.

I spin toward him, bracing my spear against my body, using myself as a fulcrum. I slash at his belly. He blocks the blow, but I catch the swinging Shackle in one of my spear's notches. I rip it from his belt. As it goes flying away, it vanishes.

Something is wrong here.

I don't have time to puzzle over it, however, because Belos lunges toward my unguarded side. I spin away, only escaping the thrust because he is slower than usual. I continue my spin until I'm behind him. I slash at his hamstring. He cries out, falling to one knee. Before I can bring my spear around to cut him again, a blue flash stuns me.

Rhode's hulking form is silhouetted against the bright light, his sword barely distinguishable. I whip my spear in a random block as I leap away to make space. My spear shudders and rings as it connects sloppily with Rhode's sword. I try to bring my spear around again, but I'm off balance.

Rhode lunges for me.

Wind tears between us, throwing us both off our feet. Dirt whips through the air, pelting my face and neck.

In the lingering glow of my Drift-light, I watch Logan shape himself from the wind. His body frays at the edges, not quite there. In a single, flowing movement, he crouches low, his right hand sweeping the ground. As he rises, a blade grows from the earth, flowing into his hand. It emerges with a deadly point, which Logan whips upward with the force of the wind. Rhode screams as the blade splits him from groin to sternum, spilling blood and entrails.

As Logan switches his grip on the sword, bringing it point downward, Rhode throws up a hasty shield of energy. Logan's sword cuts straight through to plunge into Rhode's heart.

Logan wrenches the sword free. My Drift-light paints cool blue over the blade's smooth length, which is neither pure metal nor the energy of the Drift. Logan wields the blade easily, but the energy rolling off that sword is impossibly heavy.

When Logan steps toward me, I expect the earth to rumble and crack. I breathe out a slow, relieved breath when it doesn't.

"Are you all right?" His voice is his own, shaped of the deep, rolling cadences I love.

"Belos," I say, scrambling to my feet. He is nowhere in sight.

"Be careful," Logan warns.

I nod, draw the knife from my belt, and slide into the Drift.

Horik and Jarl are engaged with Belos, their energy forms bright and lightning quick, a blur of shapes.

The knife gleams white and radiant in my hand. All I have to do is plunge it into his heart, and this will all be over.

When Horik throws Belos away from him, I get my first good look at his energy. I stare, confused. Then horror fills me.

There are no Leashes snaking out from him. Even if that had some explanation, I would still know Belos's energy, with its mad churning, all the tearing, frantic souls, in a moment's glance.

That is not Belos.

The Drift allows no illusions, no lies. It strips us all bare.

Koricus darts a sly, satisfied look at me before he flees.

With Horik and Jarl close on my heels, I speed after him. Fortunately, Koricus is too busy running to have enough focus to hide himself. He's fast, but I'm faster. I grab onto him, closing my mind to the sickening brush of his energy. I wrench him from the Drift.

He tears out of my grasp, his physical body so much stronger than mine. He makes an angry sound, shocked to have been caught. Horik and Jarl appear behind him, Drift-weapons ready.

Wind howls toward me, making my braid stream over my shoulder and my clothes strain against my body. The tall grasses of the field around us are bowed to the ground. Logan flows into shape beside me, sword in hand.

Surrounded, Koricus shapes his Drift-sword. He knows he cannot win, but he also knows we will kill him. He doesn't even try to surrender.

I don't need to ask where Belos is. The truth is a stone in my stomach. This was indeed a trap—just not the kind we expected.

"The Shackle was an illusion," I say, not needing confirmation, just voicing my anger. "You never Leashed anyone. You only took them into the Drift to make it look that way."

Koricus looks amused. "They saw what they expected, and you heard what you expected. Belos shaped you. You belong to him, to us. We know just how to use you."

A growl rumbles from Logan's chest, but I don't let the words touch me.

"We have to get back to Tornelaine," I say. "Now."

Koricus's laugh is ugly. "You won't like what you find."

"Maybe," I agree, "but you won't be there to see our disappointment."

Each of us is ready to kill Koricus. Of all the Seven, he is the cruelest. But Logan has the most anger to spend. It rolls off him like heat, ghosting over us all. Though Logan has not spoken of it, I do not doubt that Koricus tortured him, and took pleasure in it.

Horik, Jarl, and I stay back by unspoken agreement.

Logan steps toward Koricus, lifting his eerie, elemental sword.

Koricus edges away. He knows he will lose, so he strikes instead with words. "Do you feel like a man again? Because I remember when you didn't look like one."

Logan doesn't respond, but the heat bleeding from him intensifies until I have to step back.

"Does she know that you wept like a child? Does she know how you screamed?"

"Just kill him!" I shout, but Logan is frozen, unable to stop listening, unable to stop seeing himself as Koricus describes.

Koricus hisses, "Does she know that you wanted Belos to take your mind, that you liked it? We *all* knew. And that wasn't the only thing you liked, was it? Do you remember? Does it shame you?"

Logan roars, heat pouring from him. He leaps toward Koricus, bringing his sword around in a powerful swipe. Koricus tries to block the blow, to turn it aside, but his sword shatters when it meets Logan's. Logan swings again, cleaving through Koricus's neck.

Koricus's body falls, twitching, as his head rolls away. His clothes smoke faintly. His skin is blistered from the heat, cracked and oozing.

Logan stands before Koricus, his hands tight on the sword. He gasps, chest heaving, his whole body rocking. He wants to strike again, to kill him again.

I take a cautious step forward, but so much heat rolls off Logan I can't get close enough to touch him.

"Logan," I say quietly.

He shakes his head, and I hang back. Horik and Jarl are frozen, staying out of it.

Logan staggers away through the grasses. I follow a few paces behind until he falls to his knees. The sword dissolves into the earth.

He retches, his whole body convulsing with the need to expel something. But there is nothing in his stomach, and what he wants to get rid of can't be thrown up anyway. I crouch beside him and lay a cautious hand on his back. He still burns with inhuman heat, but at least I can touch him now.

The swishing of grass behind me announces Horik and Jarl's approach.

Horik says in a carefully neutral voice, "We have to get back to Tornelaine. Jarl and I will go. Meet us there when you are able."

I nod, and they both vanish into the Drift.

Logan pushes to his feet, breaking from me. His face is angled away. I want to say something, but nothing sounds right in my head.

"I'll meet you there," he says, his words uninflected, emotionless. Already he is dragging everything in, hiding from me.

"Take me with you. We'll travel together."

"I don't think I can manage that. Not right now."

I decide not to give him a choice.

Relaxing my mind enough to feel the currents of air around me isn't easy, but my need is greater than my resistance. Logan feels me do it, and his agitation filters into the air. I use it, letting it become my own. As I rise up, dissolving, Logan bleeds into the air around me. I brush against him, my diffused energies flowing through the chaotic heart of his. For a second, I am afraid. I fear he is broken, unable to focus. Then he grabs hold of me.

With an explosion of speed, we tear across the grassy plain, ripping a trench through the earth. We gain height just as we reach the village, ripping shingles from several roofs as we barrel upward. I have no power over this. I am a leaf caught in a hurricane.

We streak south toward Tornelaine and the disaster we know we will find there.

CHAPTER 15

The air around Tornelaine crackles with energy. I sense the Old Ones around us, moving through the air and the earth below. Their curiosity brushes over me, but it's Logan they're most interested in. They skim around him, seeking, grasping, possessive. Logan ignores them.

We soar over the city. The currents spiraling away from us whip around the buildings and through the streets. People flee, screaming. A few roofs have been ripped away, some buildings toppled. But the damage doesn't become severe until we near the castle.

The bridge from the city to the castle is gone, the broken stones scattered and mixed with the debris of shattered buildings. The gates and the courtyard wall have fallen into the trench that the bridge once spanned.

When we reach the rubble-strewn courtyard, I feel Logan draw away from me as my body solidifies. I stumble over the ripped earth, scrambling back from the crater in the courtyard's center.

Wind swirls and eddies around us.

"Help us," Logan calls to them. "Belos will bind you, too, if he can. Help us free Kronos."

The wind drifts away, and Logan's jaw tightens.

"Will they help?"

"I don't know."

I survey the damage to the castle. Some of the upper towers have been broken off, several walls ripped away. Beyond, the ocean crashes with unnatural anger against the cliffs. The wind howls overhead. A boom of breaking stone sounds from the east wing. The ground shudders under my feet as the whole wing crumbles into the sea as though the castle is made of nothing more than sand.

"I have to go," Logan says. "I'll try to stop him."

I slide the knife from my belt. "Maybe you won't have to."

For the first time since he killed Koricus, Logan looks at me fully. "Please be careful. I cannot lose you, Astarti."

My throat tightens. "I can't lose you either."

For a second, I see doubt in his eyes, then he nods. Wind stirs around him. His body dissolves, and he swirls away.

I force my thoughts away from him. I cannot worry about him right now. He's on his own, as I am. I tighten my grip on the knife and slide into the Drift.

The physical world fades to dim outlines. What I see from the Drift is the chaos of human struggle—and the chilling sight of Heborian's barriers ripped to shreds and hanging like broken spider webs. I tune out the frenzied movement at the edges of my sight as people flee the battle within Heborian's crumbling walls. If I focus, I can feel the roiling elements beyond the Drift, but I ignore all that. I pass through stone walls, their immerse weight and power nothing here in the Drift.

The glowing forms of Drifters and human soldiers batter one another in the hallway near the throne room. Dimly, I see the shattered walls and broken columns.

No one is within the Drift right now, all of them preoccupied with their physical struggles. I take stock of the battle, looking first for Belos. I easily spot his tumultuous energy and the blackened Leash snaking from him to disappear in the direction Logan went to seek Kronos. All his other Leashes are gone. So. He has Taken them all, gathering into himself every bit of energy he can command. This is his desperate push, and I have no doubt that his goal is to Take any Drifters he can. His energy drains constantly into that Leash. He pours himself into it to keep his fingerhold on a power much greater than his own. The Shackle dangles from his wrist, ready to be clamped onto anyone he can subdue.

Heborian sends a powerful blast of energy at Belos, knocking him back. Wulfstan follows that blast with one of his own. Closer to me, Horik swings his axe at Straton, and Jarl strikes at Theron before Theron can stab Horik in the back. Heborian's human soldiers skitter through the conflict, helping where they can, and dying far too easily.

I start to skim toward Belos, knowing that killing him is the surest way to end all this, when I spot Rood pinned under Maxos's sword. Rood's face contorts with pain as Maxos wrenches the blade from his shoulder. From the corner of my eye, I see Heborian turn and yell.

I speed over to Maxos as he raises his sword for a killing blow. He never sees me, never knows he is about to die. Maybe he won't even feel it.

I drive the knife into his heart.

His energy explodes like sparks bursting from a fire. I am blown backwards by the force of it, cringing as the sick energy washes over me. The sparks swirl and fizzle and fade.

The dim bulk of his body falls to the ground, barely discernible from within the Drift.

I scan the conflict for Belos. I jolt when I see him staring in my direction. Or rather, in Maxos's. Belos is clutching his chest as though in pain. His energy shudders. In fact, all of the remaining Seven looked staggered, and they are briefly unable to defend themselves.

I push my puzzlement aside and streak toward Belos to seize my opportunity.

Wulfstan also sees the opening and lunges. Belos turns to meet him, but instead of bringing up his sword, he brings up the Shackle. He lets Wulfstan's blade sink into his thigh.

In the moment Wulfstan is exposed, Belos clamps the Shackle onto his wrist and wrenches him into the Drift.

Wulfstan tries to tear away, but Belos drags his energy through the chain. Wulfstan crumples, fading. I dive for Belos, but Straton bursts into the Drift, blocking my thrust with his sword. Pain slides through my wrist, and I almost drop the knife.

I cannot let go of the knife or put it aside to shape my spear, but it is a terrible weapon to use against someone with a sword. I dodge Straton's swings, skimming away, hunting for an opening to get to Belos.

The Drift explodes with chaos as one combatant after another follows the fight. Blades flash all around me. I duck and slide, trying to work my way to Belos.

Guarded by Straton, Theron, Ludos, and Devos, he stands calm and exultant, sucking the last of Wulfstan's energy away. There will not even be a body to bury; Wulfstan simply vanishes through the Shackle until the cuff swings free. The new energy flows through Belos's form, struggling but forced to submit. The dark tear in Belos's leg begins to close, filled with fresh energy.

I have to get to him. Devos is closest to me, most in the way. He makes a vicious uppercut at Jarl, who dodges the blow and swings his sword low to catch Devos in the leg. When Devos reels, I seize my opportunity. I dive, skimming past Jarl to drive the knife into Devos's heart.

Devos's energy explodes, and this time I pay more attention to what happens to Belos and the others. Light flares briefly before dimming within them. Belos sags, clearly weakened.

Understanding seizes me with icy fingers.

Belos has lodged a sliver of himself in each of his men.

I shake off the numbing grip of horror and gather myself to charge. I spring for Belos as his Leash flares. I'm so focused that I do not begin to guess what it means. I fly at him, the knife held before me, an extension of my arm, of my body, of my sole purpose.

Kronos explodes into the Drift.

The wind that screams from him has all the fierce madness of the Hounding. It howls around me until I can't think, can't see. I will be blown to nothing, scattered through the Drift like the dust.

A familiar, wild presence surrounds me, and I slowly gather my thoughts, remember myself. The hands that skim my energy form move with a strength I know well. I focus on Logan, let him fill my sight. He is so beautiful here, stripped bare, nothing but wild and ferocious power.

His eyes, bright with color even here, study me. I smile at him, and the worry fades from his face. He looks over his shoulder, and I follow his gaze.

Horror jolts through me, and I whip past Logan to speed after Belos and his remaining men. I have always been fast in the Drift, and I quickly catch up with Heborian and Horik. Heborian's face is stark with terror, and I soon see why. Ahead of us, bound in ropes of energy, Rood is towed through the Drift by Belos. I ready the knife again and strain for speed.

When Kronos blasts into me this time, I'm prepared, and I hold my mind together even as his power tears as me. He is incorporeal, and I slide through the wild torrent of his energy.

Time slips and slides around me. I am barreling forward, chasing Belos. But I'm not. I am a child, learning the Drift. Belos looks over his shoulder and smiles at me. He is proud of me. I chase after him, smiling, loving this game.

No.

No!

That is not what's happening.

I force my thoughts to solidify. I must get to Belos. I must get Rood away from him.

Kronos screams as another wild power pummels us. For a second, I'm freed, flying after Belos.

Then Kronos howls through me again, as terrible as the Hounding. He *is* the Hounding. I try to hold myself together, to focus on the knife and remember what I have to do. But my hand dissolves, vanishing before my eyes, and the knife is ripped away. The pain sears me. My mind splinters with that pain and with the overwhelming power that envelopes me. I break into a thousand pieces. I am nothing.

The world fades.

CHAPTER 16

My hearing returns first. People arguing, some crying.

My legs are resting on cold stone, but my back and head lean against something warm and solid with the firmness of muscle, not stone. I open my eyes.

Logan's are a riot of color, staring down at me. A huge breath goes out of him. His eyes squeeze shut. When he opens them again, they are calmer. I watch him for a while, not thinking, just soaking in the sight of him.

He says, "I didn't mean it, you know. When I almost said maybe we shouldn't be together. I didn't mean it at all."

"I know." My voice comes out croaky.

His arms tighten around my torso. I try to hug him back, but my right hand is numb.

I sit up with a start, staring at my limp, empty hand. "The knife!"

"Kronos took it from you. I had to choose, Astarti. I couldn't fight for both you and the knife. Now Belos surely has it."

The fight comes back to me in pieces. Logan waits while my mind catches up. I squeeze my eyes shut. "He has Rood."

"The boy is surely dead by now. Or worse."

"Belos is smarter than that," I insist. "He'll use him as bait, as leverage. He's worth more that way." Logan looks skeptical. "I know him, Logan. Trust me."

"I *do* trust you, Astarti. You know that, right?"

There is more to his words than simple agreement—something deeper, more important. I wish I could talk to him about it, but there's no time. Instead of answering, I squeeze his forearm with my functioning hand. I start to get up, and Logan lifts me to my feet.

I get my first good look at the hall. Fire burns in the sconces where the walls still stand, casting warm light over fragmented stone and dust. The dead, numbering at least two dozen, have been dragged to one side. They lie in a neat row, where they will wait until time and thought can be spared for their burial. Logan makes a sound of protest when I start picking my way through the debris to see them.

I walk along the row, giving them the only thing I can, my acknowledgement of their sacrifice. Most of them wear the black uniform of Heborian's castle guard. Most of them are far too young to be lying here so cold.

One of Heborian's Drifters, Ordan, lies at the end of the row. Blood stains darken his tunic and trousers, but the fatal wound is a deep cut across the back of his neck, where a sword bit through muscle and bone. I recognize that signature wound. Theron did this.

Of course, there is no body for Wulfstan. I shudder at the memory of his energy being sucked through the Shackle. Is he still aware, I wonder, within Belos?

Belos always said it was best to Take someone when they were within the Drift. That way, he could get the energy of the physical body as well. "Waste not, want not," he once told me, smiling at his own joke. By that time, he had already given up on me and had begun instead to delight in my horror.

Maxos and Devos lie a short distance away, thrown carelessly into a heap. We killed four of the Seven tonight. It's a shame it doesn't feel like much of a victory.

"What's wrong with your hand?"

Logan's question surprises me into glancing down. I've been unconsciously rubbing the numb one with the other.

"Damage to your energy in the Drift is real, even if there's no mark to show for it on your body."

Logan takes my right arm, cradling my elbow with one hand and gently exploring my fingers with the other. He asks worriedly, "Is it permanent?"

"Probably not, but it will be a while before I can wield my spear again."

"It doesn't hurt?"

"I can't even feel it."

Logan's jaw tightens at that.

I ask, "How did you pull me out of the Drift?"

"I didn't. Heborian pulled us both out."

"But you got in somehow."

Logan gently lowers my arm. "I didn't understand it. I followed Kronos. I don't think I could have done it on my own."

"What happened with him? Did the other Old Ones help you?"

"Not really. They darted around, unsure what to do. They didn't want to fight him. I'm not sure they understand what's happened to him."

Fear closes my throat. "I don't see how we can free him now. I lost the knife."

"We'll just have to get it back."

"You're not angry with me?"

His eyes flash green. "I am now, when you ask something like that."

"But I lost the one thing—"

"And I could have chosen to fight for it. But I chose what means the most to me." He adds tightly, "You can call me selfish. Heborian already has. You can shout it if you want, like he did. But I couldn't...I just couldn't—"

I slip my good arm around his torso. I press my face to his sternum, where I can feel his heart pounding with remembered fear—fear for me. He lets out a shuddering breath and lowers his chin to rest on top of my head. His arms tighten around me almost painfully, but it feels so good. I don't want him to ever let go.

The sounds of voices and footsteps begin to intrude, reminding me that beyond this protective circle of Logan's arms lies death and destruction and a fight yet to be finished. Reluctantly, I pull away and give myself over to it.

Logan follows me down the hall to where Heborian is issuing orders to what remains of his guard. A disheveled and shaken Captain Inverre nods smartly to Heborian and sweeps away with his remaining men.

Heborian's eyes have all the same impassivity I'm used to seeing, but there are subtle hints that call it a lie. His arms are crossed, as they often are, but they're crossed too tightly, as though to hold himself together.

"Glad you could join us," he says. Normally, he would make such a comment wryly, but the words come out sharp.

Horik steps toward me. "Are you all right?"

"Fine. You?"

"Nothing can cut through this thick flesh." He tries to give me his usual grin. It's not quite convincing, but I'm still grateful for it.

I take note of our gathering. Lief and Jarl look shaken and weary but uninjured. A terrible thought occurs to me.

"The east wing," I say. "The Healers."

Logan assures me, "They're fine. They helped gather the injured and moved them to an intact part of the castle."

"And your brothers?" I hold my breath, fearing the worst.

"Alive."

Heborian interrupts, "And their concerns lie here while ours lie elsewhere. We must act quickly. What is wrong with your hand? Can you fight?"

"It's numb. I can manage a blade left-handed, but I won't be able to use my spear."

"We'll have the Prima—"

"Healing mends the body. This damage is only in my energies. She won't be able to help me."

"Very well. Then this is what we'll do." Heborian begins to sketch out a rough plan focused on killing Belos, but he doesn't get far before I cut him off.

"I don't think you understand. Belos has lodged fragments of his soul in each of the Seven. Well, the three that are left."

"You're sure of this?"

"Unfortunately, yes. Even if you managed to kill his body, he could slip into one of his men. I don't know if he'd still have control of Kronos, but we should assume that he would. Our first priority must be to free the Old One. Belos has exhausted himself and his men, but we must take away his greatest weapon before he will truly be vulnerable. Of course, none of this is possible without the knife."

"Actually," Heborian says, "it is."

CHAPTER 17

I don't like Heborian's plan. Too many moving pieces, too many opportunities for things to go wrong.

Not that there are any better options.

I skim through the Drift, giving Avydos a wide berth until I'm well south of it, beyond Belos's notice. The weapon hums with power in my hand, but its balance is off, making it heavy and awkward. This is not a weapon designed to be wielded. It was made to be launched.

I understand, now, Heborian's interest in the whaling ship that Logan and I brought into harbor. I understand why he wanted such large pieces of bone.

I grip the harpoon behind its barbed head. The shaft extends behind me, and the chain trails like a snake's listless body. I have to hope this thing can cut Kronos free, even if that isn't what it was made to do.

But what *was* it made to do?

"A last resort," Heborian called it, and there was no time to argue or question him further. When this is over, I will force him to explain that.

Heborian makes another wide circuit around me, scouting. We must not be detected. Anything that gives us away endangers both our mission and Logan's.

We skim toward Avydos's southern shore, then slide from the Drift onto the sandy beach, softly lit by the rising sun.

I scan the hills behind us with their green tops and black hollows. The fire damage is less than expected here. Every dip and hollow of ground is choked with what looks like hardened black mud, but the higher ground is largely untouched. Rain and wind have already washed away much of the ash, exposing tufts of grass and young, healthy branches of brush.

"Five minutes, Astarti," Heborian reminds me. "Then my backup plan goes into effect."

I run my eyes across the sand, filled in one low trench with the black mud, and face the clean blues of the sea.

Logan could do this better than I. I tried to argue for that, but no one supported me, especially not Logan. I know why. His task is more dangerous, and he did not want me involved in it. My numb hand was such an annoyingly convenient excuse.

"You feel nothing?" inquires Heborian.

I say waspishly, "Like I told you, he's not drawn to me like he is to Logan."

Heborian doesn't bother arguing.

I hand him the harpoon, not wanting it to weigh me down. I take a deep breath and try to relax my mind. I feel for the small currents of air, attune myself to them. My body falls into rhythm with the air, and I rise through it, dissolve into it. This is getting easier for me. Watching Logan helps. I see how he just lets himself go. I see the relief in him when he doesn't have to hold himself together anymore. That has helped me better understand the need to surrender. But I don't let go as fully. I don't need to because I don't have to hold myself together with the effort that it takes Logan. For me, this is about balance.

I think that is what kept me sane and helped me remain myself through all those years with Belos: balance. Finding small ways to be *me* even while I obeyed him. He allowed me my small defiances so long as they fell within my larger compliance. Because I never really fought Belos, I never broke myself against him.

For a second, that makes me ashamed. There is something noble and appealing in the idea of fighting until you're killed, or at least until your strength gives out. But I always hold something in reserve. I slide through, slide around, balance myself against my world. It has polluted me, in a way. I have accepted a measure of evil, found ways to balance even that. I do not know if that is right or good, but I know it is true of me.

Logan is not like that. In some ways, he is cleaner, more pure than I am. He fights more than I do, refuses to accept what he doesn't like and what he doesn't want to be. I respect that, but it worries me. He doesn't know how to find his balance. He doesn't know how to handle all the incongruous parts of himself, what to accept, what to reject, how to fit them together. He certainly doesn't know how to handle what has happened to him. He drives everything he doesn't like—every feeling, every memory—deep inside himself, as though that gets rid of it. But it just makes it more a part of him. He doesn't realize that it's all right for him to be angry, to feel hurt, to need healing. He closes that off, hides it from me, hides it even from himself. I have long suspected that releasing himself into the elements must be a little like dying: a relief to let go.

Until the moment of my death, I will never know that kind of absolute freedom, but I also won't spend the time in between suffocating myself as Logan does, trying not to seize it.

I am a survivor, a scrapper. Less noble, perhaps, but I accept that. To me, that is balance. Oh, I'm willing to risk my life, willing to die. But not on principle. It would have to be for a reason.

And so I am able to perform this search, to float along the shore, giving in to the currents of air, but also using them to get where I want to go. I skim along the surface of the water, brushing against it, alert for any disturbance, anything that disrupts the natural, mindless currents.

I circle back to Heborian, where he waits impatiently on the shore. I draw myself together, slipping away from the air currents with increasing ease.

"Well?" he prompts.

"If he's out there, I can't feel him. I'll travel inland."

"I'll follow from within the Drift. I'll need you to step out periodically so I can track you. I can't see you when you've got no body."

His voice is tighter than usual. The casual confidence I'm used to seeing in him has been replaced by a studied one. I wonder if it's hard for him to not be in the group going after Rood. I wonder if he would, in the end, let his son die in order to achieve a larger victory. Part of me thinks that he would, even if it destroyed him to do it. I don't know whether to be awed or horrified.

I slip into the wind, channeling myself toward the looming peak of Mount Hypatia. The mountain no longer belches great clouds of smoke, but particles of ash and dust float along the currents around me.

I shape my body now and then, on hilltop after hilltop, then at the blackened base of the mountain. My skin crawls at not knowing what may be happening in the Drift, so I slide into it. Heborian hovers near, the gleaming harpoon in hand. I turn to look for other energy forms, but no one is close enough to be seen. When many are gathered together, as in a city, the glow is visible from a great distance. When only a few are gathered, and especially if they're hidden on the other side of a dim, looming mountain, they cannot be seen. Even though that means Heborian and I also are not visible, I wish I could have caught a glimpse of Logan and the others. Heborian shakes his head, reading my delay. Unhappily, I press through my mooring to stand on the desolate mountainside again.

I'm surprised that the other Old Ones are keeping away. I thought the harpoon would surely draw them, but there is no sign of their presence. Perhaps they will not come so close to Belos.

I let myself filter into the air again. I ride the currents up the mountainside and soon feel a heaviness in the air. Logan, no doubt, would have sensed it from a greater distance, but it doesn't become obvious to me until I'm very close. I brush the craggy, blackened face of the mountain, letting the immense weight of stone fill my awareness.

Kronos lies deep in the body of the mountain. I feel the weight of his energy. I feel the sorrow. For a moment, I am stunned by realization. Of course I knew he was a feeling being: sentient, sensitive, able to suffer. But he is also so powerful that I have regarded him largely as an obstacle. Now, seeping through the bones of this mountain, blending for a moment with his pain, I am moved to pity. He is trapped, abused, as Logan has been, as I have been, as so many have been.

He stirs at my touch, surprised, perhaps, to find me here. I silently beg him to emerge. I cannot cut his Leash from here. I need him to enter the Drift, and I don't know how to communicate that without words. When he feels my silent urging, he draws away, like an animal that does not want to be touched. I try to be patient, but I don't have much time. I tug at him more insistently, but he only buries himself more deeply in the warm heart of the mountain. Soon he is only a dim presence.

Frustrated, I withdraw, easing myself between the heavy stone until I break the surface and shape myself from the earth. The sensation reminds me of the sword Logan drew from the ground. I had no chance to ask him about that.

Heborian appears beside me, harpoon in hand.

"Well?" he says, as he did before. He reads my frustration and nods. "I'll try to find them."

"I don't like it."

"I don't care whether you like it. We should have done it from the first instead of wasting time."

"You think finding them will be any easier?"

"Yes. I do."

I don't understand his certainty. There's something he's not telling me, but there's no time to argue.

"Fine," I say. "Let's go."

"You will wait here. I'll bring them."

My skin creeps with distrust. "Why?"

"Because I don't trust you to be calm and logical in their presence."

Some of my distrust eases. He's right about that. I want them dead for what they did to Logan. I certainly don't want their help.

Heborian seizes on the thread of understanding in my eyes. "I'll be back as soon as I can."

With that, he vanishes into the Drift.

Chapter 18

LOGAN

I sweep up the mountainside, lifting swirling clouds of ash and dust into the air. I keep a fragment of my attention on the Drifters I carry, but mostly I focus on control. As always, the temptation to indulge in mindless freedom itches through me. More than that, emotion distracts me. I'm worried about Astarti because I cannot see her. I'm worried for the boy, though that concern is more distant because I don't know him. Mostly, I am furious with Belos.

For endangering Astarti.

For so much else.

With Koricus's words sticking like tar inside me, the faintest touch of Belos's sick energy vibrating through the air is nearly unbearable.

I force myself into the present, into my task. I don't have time for those other thoughts.

I sense Kronos buried deep in the mountain. I hope Astarti can draw him out. If she fails, we may still achieve something, but it won't be enough to save us. Tornelaine is vulnerable now. It won't survive another attack.

Belos and his men, along with the boy, wait on a rocky ledge near the top. Astarti was right. He's using the boy as bait; he knew we would come.

There is desperation in his actions. Tornelaine may be vulnerable, but so is he. He's stretched himself too thin, grabbed at too much. He needs more power to hold the power that he's already taken. The boy is Heborian's son, a strong Drifter. If Belos wants more than Rood can give, there's only one of us he's likely to trade for.

As planned, I stop down the slope. We need Belos in sight so that if Astarti succeeds—or fails—we know to act and can do so quickly. But we also need to buy her some time.

I shape myself from the wind and let the Drifters' bodies settle into their own forms. Dust billows away from us. Not my smoothest landing. Lief and Jarl stagger away from me, visibly shaken. I doubt anyone likes having another control their body. Horik, who has traveled the wind with me before and is remarkably difficult to rattle, just brushes ash from his tunic— smears it really—and gives me a stern look.

I close my eyes for a moment, willing myself to calm down. Too much depends on me right now. I must be in control. I feel the wind die, feel a sudden weight to my body that tells me I wasn't quite here a moment ago. When I open my eyes, Horik nods. *Better*, he seems to say.

I glance up the blackened slope. We're close enough that I can see five distinct bodies but not close enough for me to see who is who. Two vanish.

Straton and Theron appear before us, the faint blue glow of the Drift lingering around them. They are both pale and exhausted-looking.

"Where is Astarti?" Straton asks in his sly voice.

Because I'm a terrible liar, I do as planned. I glare at him like I want to rip his face off. It's easy because I do want that. I see what Astarti means about lying: find the grain of truth and build around it.

Horik rumbles, "We lost her."

"What do you mean you 'lost her'?" Theron sounds genuinely concerned, and that annoys me. What right does he have to know anything about her, to care?

"In the Drift," Horik says. "She went after Kronos. You didn't see what happened?"

It seems like a good lie to me. Simple, partially true.

Theron and Straton share a look. I'm not sure if they believe us, but they drop the matter.

Straton says, "You've come for the boy." When we don't confirm, he says, "Belos will trade."

"For whom?" Horik asks.

"Whom do you think?" Straton sneers.

Horik states our terms. "If the boy is Leashed, he will first be cut free. I assume Belos has the knife?"

Straton's smirk is answer enough.

"Furthermore," Horik continues, "We will be allowed to get him away before you start on Logan."

Straton counters, "The boy will be free after the trade is complete. As for getting him away, you won't be there. You three will wait here, in sight at all times. Should any of you step into the Drift, the boy will be Taken. Should Logan attempt to resist or escape, the boy will be Taken."

Lief and Jarl shift uncomfortably. We didn't anticipate this.

"No," Horik answers.

"Fine." Straton begins to turn away. "He will Take the boy then come after you. Prepare yourselves."

"We accept the terms," I say.

Horik makes a warning sound, but I ignore him.

Straton turns back to me. "Good. But. There is one more thing Belos requires you to accept." He elbows his cloak open and holds out the Shackle, one cuff already on his wrist, the other dangling from his grip. I recoil before I can stop myself, and Straton gives me sly smile. "No? If that's how you feel…"

He begins to turn away again. I think frantically. I knew that thing would end up on me at some point today. Does it matter if I have to wear it a little longer than expected? Belos is doing this to mess with my head, that's all. If I refuse, will he Take the boy to prove his point? Astarti might know, but I don't. I can't take the chance.

"All right," I bite out. "But only if we walk. I won't go into the Drift with you. That's final." What better excuse, really, to buy Astarti more time?

"You're more reasonable than expected," Straton comments. "I don't remember you being like this at all."

I stiffen as he steps into my space, but I don't allow myself to move back. When he holds out the smooth white cuff expectantly, I extend my left hand. Horik makes a sound of protest, but there's nothing to be done. When the cool cuff clicks shut on my wrist, a shudder creeps through me, but I swallow it back into myself.

"Let's go," I say.

Straton looks briefly disappointed, then he gestures grandly up the slope. The liquid fire cooled in bumps and waves, like wax that spilled down the mountainside. In places where the rocks protrude more, the burning gush passed around, leaving the brown and gray stone exposed. A white flower, growing from a cleft in one protruding boulder, dances in the breeze.

"So," Straton says as we begin to pick our way up the blackened slope. "Astarti is dead then."

Either he is taunting me or he's testing for the truth. I don't trust myself to lie well, so I say nothing. Maybe that's what gives me away. If Astarti really were dead, what would I do?

I would lose my mind. I would kill them all, no matter the consequences.

"He's lying," Theron hisses, the inflection of his voice not his own.

My skin crawls, but I make myself look at him. The tilt of his head, the way he walks—all of it is Belos. The Shackle seems to hum on my wrist, and it's an effort not to wrench my arm away from Straton.

Theron shakes his head, and his body language shifts subtly. He stares ahead, scowling, his expression once again as I remember it.

"How can you stand it?" I ask him, unable to keep the disgust from my voice. "Why did you ever let him do that to you?"

Theron ignores me, but Straton snaps, "It is not for *you* to question *us*."

"You hate it," I say, only half-guessing. Straton seems too proud, too haughty to bear such a thing gladly.

His lip curls, telling me I'm right. He gives the Shackle a yank, trying to remind me of my situation.

I glare along the length of it to where the other cuff encircles his wrist. "I would have thought you all had learned by now: power travels both ways along a Leash."

Now Straton ignores me too, and we make our silent, awkward way up the slope, the Shackle chain swinging between us.

I feel in control, anchored in myself and my purpose, for most of the climb. The exercise helps, lets me focus on walking. I fixate on the dull ache in my bad knee. The joint clicks annoyingly with every pushing step.

Belos's slick, oily energy washes at me. Anyone who says that memory is only in the mind is wrong. It is physical too. I *feel* the slide of his energy through me, violating every fiber of my being as though I am still bound to him. Sweat breaks out all over my body. *Focus*, I tell myself, *on each step, on the plan. You are here of your own volition.* I squeeze the fear and revulsion into a tight ball and drive it deep inside myself until it is small, distant, buried.

We reach the ledge where Belos stands with the bone knife pressed to Rood's throat. Ludos lurks behind them. I look the boy over. Blood stains his doublet at the shoulder, but he's standing on his own. His dark eyes are wide and wary, but his fear is under control. I shouldn't be surprised. He is Heborian's son.

Belos, gaunt and hollowed by strain, looks me over. His lips pull back in a cadaverous grin. "I should have known from the beginning what you are."

Only then do I realize I'm fraying at the edges, beginning to dissolve. I force my body to obey me. I *will* be in control.

"You think you can win," Belos says. "You think you're stronger than I am."

I want to ignore him, to pretend his voice doesn't creep under my skin. "Every bit of your strength is stolen. None of it is you. All of it is someone else."

He smiles, delighted to debate with me. "You know better than that. Everything I have taken, I had the strength to take." When I don't react, he adds, "I think you know, quite intimately, that I have made all that strength and power my own."

I force myself to be still and silent. I can't argue with him. He's better at it than I am. He will use it to unsettle me, to weaken me.

He smiles a little, understanding my silence. "I will use that strength now to take yours."

"You will try. That's what this trade is. Rood, for your opportunity."

He gives me a look that, if it weren't so perverse, would be tender, and it makes bile slide up my throat.

"Oh, Logan," he croons. "Let us not lie to one another. I know you too well for that. Deep down, you want to be Taken. You want to let go. Don't you realize? It was the key to unlocking you. You wanted it, Logan, what I did to you. You resisted, but you wanted it."

I hear the Shackle chain rattle and realize I'm shaking. So easily he gets to me. My hands tighten into hammers. I want to break him apart. I want to smash his face until he doesn't even look like a person anymore.

I can't. As always, he has the power, the leverage. It is horribly familiar, glaring at him with my impotent rage. I think, *Nothing has changed. I've never been free of him. Every small victory has been a lie, a delay.*

Belos inhales deeply, as though he smells my reaction, as though he is savoring it. "Don't you remember how good it felt when you finally gave in? I was there. I felt your relief."

I rock toward him, burning with the need to shut him up. The Shackle jerks my wrist, and Belos presses the knife harder against Rood's neck. The boy sucks in a breath.

I growl, "Enough! Let's get this over with!"

Belos's lips quirk in a smile. "With pleasure."

CHAPTER 19

I'm twitchy with impatience. Heborian is taking too long. I slip into the Drift every few minutes, looking for him, making sure no one is sneaking up on me. I massage and slap my numb hand. A little feeling is beginning to return. I keep at it until my flesh is red and I feel a tingling in my fingers. Relief makes me light-headed. Despite my assurances to Logan, I've been terrified of not regaining the use of my hand.

I shape my Drift-spear in my left, which feels horribly awkward. I work through some forms, forcing my left hand to lead the movements. My right is still too numb to grip, so I use it as a pivot point. I am slow, careful, teaching my body this new movement. I manage a swipe and turn before the spear slides off my numb wrist to skitter and screech across stone. Annoyed, I rebalance the spear and try again.

When Heborian appears from the Drift a few feet away, I whip my spear toward him automatically. I'm already slowing the weapon when he blocks me with his Drift-sword, a blade covered in Runish symbols. He raises a dark eyebrow as I lift my spear away. He holds the harpoon in his other hand, the chain coiled around his arm. That thing is far too much like a Shackle. What purpose can a chain have but to bind and control?

"Did you find them?"

"They're coming."

"And they agreed to help?"

Heborian makes a sound of confirmation.

I narrow my eyes with suspicion. "How did you convince them? And do they understand exactly what we need them to do?"

Before he can answer, the Ancorites come whispering toward us. They're as insubstantial as smoke. My skin tightens, and the fine hairs on the back of my neck lift.

Bind, seize, hold.

Their voices are dry leaves blown across stone.

There are three of them, ghostly, their bodies semi-transparent, their colors subdued. They flitter across the mountainside, whispering, *Find them, bind them.*

A rocky hand and arm, larger than my whole body, grows out of the mountain. Kronos snatches at the Ancorites, but they dart away like flies. And, like flies, they return, whispering. Kronos emerges further: shoulder, collarbone, head. He leans out of the mountain, both part of it and not. It is an eerie sight, not unlike the sword Logan drew from the earth. Starting at his face, stone begins to soften into skin. This is my first good look at him. Though he does not look old, age radiates from him. He is handsome in a rough way, his features blunt, carved from stone. He grabs again for the Ancorites, but they dart out of reach.

I slip into the wind and swirl toward him. "Kronos!"

His eyes, swirling with color, lock on me. His expression hardens. He begins to withdraw, stone closing over his shoulder and neck.

"I can help you!"

The Ancorites sweep near. *Bind, bind, hold.*

Kronos swats at them angrily.

I extend my hand from the wind to touch his rocky shoulder. Time slows, plays tricks. We are somewhere else, on another mountainside. Snow drifts through the air and lies thick between the protruding rocks. Kronos looks at me and says, in a rocky grumble, "Child."

I jerk my hand away, shake my head to clear it. I cannot afford distraction.

"Please," I beg him. "Trust me."

Little by little, Kronos emerges from the mountain, simultaneously growing from it and shrinking to a more human size. I withdraw from the wind, and we stand on the mountainside together. The last of the stone fades from his body. He looks almost human now, though this is only a form he is choosing for a moment. He is still the mountain.

And the sky and all the world.

But none of that matters because there is no power in the world, no amount of strength that cannot be overcome. Kronos has spent ages learning that lesson, and I see the pain of it in his ancient eyes when he says, "Child. Help me."

CHAPTER 20

LOGAN

Without warning, I am yanked into the Drift. The vastness spreads out in all directions. I am instantly exposed, everything I can hide in my physical body laid bare. In the moment it takes to orient myself, to overcome the instinctive fear of exposure, Belos betrays the deal, as I knew he would.

The Shackle glows brilliant white, vibrating against my wrist. I wheel on Straton, lunging for his throat, but it's not him anymore. Belos's black will floods through him and down into the chain. I make a useless, automatic attempt to scrape off the cuff; my fingers swipe through it.

The black stain seeps through the cuff into my hand. I recoil at the familiar, sickening slide of Belos's will. For a moment, I am back in the Dry Land, Leashed, possessed, clinging to a fragile thread of sanity.

No.

No.

This time is different. I am not Leashed.

And I have beaten him before.

Rage burns through me, sparking my energies to blazing life. How could I have let him take me back into that fear even for a moment? I will never, *ever* be overpowered by him again.

Weapons slash at me. Straton, Theron, Ludos, and Rood circle and jab, all moving in synchronicity, each of them an extension of Belos. I wheel, roaring, and my energy explodes outward in a gust of wind.

Their energies fray under the force of it, and all of them are briefly stunned. I thrash at them, with wind, with my fists. Part of me realizes I am losing control, but I don't know how else to fight him.

His energy surges through the Shackle and with it his voice, paralyzing me. *You want this. Relax, give in. You want this.*

The others leap on me, slashing and punching, ripping at my energies. Astarti says you can die here. I will make him kill before I let him take me. I don't know how to get out of the Drift on my own. This isn't how this was supposed to go.

Horik, Jarl, and Lief, realizing that something has gone wrong, flash into the Drift. Theron, Ludos, and Rood spin away to meet their attack.

I gasp relief, but a moment later Straton—Belos, really— plunges a hand into my chest. My mind shatters at the crippling pain, the sickening violation. I can't get my bearings, can't focus.

You are weak. You are broken. Give in. It will be easier.

I am crumbling under the weight of that truth.

He is beating me. This time, he is winning.

An axe flashes in front of me, and the hand is ripped from my chest. I stagger back, stunned by pain and sudden lightness.

Someone grabs my arm, and I am wrenched through my mooring.

The physical world explodes around me, battering me with the return of my senses. The sharp ache in my chest is the center of my awareness until the cuff jerks my wrist. I frantically scrape it off, barely feeling the tearing of skin.

An axe whizzes past my ear.

Straton shapes a shield of energy, and Horik's axe dissolves against it.

The others appear from the Drift, scrambling, fighting.

I can barely breathe around the pain in my chest. I forcefully drag air into my lungs. Horik shouts at me, but I can't make sense of the words.

Something slams into my thigh. It takes a moment for the pain to register, then it blazes white-hot.

Rood wrenches his sword free, his eyes dead and black. He swings again, but I dive inside his guard. I barely feel the blade slicing my arm as I tackle him.

He's just a boy, with a boy's strength, and even with my chest burning and my lungs not quite working, I easily pin his arms to the blackened ground. He tries to bring his knee up into my groin. I jerk away only to catch the blow against the wound in my thigh. Pain explodes, but I hang on.

Somewhere up the slope there is a scream of rage, and Rood goes limp under my hands.

"Wh-wh—" he mumbles, his eyes starting to clear.

I catch movement from the corner of my eye, someone diving down the slope toward us. I look up just as Horik, face and neck bloodied, slams into me and Rood. The bone knife is in his hand. We tumble down the slope, banging over stones. I don't have the presence of mind to let go. I'm still clinging to the boy when Horik rips him into the Drift.

Chapter 21

I am turning to call Heborian, to have him bring the harpoon, when Kronos growls. It's an animal sound, terrifyingly primitive. Hair rises all over my body. I don't dare move as I shift my eyes to Kronos's face. His are pools of black, and they startle me into movement. I scramble away from him, sloppy and useless in my fear.

But he's not coming for me. He rises into the air, his body fading and dissolving.

Something whizzes past me in a streak of white, propelled by faintly glowing Drift-energy. Kronos vanishes as the harpoon pierces the air where he just was. He tears up the mountainside, raising a column of dust.

The harpoon clatters and skitters across the hardened black crust. I trace the chain, which expands strangely with Drift energy, back to Heborian. He braces, clinging to the last link. The Ancorites are threading along the chain, swirling around and through it. And through Heborian.

I don't have time to confront him. I let myself dissolve, and I leap into Kronos's wake.

I blow over the blackened, craterous peak of the mountain. The currents swirl in the depression, and I have to struggle against the downward pull. Kronos draws ahead of me, far faster and more powerful than I am.

A fight rages on the slope below, but the combatants are shielding themselves against the whipping dust as much as against their opponents' weapons. I can't spot Logan. I identify Belos and angle toward him, but the windstorm is too much. I get blown off course, tumbling away through the wild currents. By the time I balance myself against the wind and get back to the slope, Belos is gone.

Dust clouds the air.

I touch down beside Jarl, who is bent double, coughing. I bury my face in the crook of my arm, breathing through my linen sleeve. I blink through tears to see Lief thump down onto a boulder. A body lies crumpled beside him.

"Where's—"

Logan, Horik, and Rood appear from the Drift ten feet from me. Horik drags the back of his sleeve across his bloody mouth. The knife is clenched in his fist. Rood collapses at his feet, gasping. Logan staggers away, sucking hard for air, then coughing on the dust. His head whips one way then the other, hunting.

"Logan!"

His head snaps in my direction.

I run to him, and he grabs me into his arms. I pull back, desperate to look him over, to know whose blood soaks his pant leg and sleeve. He winces at each sharp breath as though his chest hurts. His eyes rage with color.

He tears away from me, staring from Lief to Jarl. "Where is he? What happened?"

"The wind," Lief says. "It took him. All of them."

Heborian appears from the Drift, harpoon in hand.

"Father!" Rood cries, and Heborian rushes to him.

Heborian drops the harpoon and takes Rood's face in his hands. "Is it you? Is it you?"

"He's free," Horik assures him. "We have the knife."

Heborian sags with relief and gathers Rood into his arms in the warmest gesture I've ever seen from him.

Horik suggests, "We should rest, make a new plan."

Logan shouts, "What plan can there be but to go after him? He's weakened!"

"So are we."

"Logan," I say. "Let's just figure this out." He's going to do something rash; I can feel it.

"We can't track him through the air," Heborian adds, but Logan counters, "*You* can't."

I say sharply, "Don't even think about it."

Logan turns, limps a few paces away from me. I follow cautiously, unsure of what's happened here, unsure what he'll do.

He says in a low voice meant only for me, "He almost had me. How can I have let him get to me again?"

My blood chills. "What happened?"

He doesn't seem to hear, and when he speaks again, he seems to be speaking more to himself than to me. "He *cannot* have power over me."

"Logan—"

Already his body is fading. "He says I want it, but I don't. I *don't.*"

"Logan!"

I snatch at him, but my hand passes through his dissolving form. He rises up and streaks away, raising a new cloud of ash and dust.

I wheel on Horik. "What happened?"

Horik gives a brief account. I close my eyes when he reports on Logan wearing the Shackle. I know what that feels like. When Horik describes the fight in the Drift, I demand, "Belos tried to Leash him again, didn't he?"

"I was a little busy at the time," Horik says dryly, "so I can't say for sure, but, yes, I'm sure that's what was happening."

"It's horrible," mutters Rood. He's sitting on the ground, limp, rubbing at his chest.

I crouch beside him. When someone has been Leashed, especially possessed, you don't ask if they're all right. They're not.

Rood meets my eyes. I'm glad that he's able to. I want to touch his shoulder, to tell him with my fingers that I understand, but I don't feel comfortable. He gives me a grimace that I think is meant to communicate that he's all right. I nod, wishing I had the courage to do more.

I have to get to Logan. He's injured, exhausted, not thinking clearly. He can't possibly win against Belos, Kronos, and whatever remains of the Seven, especially if—

"Does Belos still have the Shackle?"

Horik confirms with a grim, "Yes."

I curse. "And the Seven?"

"Just two of them left," Lief says. "This one"—he nudges the body at his feet, and it groans. Lief bolts up, scrambling away.

Drift-weapons flash into everyone's hands, and I'm sure we look ridiculous stalking so cautiously toward someone barely conscious.

"Thought he was dead," Lief mutters.

Horik uses his boot to shove the man onto his back. Theron moans. A huge gash runs from his belly into his ribs. White fragments of bone are mixed with the bloody mess of skin and muscle. He should be dead, but the unnatural energy within him seeks even now to repair the fatal damage.

Horik lifts his axe.

"Wait!"

"Astarti, he's—"

"Linked to Belos. He can tell us where Belos is."

Heborian scoffs, "He won't. He's dead, and he knows it."

"Of all the Seven, he might. I know them, Heborian. You don't. You can at least let me try."

Heborian makes an impatient, get-on-with-it-then gesture. Horik lowers his axe, and I crouch beside Theron. I start to reach for his face, but I'm too conscious of everyone looming over me.

"Do you think I could get some space?"

"Be careful," Heborian warns, and everyone moves back a short distance. They're still watching me, but I can almost pretend they're not.

I touch Theron's cheek, and his eyes flutter open. He stares at me, trying to focus, then wheezes, "Astar…"

He would know the lie in my smile, so I don't try to pretend. Theron has done terrible things. It's hard to deny that he is a terrible person, but, of all of them, he is the only one I can imagine might have been something better in another life. He is the only one I don't hate.

"I need your help," I say quietly. "I need to know where he is."

Theron can't move his head, but his eyes shift away. His breath rattles, sucking and bubbling through punctured lungs.

"You will die today, Theron. How would you live your last moment?"

His eyes come back to my face. "As a…traitor? Is that"—he breaks off, wheezing—"what you want?"

"I want you to help me. To do something for a friend of your own volition. To choose to help me, as you wanted to so many times."

"Friend," he rasps.

"We could have been. We were sometimes."

"I...loved you." Even through the pained wheezing, I hear the bitterness.

"I know."

I could lie to him, pretend that I loved him, too, but I won't lie to a dying man, not even this one. Besides, he would know.

"How?" he asks, and I hear the unspoken remainder of the question. How did I do it? How did I free myself?

"Someone told me I could remake myself, and I believed him."

"And—have you?" There is no sneer in it. He genuinely wants to know. He hopes that I have. That, more than anything, makes me mourn him. Not his impending death, which he deserves, which is necessary, but the loss of what he might have been had he not succumbed to Belos.

I tell him, "I'm still working on it. But I think it's possible."

He rasps, "I was...glad. When you got away. You are...more. Than me."

Honesty at the moment of death is terrible to witness. It is too late to remake yourself. All the lost opportunities string out into the past. In the end, we all die—every choice leads ultimately to this moment. How awful it would be to face it with regret, with sudden, useless realization.

Because I am merciless—because I am, in a way, still what I have always been—I press him toward that even more.

"Do one good thing, Theron. Help me."

He looks at me for a long time, the pain of his choices in his eyes, the understanding that if he helps me now, he will be admitting that all he has done is wrong. I don't know if he has the courage to face that, but in the end he says, "All right."

CHAPTER 22

LOGAN

I tear through the wind, moving faster than I ever have. Water lifts and sprays in my wake. None of the logical reasons to go after Belos matter to me right now. I just need to see his face when I overpower him. I need to see him acknowledge that I didn't want his control. Why does he think that?

His words eat away at me.

It's like I never beat him back, like that was a fluke, a lucky victory.

I can't accept that.

I catch up with them on the western coast of Kelda. Kronos reaches back to me. His relief is palpable. He lets me in just enough that I can distinguish the energies of Belos, Straton, and Ludos. Belos scrambles for control, but I slide around him. I make myself a barrier between him and Kronos. Kronos seizes his opportunity and slips away into the Drift.

For a glorious moment, Belos, Ludos, and Straton are within my power. I wonder if I could rip them apart like this, blast their energies to nothing, let them scatter through the wind. But that's not what I want.

I want to feel this with my body.

I let go of their energies, letting their bodies reform. The three of them bump and tumble across a rocky shore. I force my own body to draw together. The returning pain in my thigh is sharp enough to stagger me for a moment, then I seize on it. It tells me that I am fully here. I will do this as a man. He *will* see me that way.

I draw stone and thin veins of raw metal into my hand, letting the sword take shape.

Belos, getting to his feet at the water's edge, watches me approach. The Shackle dangles from his wrist, and my temper boils at the sight of it. When Belos shapes his Drift-sword, I feel a surge of satisfaction. Good. This is exactly what I want.

And that's how he fools me.

I swing hard, realizing mid-stroke what is going to happen. He never raises his sword. He never intended to fight.

My sword cuts through air as he vanishes into the Drift.

I yell, and the wind sweeps out from me, a furious gale that feathers the ocean and sends Straton and Ludos flying like leaves.

Before they can pull the same trick as Belos, I seize them, every fiber of their bodies responding to my will. They are, after all, nothing but air, water, earth, and fire.

I strip the elements from them. I draw the air from their lungs until they can't find breath even to choke. Their mouths gape uselessly. I strip them of water next, drawing it out through their skin, letting their bodies' heat consume them. They shrivel like desiccated fruit, wrinkling and cracking. I increase their body heat further until they flake away bit by bit, fire burning the earth to nothing. When they are nothing but dust, I let them go, and the wind carries them away.

CHAPTER 23

As we skim through the Drift, Theron dissolves in my hands. He can't speak here. Even in the physical world he might be beyond that. His eyes don't seem to see me anymore. As his energy drifts into the distance, fading from sight, I can't help but wonder if that is all there is to death: dissolution.

We continue in the direction Theron indicated. Just when I start to worry we've lost the trail, Kronos explodes into the Drift.

The wind rips and tears, and for a moment I can only concentrate on holding myself together. I try to steady myself, balancing against the air here as I would in the physical world. When I look for the others, I spot them far behind me. I skim back to them, sped by the wind. Horik is struggling in my direction but not making much progress. He is trying to bring me the knife. I grab it from his hand and wheel about. I press into the wind, sliding between the currents.

Ahead, at the heart of it, light blazes. The form is shifting, fluid. At the center of it burns the white Leash. The wind scours me, but I will myself into it further, closer.

The Leash brightens as Belos appears in the Drift. He hauls on the Leash. He doesn't see me yet. The Shackle swings free from one of his wrists.

As the wind dies a little, I press closer.

Belos notices me and drops the Leash. Swords flash into his hands. The knife may be more deadly than his swords but only if I can get close enough to stab him.

Of course, that's not my goal right now.

Belos seems to realize this and starts backing off, dragging at Kronos, trying to haul him away. But Belos is weakened, and Kronos is resisting. The Leash floods black, bleeding Belos's will into Kronos. He turns to follow Belos, but I am almost there.

The wind streaming from Kronos scrapes through me. As before, time slows and bends. My mind fills with the silly joy of youth, the joys of running and laughing, and I don't know whether it is my childhood I am caught in, or one I might have had in another life. In the same moment, age washes through me, and I am an old woman, content to watch and laugh as the children run. I am rocking in a chair on a wooden porch overlooking a smooth beach. The sea lies beyond. I look at the man beside me, and it is Logan, weathered by age. He smiles at me, and I see what I have always wanted to see in him: peace.

Time speeds up again, and the reality of the Drift consumes me. I must focus. I must be present. The Leash seethes before me, coiling away like a snake. Belos swings toward me, swords flashing. I still have only one good hand. I can't shape a weapon of my own without losing the knife. But the Leash whips toward me. If I ignore Belos, if I let him cut me, I can get to that Leash.

I said I would die for a reason. Is this not a good one?

The bone blade presses into the cord of energy, which frays like a thousand threads. I have never seen a Leash so thickly woven. Before I can finish my work, a huge hand wraps around me, jerking me away from Belos's falling sword.

I cry out silently and struggle for freedom, but Kronos holds me close, and the wind eases around me. He is shaped much like a man now but brighter, greater. He reaches out his other hand to the frayed Leash and tugs. The last threads give way.

Belos staggers back. Kronos swipes at him, scraping a hand through his energies. Belos screams, and the sound echoes through the silent Drift. The swirling chaos of Belos's energy streams from the rent. It takes me a moment to realize: he is bleeding out all the souls he has Taken. They scramble toward freedom. One face then another forms briefly before dissolving with relief into the Drift. It seems to go on forever. There are dozens, hundreds maybe.

I wait for Belos, too, to dissolve, but he doesn't. All that leaves him is that which never belonged to him in the first place.

In the end, he is left reduced to his own bare self, sagging and exhausted, his energy pulsing with sluggish horror.

Kronos grabs hold of him and drags us all out of the Drift.

I smell the ocean before I see it. I feel rocks and pebbles under my hands and knees. Cold water licks at my boots. Something bumps rhythmically against my right foot, and I glance back to see Belos's prone form rocked by the tide, his hand nudging my boot. I scramble away and push shakily to my feet.

Wind curls and eddies around me. It lifts and tangles my hair. It is curious and uncertain. Another breeze joins the first, and I know Logan's presence at once. He brushes over me in disbelief, moves with hesitation around Kronos.

Kronos gathers himself from the wind, taking shape beside me. For all that he looks human, no one could mistake him for that. His otherness shivers over my skin.

Logan gathers himself into his body next to us. Kronos raises a curious hand to Logan's face, and Logan startles at his touch.

I hear the rushing whiz of displaced air. I only have time to gasp as the harpoon speeds past me, a blur of white.

But Kronos is already gone, a gust of wind tearing away over the sea.

Logan and I wheel on Heborian.

I shout, "What are you doing?" but Logan has no use for words.

He charges even as Heborian is reeling in the harpoon. He tackles Heborian, slamming him onto the beach. Logan rears back with his arm cocked, ready to smash Heborian's face, but Horik and the others grab him and haul him back.

I start to run after them, but something trips me. Hands scrabble up my body, and I thrash instinctively.

Belos flips me onto my back. He tries to shove the Shackle cuff onto my wrist. I shape my spear, but Belos has my arm pinned, and the spear with it.

Someone dives over my head, and Belos's weight vanishes. I sit up as Logan shoves Belos under the water. Belos flails, but he has no power to use beyond his inherent earthmagic and his body. He is no match for Logan in either.

Heborian shouts orders, and the Drifters grab Logan and haul him back. Belos surges up from the water. He crawls to the shore, hacking water from his lungs.

Logan tries to tear out of the grasp of Horik and the others. It's not that I want to save Belos, but someone is going to get hurt. I step into Logan's line of sight. It takes him a moment to register me, then he starts to settle. Horik eases his grip, and

Logan rips away from him. His chest is heaving, and his eyes are wild with color. He glares over my shoulder.

"What are you doing?" he snaps.

I spin to see Heborian hauling Belos up by the Shackle.

"You're not the only one he's hurt, Logan. His death doesn't belong to you alone. It belongs to all of us."

"What are you going to do with him?"

"I will show Tornelaine that we have defeated him. I can't let you waste that opportunity."

I can't argue the logic of that, and neither can Logan. He angles his face down. He tries to breathe steadily, to calm himself. The others move away to join Heborian.

I say, "We'll be behind shortly."

Belos raises his head a little. "What's this, Astarti? You would miss the parade?" His voice may be weak, but all his usual sneer remains. How can he hold onto that even now?

"Just take him."

Everyone but Horik vanishes into the Drift.

"Do you need me?" he asks.

"Leave us, please."

When Horik vanishes, I take a cautious step toward Logan.

"I'm not going to hurt you," he snaps.

"I know that. I just don't know if you're ready for me."

That makes him look up. The dark smudges under his eyes are stark against his paled-out skin. I glance down at his leg, where the blood stain has spread from thigh to ankle. His arm is cut also, but there's not as much blood. None of that is what really worries me.

His chest jerks with his harsh breathing. He takes a deep breath, trying to slow it, but he goes right back to panting. "I didn't get—and your father—and then—"

"Sit down," I say firmly.

"I'm going after him."

"Kronos?"

"Who else?"

"Logan—"

"Don't. *Don't.* I know that tone. I will not calm down or be reasonable or—"

"Sit *down!*"

"No!"

"Logan, please, you're scaring me."

He freezes. The horror in his face tells me he misunderstands that. I'm not scared he'll hurt me. I'm terrified he will hurt himself.

He sits slowly, and the motion would be silent if not for his leg, which makes him grunt. He draws up his good knee and laces his fingers around it. He lowers his forehead to his knee. I hover uncertainly, unsure whether to touch him. He goes still, dragging everything in as I have seen him do so many times.

I crouch beside him. "Are you ready to go back? Your leg needs to be treated."

"I want to find him."

I grit my teeth in frustration. "How?"

"If he's close enough, I'll be able to sense him."

"And if he's not?"

He pushes awkwardly to his feet, forcing his injured leg to comply. "I'll return to the city later."

"You're not going anywhere without me."

His eyes flash green. "I have to go alone."

"No, you don't. If you refuse to return to the city now, take me with you, or I will follow."

"Astarti, I need—"

"I'm not leaving you alone. No matter what you want."

He makes a sound of frustration. He turns partially away, then back to me. I seize on this small sign of acquiescence and slip my arms around him.

He takes us into the wind.

We streak out over the ocean, where the morning light sparkles on the waves. It's hard to believe it's still only morning. It's even harder to believe the day is so beautiful. We range along the shore, heading north for miles before turning inland. We fly over the farmland of Kelda. The trees are in full summer leaf, and the crops are starting to ripen.

I can tell Logan is about out of strength when we start brushing treetops and skimming the hills. We dip dangerously, streaming through the tall grass of a hillside. I try to slow us down, but I still don't know how to manipulate anyone's energy but my own. I wrench away before the crash, balancing myself against the currents, but I can't save Logan.

He plows into the hillside, digging a trench in the soft earth as he skids to a stop. I stumble from the wind, clumsy in my hurry. I land with an elbow in his stomach, driving a "whuff" of air from him. He lets his head drop. His eyes are closed with exhaustion.

I straighten his legs so I can get a better look at his injury. I shape a Drift-knife and cut open his pant leg around the wound. It's swollen and still bleeding. I cut off a portion of my shirt's hem and wad it up. When I press it to the wound, Logan's eyes fly open. He looks at me in surprise then lets his head drop again.

"Are you done yet?"

He closes his eyes. "Yes." He sounds embarrassed.

"Can I take you through the Drift?"

He doesn't answer.

"I could just wait until you pass out. That way you wouldn't even know." I'm sort of teasing.

His eyes slit open. He watches me for a while. I don't like to be watched by other people, but it doesn't bother me with Logan.

168

He asks, his voice barely above a whisper, "Why do you stay with me, Astarti?"

How can he ask that? It almost makes me angry. But sometimes we need to hear the words, so I give them to him. "Because I love you, Logan."

Those words don't make sense to me with anyone else. They are another thing that, with Logan, I just understand.

His expression is pained, like he has something to say that he doesn't like. That means I probably won't like it either.

"I want better for you. Than this."

It frustrates me when he says such things, as though I can't decide for myself, as though my decision is wrong. As though there is even a decision to make! But I know that what he says comes from doubts that have nothing to do with me.

I could argue with him, try to reason, but he's too tired for that, so I tease, "You know what they say: you can't account for taste."

He gives a surprised laugh, and it makes me smile until he grows serious again. "I love you, too, Astarti. That's why I want better for you."

I can't bring myself to be flippant a second time, but I won't entertain his doubts. I tell him firmly, "You are going to get better, and that is all I need. Do you hear me? You just need to let yourself heal."

He only looks at me, not believing.

CHAPTER 24

Logan doesn't let me take him through the Drift. By the time he reshapes us from the wind in the shattered courtyard of Heborian's castle, he's swaying with exhaustion and barely putting any weight on his injured leg. Raised voices in the city beyond make me tense for conflict, then I realize: they're celebrating.

Can this be real?

I gaze across the crater of the courtyard, scanning the fragmented walls and the broken ends of the bridge that once led into the city. The castle itself shows equal damage. At least a quarter of the structure has crumbled into the sea. Several towers have toppled. In this quiet moment, I have time to wonder just how many people died yesterday. Yet, despite that, I suppose it *is* a day to celebrate.

The guards at the castle doors have recognized us and are picking their way through the rubble. Logan is limping badly enough that one of the guards tries to draw Logan's arm over his shoulder to support him. Logan pulls away. He doesn't like to be touched by people he doesn't know.

As we make our way to the temporary infirmary, we pass dozens of servants busily clearing rubble from the halls. At first this startles me, but maybe people are better off with work to do. I would be, if I weren't so tired. Frankly, it's a relief to see so many uninjured.

The Healers have established themselves in what looks like a recreational room. Racquets hang from pegs on one wall, and a net lies folded under them. In the open spaces between cots, the floor is marked with colorful lines. Most of the cots are occupied. Renald, the royal physician, and several young people who seem to be his assistants move from bed to bed. They check bandages and offer steaming cups to their patients. The Healers are occupied at the far end of the room, where the worst injured are gathered.

I guide Logan toward an empty cot. "Wait here. I'll get one of the Healers."

Logan sits on the edge of the cot but catches my hand. "No. I'm sure others are in greater need. I'll wait my turn."

I accommodate Logan only in part. I seek out the nearest assistant, waiting in the open space of the aisle while she finishes rubbing a salve into the gnarled fingers of an old man. Before I can get the girl's attention, Renald spots me. He is a slight, balding man, and his movements are quick and businesslike as he hurries to meet me. Fatigue pinches the corners of his eyes. It was a long night for everyone.

"Astarti," he says in surprise. "Are you injured?"

There's nothing he can do for my hand, and the pinpricks of returning feeling give me hope that it will soon be back to normal. It's rather bizarre, really, to have come out of this without so much as a bloody lip.

"I'm fine, but please come look at Logan."

When we get to where I left Logan, he is leaning against the wall behind his cot, eyes closed. His good leg extends off the bed, foot on the floor. The injured one is stretched out before him, smearing the sheet with dirt, ash, and blood.

Logan doesn't stir when we approach. I touch his shoulder so Renald doesn't startle him. His eyes fly open.

Renald uses a pair of small scissors to cut off the cloth I wrapped around Logan's leg. He examines the wound.

"It's too swollen to stitch, and I suspect one of the ladies"— no need to ask whom he means by that—"would singe my ears if took a needle to you anyway. Dela," he calls. "Warm water, soap, clean cloth." He turns back to Logan. "I'll clean it to make easier work for the Healers, though I'm sure they'll be over as soon as they catch sight of you."

"I can wait if—"

"Don't be absurd."

Logan looks faintly surprised at Renald's brusque tone.

I grin. "A firm hand, I see. Thank you, Renald, for setting that example. Now I know just how to deal with him."

Logan snorts. "Don't even think about it."

Renald, however, is busy pulling out a small table for his assistant as she approaches with a steaming bowl of water in her hands and white cloths draped over her arm. She freezes when she gets a good look at Logan, and water sloshes over the side of the bowl to splatter on the floor. That's when I recognize her. Dela is the Earthmaker girl Logan brought back from Avydos. The one who was terrified of him.

Renald makes a sound of annoyance at the spilled water. "Dela," he says firmly. "Patience, attention, a steady hand. Remember?"

"Yes, sir. Apologies." She proceeds toward us, eyes flicking to Logan and away.

"Good girl," Renald says with equal firmness as she sets the bowl of water on the table. "You see to his arm while I work here."

Dela's lips pinch, but she nods.

Logan says woodenly, "She doesn't have to. She's frightened of me."

"She is under my command, not yours," Renald says without looking up from the cloth he's wringing out. He hands it to Dela, and she quietly moves around the foot of the bed to get to Logan's injured arm.

Logan doesn't look at her as he shrugs his shirt up. He leans forward to pull it off.

"Dela," Renald says inflexibly, and she grabs hold of the hem of Logan's shirt and tugs. She gasps as she catches sight of Logan's back in the moment before he leans against the wall again.

Logan pretends not to notice, staring down into his lap as Dela leans near with her cloth. The cut runs from his forearm, along the outside of his elbow and halfway up his upper arm. She dabs cautiously. When Renald begins to scrub at his leg, Logan makes a hissing sound that sends Dela skittering back. She returns to her work with a determined expression.

Personally, I'm a bit annoyed. Logan did save her life and got her away from Belos. I realize she's very young and probably not used to the fear she experienced, but still.

"I'm sorry," Logan says quietly. "That I hurt you."

She pauses in her work. She looks up at him, drawing back a little at the sight of his eyes. He looks away. She continues to watch him, and I see the moment he becomes a person in her eyes. It's in the parting of her lips, the faint confusion. She glances at the wound in his thigh, where Renald is busily wiping away blood and fluid. Her gaze returns to the cut in his arm.

"I'm sorry, too," she says, her voice barely audible. "That I was so frightened."

Logan's head snaps toward her, then he slides his eyes away to spare her the sight of them. "You don't need to apologize for that."

"You took me away from there. Thank you, Primo Loganos."

Most people don't use his title. It surprises him as much as me.

Dela returns to gently cleaning the wound. I know it must hurt, but Logan holds himself still and silent. Even when Renald uses his cloth to scrub dirt out of Logan's leg, he only freezes more, trying not to startle the girl again by reacting. When Dela is finished with her work, Renald dismisses her to attend other patients.

Logan notices me glaring after her and says, "She only a child, Astarti."

I sniff loudly.

"At least she didn't scream this time."

There's a hint of humor in his voice, so I joke back, "Progress."

"I take what I can get."

His humor vanishes when Renald dabs at his leg with antiseptic. Logan's eyes widen, and he makes a choking sound.

I grimace in sympathy, but Renald says unapologetically, "The more I do, the less strain there is on the Healers. Amazing magic, you know. I don't tell them that, and they could stand to pay more attention to the principles of medicine, but—"

"Astarti! Logan!"

The voice is Korinna's, and she comes hurrying down the aisle, blonde braid flying behind her. She slows to a more sedate pace under Renald's withering glare.

"Miss Korinna," Renald chides, "what have I told you about running in the infirmary?"

"Oh, posh," she mutters, and I grin. She gives me a sly smile as Renald returns to his work, shaking his head in irritation. "Horik told us to expect you."

Something in the way she says Horik's name makes me eye her. Spots of pink appear on her cheeks. Logan, oblivious man that he is, notices nothing. Of course, his thoughts are probably focused on the forceps Renald is cleaning.

"What're those for?" I ask.

"As I said, Astarti, the more I do, the less strain there is on the Healers. We have a system now." He puts his hand firmly on Logan's knee. "Hold still. There's a piece of rock in here."

Though Renald is skilled and efficient, Logan's face whitens as Renald digs into the wound. I have a pretty strong stomach, but even I have to look away. Korinna winces slightly.

"There." Renald holds up the bloody forceps to show off a fragment of stone. "This, Korinna, is what I keep trying to explain. The more you can do mechanically *before* Healing, the less energy you will expend. Always clean the wound first. Always take the time to—"

Once again, Renald is cut off by the rush of one of the Healers through the infirmary. He doesn't, however, chide Gaiana as he did Korinna. With a sigh, he drops the forceps and bloodied cloths into the bowl. He nods to Gaiana and retreats.

Gaiana looks as tired as everyone else, perhaps more so. Logan notices.

"Mother, this can wait."

Without a word, she seats herself on the edge of the cot and presses her hands to the wound. Logan tenses at the pain then slowly relaxes as it disappears. He turns a startled gaze to Korinna as she draws away from his arm, leaving the flesh whole. Korinna darts a look at Renald and looks relieved to find

175

his back turned. Apparently, only major wounds are to be Healed. Logan raises a wry eyebrow at her. She winks, then hurries off to return to her duties.

"Why did you not come back with the others?" Gaiana asks softly.

I don't expect Logan to answer, but he says, "I didn't want to lose him."

"Did you speak with him?"

"No. He was gone."

"I would like to ask you to let him go, but—"

"But you won't ask that. You've no right to."

It is the firmest I've heard Logan be with his mother. She lets out a barely perceptible sigh.

Logan adds, "Especially after *you* went after them. What were you thinking that day, following them into the ocean?"

I anxiously await her answer. I've wanted to know this myself.

Gaiana frowns slightly. "I wasn't thinking. I felt them, and I wanted to go. That is all."

That doesn't make a lot of sense to me, but Logan nods, accepting it.

"There you two are," comes Bran's voice from the doorway. "I heard you'd been seen. Thank the—" He cuts off the familiar expression with a slightly baffled look, finishing instead, "I'm so glad you're both all right."

I tell him, "You can say, 'thank the Old Ones.' It was Kronos who stripped Belos of power, not us. I haven't the foggiest idea how he did it."

Bran comes to the foot of the bed. "He's in the dungeon, you know."

I shudder. Somehow my mind hadn't made the connection between Heborian bringing Belos back to Tornelaine and him actually being here, a few floors below.

Bran says, "Heborian brought him through the main streets. He had him contained in a…bubble? of Drift energy. I thought there'd be a riot. But you know what? When they reached the castle, Belos looked, if anything, bored. What do you make of that, Astarti?"

I shrug. "Either he thinks he's got some card left to play—though I can't imagine what—or it's just another lie. You can never trust anything he says or does. He's called the Liar for a reason."

Logan is frowning at his hands, and I'm reminded of his words when we stood on the side of Mount Hypatia. *He says I want it, but I don't.* Logan was desperate to prove wrong whatever Belos said to him. What did Belos say Logan wanted? And what was the grain of truth in it? I know Belos well, and I know much about lying. Lies only work—they only hurt us—if there is a grain of truth in them, however much that truth may have been distorted.

Koricus said something similar. That Logan wanted his mind taken. Does Logan believe that? I know little of what happened during his imprisonment, so I don't know what these things mean to him.

Dela approaches shyly with a tray laden with bread, dried meat, cheese, and cups of water.

"Thank you, child," says Gaiana as Dela sets the tray on the small bedside table.

Dela dips her chin and hurries away again.

Logan hands me a cup of water, which I drain in seconds, finally washing the dust and ash from my throat. He tries to give me the second cup, but I refuse it. Why won't he ever take care of himself? He sucks down the water while Bran fetches a pitcher. We both refill our cups several times. Clearing my throat makes me realize how much dust is in my nose, but I'll wait to take care of that later. We start on the food next, and while we eat Bran tells us about the feast being planned for tomorrow.

"A feast," I say doubtfully.

"It's not a bad idea, really. Everyone needs a chance to celebrate, to realize that this is over."

I nod agreement, but I can't help wondering: is it over?

Chapter 25

After cleaning up, Logan and I sleep most of the day. Fortunately, our rooms are in part of the castle that didn't get damaged. It's fairly quiet at this end, though the rumbles of earthmagic wake me once or twice. The Earthmakers are helping clear rubble and repair damage. Clara told me, when we met her in the hallway, that the crater in the courtyard is being filled and the bridge restored. She also hinted that the upcoming feast will be a perfect time to "try a few things." She winked at me and hurried on her way, oblivious to—or simply ignoring—my look of horror. When Logan asked what that meant, I admitted to my inadvertent promise to let Clara work on my—what would you call it?—style. Logan, blast him, looked quite amused by the whole thing.

The first time the tremors of earthmagic wake me, I sit up, hunting for Logan. It's almost a reflex now, but he's dead asleep, too tired to dream. He looks young when he sleeps like this, all of the hardness gone from his face, all the tension gone from his body. He usually sleeps on his back, but right now he's on his stomach, one arm hanging off the bed, the other tucked under the pillows. I want to slip my arm under his chest, to feel the warmth of his skin, the beat of his heart, but I'm afraid to wake him. Instead, I watch him until I drift off again.

It's late evening when something other than the distant earthmagic wakes me. I sit up in the dimness, alert and certain that something is in the room. I startle at the sight of Logan crouched at the foot of the bed.

He says, voice scratchy with sleep, "They're here."

Gooseflesh rises all over my body, and I scramble out of the covers to crouch beside him. At first I think he means the Old Ones, then I hear the whispering.

Find them, bind them. Bind, Bind, Bind.

They slip through the air like dry leaves on the wind.

Even though it's useless against the Ancorites, I shape my Drift-spear. I have to have something in my hand.

One of them floats beside me, just beyond my side of the bed. I rise, whipping my spear toward it. I connect first with the bedpost, splitting it like firewood, then my spear swipes through empty air. The Ancorite whispers up my arm and over my shoulder, an icy finger gliding over my skin. In this same moment, the air grows heavy behind me. It's full and angry like a storm about to break.

Logan roars, his voice partly his own, partly that of the wind. A gust slams into my back and sends me flying from the bed. Training makes me tuck and roll, holding my spear close so I don't cut myself.

Wind rages through the room, and I come up crouched. I'm braced for attack but uncertain what to do. In the dimness, I make out movement, but I can't see what's happening. Furniture topples and fabric rips. The screaming wind blows straight at me. I duck, and it tears over my back. The bedside table clatters. The wind explodes through the window with the sound of shattering glass.

Inside, the room falls silent, but through the gaping window comes the sound of wind howling into the distance.

Cautiously, I shape a Drift-light. The room is a mess of broken furniture and scattered bedding. The sheets, torn and twisted into ropes, lie strewn across the floor. The bedside table lists brokenly against the bed, and the jagged remains of the window glass catch slivers of my blue light. Most of the glass was blown outside, but a few fragments gleam on the floor.

My heartbeat slows. I let my spear vanish, only then realizing I held it in my right hand. I flex the hand, relieved by the strength in it. I am preparing to go after Logan when he blows into the room, sending my heart skipping again. He shapes himself from the wind, standing naked before me with terrible fury in his eyes.

He turns away with a grunt, walking right through the glass. My Drift-light plays over the rigid muscles of his back as he tries to straighten the bedside table. It breaks apart when he picks it up. He hurls the remains aside and slams his fist into the wall. Stone crumbles. Cracks spread like a spider web around his fist. He wrenches his arm back like he's going to punch the wall again but stops himself.

I watch him drag it all inside. I don't need to see his face to know it's happening. It's in every line of his body. The tension seeps inward, leaving his body hard and angry but still.

He slowly turns to face me and says woodenly, "They're gone."

"Dead?"

"They fled into the city. I didn't want to…"

I nod. He didn't want to fight them where people might get in the way and get hurt. Instead, he came back here to punch a wall and turn his temper in on himself.

"I'm fine now," he snaps, as though he thinks I'm afraid of him.

It's not that; it never has been, though it must seem that way to him. I just don't know what to do. He has a right to be angry with the Ancorites. He has a right to destroy them. In fact, I hope he does. But he made the right decision to let them go tonight. How can I help him with that?

Because I don't know how to help, I order him, "Get out of that glass."

He looks down, surprised, and picks his way toward me. He sits on the edge of the bed to examine the bottom of one foot. He picks a sliver of glass from his sole, releasing a trickle of blood. He flicks the sliver toward the window with the rest of the mess.

I hunt through the rubble for something disposable or already ruined. I come back to the bed with a strip of shredded sheet. Logan takes it and presses it to his foot.

"Let me see your hand."

"It's fine," he grumbles.

"Let me see it."

He grudgingly holds out his hand. It should be broken, but his knuckles are only scuffed. It might bruise a little, but that's all. The more he uses his power, the more it grows, and the less I understand it.

He bites out, "I want to know why they're here. They've never come before."

"The last of the Old Ones is gone from Avydos. They have no reason to stay there anymore."

"So, what then? They're coming after me?"

"Maybe."

"You know something more. You have a suspicion. I see it in your eyes."

I hesitate. It's not that I want to protect Heborian, but I know that if I tell Logan what I saw on Avydos, it will start a fight. I breathe out slowly, bracing.

Better a fight than a lie.

Though his face remains still, his eyes swirl with color as I tell him what happened.

He demands, "Did he make some kind of deal with them?"

"I don't know. Don't look at me like that, Logan—I *don't know.* I didn't hear him speak to them. He was supposed to ask for their help. Like I said, they came back with him. They did what we wanted and prompted Kronos to come out. I have no idea if, when they were helping Heborian with the harpoon, it was by agreement or by their own initiative. I simply don't know what was going on."

Unsurprisingly, Logan stands from the bed. "Then let's find out."

I sigh in resignation and kick through the mess for some clothes. I find a shirt and breeches from a few days ago. A cautious sniff confirms they are acceptable.

Logan seems to find some equally passable clothes, though his shirt is badly wrinkled. We smirk at each other under the Drift-light. Perhaps someone in this relationship needs to start insisting on a bit of tidiness, but it's not looking good.

We're crossing the darkened sitting room when a fist pounds on our door. I shape my spear automatically and shout, "Who is it?"

"Lady? Is everything all right? We heard a crash."

I ignore the absurd address and open the door. The guard steps back at the sight of my spear. The guards behind him shift uncertainly.

"Everything's fine."

"Are you sure?" The lead guard darts a look at Logan behind me.

Why does everyone look at him like that? This wasn't even his fault.

I let my spear vanish. "Thank you for your concern," I say with finality.

The guard hesitates then ducks his chin and leads his men away. Logan follows me into the hallway.

Halfway to the royal wing, we run into Heborian. We're in one of the broad, main hallways. Sconces cast flickering light across the floor and walls. Heborian's shoulders droop wearily when he sees us. He's wearing clean clothes, but the tired lines framing his mouth and the dark crescents under his eyes tell me he hasn't yet been to bed. He waves off the attendant who is hovering at his shoulder, issuing a quiet order to prepare his room. I almost feel guilty, but Logan clearly does not.

"Do you want to tell me why the Ancorites"—Logan's voice lashes through the word—"are in this castle?"

Heborian's eyebrows lift. I'm quite adept at detecting false expressions, and he looks genuinely surprised to me.

"They came after you?"

"Is that what you want?"

"No, Logan, that's not what I want."

"Am I supposed to believe that? You turned on my father!"

Heborian studies Logan. "How do you know he's your father? Couldn't it be one of the others?"

Logan is taken aback, as though it should be as obvious to everyone as it is to him. "I just know." He adds angrily, "And that is entirely beside the point! Did you let the Ancorites in here?"

"Do you really think I can control where they go? Astarti? Can you talk some sense into him?"

I put up my hands in a you're-on-your-own gesture.

"Leave her out of this!" snaps Logan. "This is *you*. What were you doing firing that thing at Kronos?"

184

Logan is losing the thread of his argument, and Heborian takes advantage of it. "What is your question, son? Are you asking about the Ancorites, or are you asking about the weapon?"

Logan's fists clench dangerously. I've let this go far enough, so I say, "Heborian, don't play games."

He rubs tiredly at his eyes then drags his hands through his hair. "Listen. It's been a *very* long day. I just want to go to bed. Can we do this another time?"

Logan says sharply, "Only if you can tell me honestly that you didn't bring them here."

Heborian lets out a weary, relieved breath. "Yes, I can tell you honestly that I didn't bring them here."

Logan grudgingly accepts this, falling back, but I eye Heborian with suspicion. Heborian meets my gaze with a lifted eyebrow, then turns away without farewell and sweeps down the hallway.

I like that Logan isn't duplicitous or manipulative. I like that he doesn't think in terms of technicality or specificity. No, I don't like it. I love it. It is one of the things I value most about him: an inherent honesty that has nothing to do with speaking technical truth.

But.

It also makes him easily fooled by those who do think that way. He has no idea that he asked the wrong question. He has no idea that he gave Heborian the opportunity to answer without really answering. No, Heborian didn't bring them here. He was able to say so honestly.

That doesn't mean he didn't want them to come. That doesn't mean he won't make use of them.

   

We go the kitchens partly because I'm hungry and partly for something to do. The kitchens lie in another undamaged part of the castle, and it's a good thing they're intact because food is probably more important to the sustainment of this castle than anything else. I've been down here before, so I know to expect the large assembling room with its shelves crammed with serving ware. Logan, however, makes a sound of surprise. Yeah, this place is enormous.

Through the wide doorway lies the main room, a vast space filled with ovens and sinks and work tables, the whole thing organized as tidily as the library. Though I've had little cause to interact with most of the castle's residents, many of Kelda's noble or otherwise-wealthy families stay under Heborian's roof. None seems to call this home, but they'll come for a week, a month, maybe several. Horik says it's normal. Nobles look after their interests, and that's easiest to do if Heborian remembers they exist. Some left when the trouble started; others seemed to think themselves safer by staying. In addition, there are the scholars, craftsmen, servants, and soldiers to feed.

Even now, with evening well underway and dinner surely over, the clatter of pots and hissing of steam filters from the kitchen into the assembling room. I go to the basket on the long table that stretches along one wall. I lift up the white cloth, but there's only a single roll left. I break it in half to share.

Chewing, I approach the doorway, hoping I can persuade someone to slip us a more substantial snack, and nearly collide with Horik. I move out of the way as he edges into the assembling room looking harried. He has half a ham in one hand, a flagon of wine in the other, and a loaf of bread tucked under his arm.

"I wouldn't go in there," he warns.

"Why? What's going on?"

"Farrah, the head cook, is in a right state about this whole feast thing. Heborian said it needn't be fancy, but there are about twenty sauces in the works, and I almost got hit in the head with a pheasant. Besides, if you come within ten feet of the cake they're making, prepare to hear at least seven people scream at you."

I take an unconscious step away from the door. "Sounds terrifying."

Horik nods us toward the assembling table. "I'd rather share than send you into that war zone. Find some chairs."

Logan and I drag three chairs from a corner while Horik dumps his bounty at one end of the table and gathers plates, cups, and knives. The plates are rimmed with gold, and the knife Horik uses to hack at the ham looks like solid silver. I almost laugh at the absurdity of it all. Logan, rolling up his wrinkled sleeves, looks more like a soldier than anything. Horik has one elbow on the table and is sawing at the ham like it's a block of wood, and I've just noticed a gray stain on my shirt. And a green one. Gold-rimmed plates, indeed.

Horik drops a slab of ham onto my plate as I fill the cups. Horik drains his and takes the flagon from me to refill his cup himself. I guess I didn't pour correctly. Ah. I see. I didn't fill it *all* the way to the brim. My mistake.

"No luck with Kronos?" Horik asks.

"No," I confirm. "Gone."

Horik's eyes flick to Logan. "Sorry, Logan."

Logan concentrates on sandwiching ham between two slices of bread. I'm reminded that Horik and Logan's last interaction involved Horik hauling Logan away from Heborian, then Belos.

I start to worry that Logan is resentful of that, but he says, "It's not your fault."

Horik wants clearer confirmation. "We're good?"

"Of course, Horik."

Horik looks relieved. He swirls his wine and takes a sip. "Have you seen the courtyard?"

"We've been sleeping all day." I add, exasperated, "Hasn't anyone else gone to bed?"

"I just got up," Horik assures me. "But I did go look at the courtyard. All filled in. Looks better than it did before! And the bridge is up. These Earthmakers." He shakes his head in awe. "We should keep them around."

That makes me wonder: will they stay? Or will they return to Avydos?

I ask Logan his opinion on it, but he shrugs. "I have no idea."

"What will Aron want?"

"To go back. How soon will they do that? Who knows. And it will take longer to rebuild the islands than to repair that courtyard. You saw what the mountain did. There are no crops."

"Maybe it's not such a bad thing," I say. "Earthmakers, Drifters, humans. All of them here, working together. Maybe things will be better. You know? Maybe they'll learn to accept…" I don't realize I'm talking about me and Logan until I fall silent. Will it be better? Or will he have to choose between me and his people?

He finds my hand under the table and squeezes, telling me what his decision would be.

But I don't want him to have to choose.

Horik drops a pair of dice onto the table. "Care to reduce some of your debt?"

I don't remember how much I supposedly owe Horik after our last game of dice, but I'm pretty sure it was a lot. Certainly more than I have, which is nothing.

"You know I'm not lucky, Horik."

Horik grins. "Oh, I disagree, Astarti. You just need a broader perspective."

That makes the corner of my mouth tug up. I return the pressure of Logan's fingers under the table. "Maybe so."

We play dice in the corner of the room, apologizing profusely when one of the assistant cooks comes out and exclaims at the mess we've made. She clears away the remains of our meal, muttering all the while, but she returns shortly afterwards with a fresh flagon of wine.

"For saving the castle," she says. "But, truly, the assembling table is not for eating at."

"Apologies, Jennie," Horik says with a grin.

She blushes and hurries back to the kitchen.

"What is it with you and the girls, Horik? They love you."

Horik puts on a hurt expression. "And why shouldn't they?"

I snort. "I don't know, that terrible haircut?" Horik's hair has grown out a little, but it's still cropped close to his head.

"And whose fault is that?"

"Mine maybe," I admit, thinking of the way I accidently cut off a lock of Horik's once-long hair while learning to refine my control of Drift-energy.

"Maybe!" he objects. "Huh." He tosses the dice into the corner, and they turn up two dots.

"You're so easily riled," I tease, knowing it's the opposite of true. "So easy to put you off your game."

"Phht. You turned those over with Drift-work, didn't you?"

I stare at him, taking in the playful smile behind his question. "Is that how you win? Have you been cheating?"

He gives me a look of mock-outrage. "Of course not!"

"You have!"

He sniffs. "I guess you'll never know."

"Due to suspicion of cheating, I must declare that I owe you nothing."

Horik responds wryly, "Considering you never had any intention of paying me, you'll forgive me if I don't think that means very much."

I snort.

Logan comments, "Are you sure you two aren't related?"

"Well," Horik says thoughtfully, "Heborian is my mother's"—he ticks something off on his fingers—"third cousin's son, so I guess we are, a little."

I look at Horik in surprise. "I didn't know that."

"There's a lot you don't know about me," he says with an air of mystery.

I snag the dice from the corner. "I know you're about lose, oh, Man of Many Secrets."

Horik grins. "Man of Many Secrets. I like that."

We play several more rounds, and Horik wins, as usual. Try as I might to detect any currents of Drift-energy, I feel none. Maybe he is just lucky.

Horik teases me about still nursing my first cup, but I have no interest in feeling the effects of wine. Horik clearly enjoys those effects, growing more relaxed every time he refills his and Logan's cups. But where the wine makes Horik laugh and give me an absurd kiss on the cheek, it makes Logan quiet. I try not to worry about how much he drinks. He doesn't look drunk. His words aren't slurred. Besides, he's an adult, and I'm not his mother, not that she would try to stop him either.

Though Logan and Horik are both deliberately consuming, it's Logan's purpose that worries me. He is using it as he uses everything, to close himself in. By the time we leave the kitchens, with me yawning and ready to return to bed, he hasn't spoken for at least twenty minutes.

What is he thinking?

He won't tell me, so I don't ask.

Should I?

It's dangerous, what he's doing, turning inward like that. It scares me so much it makes me silent, a coward, and I fall asleep with more fear in my heart than I felt even as I cut Kronos's Leash, expecting to die.

CHAPTER 26

I wake near dawn to find Logan gone. I want someone to curse; I want someone to blame. I blame Logan, a little. Why didn't he wake me? Then I blame myself. I knew this was going to happen and did nothing to prevent it. Not knowing what to do is no excuse. I didn't even try.

I dress quickly and slide into the Drift. I will find him, and if he's fighting I'll do whatever it takes to stop him.

I drift through the castle, prepared to hunt all of Tornelaine when I see him. He didn't leave. He's deep underground. In the dungeon.

I have a brief, absurd thought that Heborian has betrayed us and imprisoned Logan, then I realize what he must be doing.

I slide out of the Drift at the top of the dungeon stairs. I shape a Drift-light, which casts cool blue over the damp stone walls. Warm lamplight fills the bottom of the stairwell, and I move cautiously toward it.

A guard slouches in a chair, cleaning under his fingernails with a knife. The chair is leaned back, front legs off the floor, but slams down when the guard sees me. Even though I know Belos has been stripped of power, I'm still a little shocked that this is the only security down here.

"I'm looking for my friend," I say, unwilling to speak more personally to this man I don't know.

The guard waves me toward the cells. "You're on the list."

"List?"

"Of approved visitors."

Approved visitors? If there are restrictions regarding who comes down here, why I am allowed? Logan clearly is also. I can only assume Heborian is keeping Belos alive for a public execution, so why allow those most likely to kill him to have access to him?

The aisle between cells is wide enough to walk down the center without being in arms reach of the cells on either side. Though it's a good precaution, the open space makes my skin crawl. I don't look in the cells. The guard's lamp and the burning torch bracketed at the far end of the room are enough to show outlines. From the edges of my vison, I see prisoners lying listlessly on their cots or huddling in corners. Many of the cells, however, are empty, so I'm surprised to discover that Belos is kept at the far end of the row.

I know exactly where he is because I can hear his voice, the cold, clear tones unchanged, apparently, by his fate.

"Ah, Astarti," he says when I stop outside his cell.

Belos reclines on his cot in apparent comfort, as though he doesn't notice the iron shackles on his wrists. The chains are too short for him to lower his arms, so they hang above him like he's a puppet on strings. It has to be uncomfortable, but you'd never guess that from his satisfied expression.

The reason for his satisfaction is readily apparent. Logan stands in the middle of the cell, arms tightly crossed. He is completely still, physically containing it all, but the anger

193

radiating from him washes against me even where I stand beyond the bars. He blinks twice before he seems to register my presence.

Belos says casually, "We've been having the most pleasant chat."

"I'll bet. Logan?"

He walks stiffly to the bars. The light of the torch flickers over his face, sparking in the swirling color of his eyes. His expression gives me nothing, and I won't question him in front of Belos. He fades until I can see through him, like he's a ghost. He passes through the bars and solidifies beside me. I touch his crossed arms. The muscles are knotted like ropes. He starts to move past me, but I tighten my grip.

"Please don't," I whisper.

I hold my breath until he nods.

I trust him not to lie to me.

As he walks away, his boots snapping along the stone floor, I know I should follow.

I can't.

In this moment of standing outside Belos's cell, I realize why Logan came down here, even if he didn't get what he wanted. I know, too, why Heborian granted us access, and I'm grateful for it. Just as I needed to see Belos's fortress in ruins, I need to see him that way. I need this to be my new image of him, even if he wears that smug, lying smile.

"What did you mean, 'don't'?" Belos inquires.

I take in his lank blond hair, the smear of dirt across one sunken cheek. I let my eyes linger on the iron cuffs. And so I am able to make my lips form a smug smile of my own. "Wouldn't you like to know?"

"I can probably guess."

"I doubt it."

"You forget, Astarti, I spent many weeks inside his head. I know him better than you do."

I keep my face blank. "And I know you well enough not to listen to that."

He gives me a lazy smile. "You're a good liar, Astarti. I'm sure you fool everyone. But not me. I taught you." He settles more comfortably. "Don't you want to know what got him strung so tight?"

"I won't be able to trust your view of events, so, no, I don't."

He shrugs in his chains. "No matter. I'm sure he'll tell you."

I adopt a casual posture, cocking one hip and leaning against the bars.

Belos smirks. "I'll let you off the hook. Wonderful phrase, that. So appropriate. You are a fish on a hook, caught by your need to know."

"And just what do you think I need to know?" Of course I shouldn't ask that, shouldn't give in to him, but I can't stop myself. And so he hits me with the truth, using it just when I'm braced for a lie.

"You need to know how to stop him."

"Stop him?"

"From hurting himself."

I stare. How can he know that?

"Like I said, Astarti, I know him better than you do. And I know *you* better than you think."

He sees that I want to ask. He sees that I won't. He pretends to be sympathetic. "I'd like to help you, but the truth, as I think you know, is that you can't stop him. He's going to break. It's already happening. The only question is: how soon, and what will be the final blow that shatters him into a thousand pieces?"

And just like that, I know myself for the greatest fool there ever was. Better I had kept my final image of Belos as him crumpled by the sea. Better I had not given him this chance to defeat me with words once again. They are all he has now, and he wields them better than he ever wielded a sword.

I want to say, *I hate you*. It fills my throat, beats against the back of my teeth. But he would smile. He would love it.

Like the fool I am, I grasp at the only thing I have. "You talk boldly for a man who just lost everything."

"Is that how this looks to you?"

I make a show of looking him over. "Yes, that is how this looks to me."

"Come now, Astarti. You're smarter than that. I'm yet alive."

"And awaiting execution."

"But that day has not yet come, and I have in my grasp the key to my freedom."

"And what is that?"

"You."

"Me? Have you lost your mind as well as your power?"

He ignores that last bit. "Because you want to save him. Because you still think it's possible to prevent that last, shattering blow."

I stare, unable to walk away, unwilling to ask.

He takes a deep, savoring breath. "I can find him. I am the only one who can."

I don't know how to react, so I don't react at all.

Belos goes on, "Logan wants to find him, doesn't he? His father? And you want that for him. Don't you?"

"You can't find Kronos."

"Think, Astarti. Think. Straton was always wrong about you. You *are* smart. You know the truth. You can see it."

Belos is implying that he left a bit of himself within Kronos, that he can track him by that. I'd like to scoff, but instead I feel the blood drain from my face.

Because it's possible he's speaking the truth. Because there is no way for me to prove that he's not.

I back away from the bars. No. I won't believe him. I can't allow myself to.

I wish I could throw some cutting last words at him, but nothing comes to my lips. I turn away. As always, all I can do is escape.

Belos calls after me in his cool, smooth voice, "I'll see you later, Astarti."

CHAPTER 27

Logan has kept his unspoken promise. I find him in our bedroom, shoving broken furniture into a corner. He's dressed in clean clothes now, leather breeches snug on his hips and a dark blue linen shirt tucked in.

I need his touch. I need him to help me forget what Belos said. I need to feel myself unwind in Logan's hands, to feel him unwind in mine. I need to believe that we don't need Belos.

When I slip my arms around Logan's waist, he returns the embrace, but he's not really there. We might as well be across the room from each other. It freezes me, makes me draw away. Logan doesn't seem to notice. He picks up a broken chair and tosses it out of the way.

I rub my arms, chilled in spite of the warmth of the room. Belos is right: I am going to lose him. Those may not have been his precise words, but they are, I fear, the truth. I want to save him, but I don't know how.

He won't let me.

When someone knocks on the sitting room door, I'm almost relieved.

"Korinna," I say in surprise when I open the door.

She reads my tension. "Is this a bad time?"

"Not at all."

"I have a message and a request. The message is for Logan." She looks over my shoulder, and I glance behind to find Logan standing in the doorway between the bedroom and sitting room.

"Message?" he says. "The only one who sends me 'messages' is Aron."

Korinna lets out a huff of surprise. "Good guess. He asked that you come to his rooms."

"Is it just him?"

"And the Polemarc."

"Hmm. All right."

I ask, "Do you want me to come?"

"No," he says, "It's fine."

Fine. I hate when he uses that word.

"Oh, good," says Korinna. "Then maybe you'll be interested in my request. I'm going into the city. Kind of a goodwill venture. I'll go through the camps and visit some of the local physicians. The worst wounded were brought to the castle, but there may be many that should be evaluated. I was hoping you'd come? I warn you, though, Renald is coming also. It was his idea actually. Interested?"

I've already made one cowardly escape today. Why not another?

℘ ℭ

Half an hour later, Korinna, Renald, and I are approaching the neat rows of canvas tents that occupy Tornelaine's market square. A few hawkers cry their wares at the edge of the encampment. Earthmakers and Keldans alike filter toward the carts of hot bread and roasted meats.

"Honey cakes!" exclaims Korinna, a hand flying to her lips. "I can smell them. Renald, sir…"

"Oh, all right. But only if you bring me one."

Korinna grins and nods for me to follow. We make our way through the crowd to one of the more popular carts. I shift uneasily in the line. So many people. And not only that, but…

"Korinna, I don't have any money."

She looks at me aghast. "Really? You're the king's daughter! Surely you're entitled to something."

"Entitled?" I find that an uncomfortable word.

"Owed, then. Good gracious, a soldier's pay if nothing else!"

I never thought of that. Not that I particularly want money, but it would be nice to be able to buy, well, honey cakes and such. I wonder if I'm going to have to start thinking about things like that now. I've never had a…job.

Korinna offers, "If you don't want to talk to your father about it, I'll mention it to the Prima, and she'll mention to the Arcon, and he'll mention it to the king."

I give her a sidelong look. "Is that how things work?"

She returns my look with one of surprise. "And I thought I was hopeless at politics. Of course that's how things work."

We get to the front of the line, and Korinna trades three coppers for three cakes. She hands me one. It's warm and sticky, and when I bite into its sweet bliss, I decide that, yes, I need money for honey cakes.

By the time we get to the tents, my cake is long gone, and I'm licking my fingers in, I'm sure, a quite unladylike way. Korinna, I notice, is doing the same. Renald, on the other hand, wipes his fingers surreptitiously on his pants. I'm not convinced that is any more proper, and it's certainly a waste of honey.

Renald stops at the first tent to inquire if there are any wounded or ill. As part of his inquiry, he announces himself as "the king's physician." Renald is not generally pompous, so I have to assume this venture is as much about making a show of Heborian's generosity as it is about tending the sick. Maybe I'm unfair. Heborian *has* been generous and has asked for little in return. Of course, he's put himself in a position to receive plenty from the Earthmakers, like all the repairs to the castle.

Sneaky bastard.

I turn such thoughts aside. I hate being cranky.

We're directed to a large tent at the center of the camp. The front flap is tied open to let in the fresh air. Renald enters first, announcing himself once again as the king's physician. He waves me and Korinna in behind him.

The interior space is clean, if cramped. Several cots, three of them occupied, are pushed against one canvas wall. A worn rug lies underfoot to keep out the chill of stone.

An Earthmaker woman dressed in robes that were once fine but are now worn and stained greets Korinna and me. "Thank you for coming. I've done my best, but I'm no Healer. We have nothing too serious here. A few colds. A difficult pregnancy."

Renald makes his way to the pregnant woman, and I can't help staring after him. He seems to feel my eyes on his back.

He turns and says, "What, you think I've never attended a woman who is with child? Who do you think helped bring you into this world?"

I jolt.

Renald gives me an I-know-something-you-don't smile. "You were *such* a screamer."

I will never get used to way the past slams into me, the way that things I learn about myself feel so bizarre.

"Do you want to know what your mother said about that?"

That hits me with even greater force, but instead of being bizarre, it's painful. I'm not ready to think about her. I may never be.

Renald doesn't seem to notice my discomfort. "She said, 'Good. I don't want her to be quiet.' A strange woman, was Sibyl, but she knew her own mind. I respected that."

Renald turns back to his patient, and I follow Korinna to another of the cots, where a boy of perhaps nine lies sniffling into a handkerchief. I'm still trying to shake off the unexpected thought of my mother when Korinna nudges me with her elbow.

"Do you want to try?"

"Try what?"

"Healing."

I gape at her. "I don't anything about Healing."

"It's a blending of the five elements, and you can use all five. There's no reason you can't do this."

"You really think so?"

"Of course! Let me try to explain. Healing is about being in tune with the other person. It's a certain…empathy, a connection to what the other is experiencing. That is why touch is so important. You bring yourself into contact, you *feel* the injury. You…understand it." She chews her bottom lip, clearly seeing that she's lost me. "Never mind. Don't worry about that. You'll know it when you feel it. Maybe start with this: Healing requires an awareness of how the body is built of the elements, how they interplay."

"I think I understand that. When I blend with the elements, I'm using my body's affinity to them, finding the way we are alike."

"Yes! Good! To Heal someone, you find that affinity."

"All right, but how do you get from affinity to actually, well, *healing*."

"That comes from giving of yourself. Letting a portion of your energy—the energy that lies in all the elements within you—flow into the other person. It's hard explain because it's not a procedure like stitching a wound. It's flexible. Each person is different, and you must seek compatibility with them. That will open the door, so to speak."

I mull that over as the boy sneezes into his handkerchief.

"What's your name?" Korinna asks him.

"Melus," he says, the name garbled by congestion.

"Astarti?" Korinna prompts.

Awkwardly, I put my hands on the boy's head. He lies still, trusting me. I try to let my mind dip into that place where I'm aware of the elements, but I feel it only in my own body, not in his. I don't know him. How can I have an affinity with someone I don't know? Feeling foolish, I take my hands back.

"You have to let yourself be comfortable," Korinna explains. "Here, watch me."

She lays her hands on the boy's face. She smiles slightly and closes her eyes. When she takes her hands away, Melus blinks in surprise.

"Better?" she asks.

He sits up. "I've never been Healed before." His voice is clear and full of wonder.

Korinna chucks him under the chin, which seems to surprise him as much as the Healing did. I am reminded that most Earthmakers are firmly inexpressive. I like Korinna's way better.

"Go on," she says. "Go help your mother. But, Melus?"

He pauses halfway out of the cot.

"Do me a favor? Find Kassandra Irenos and tell her that her daughter is here."

"Yes, of course," he says with a serious expression, for all the world like a thirty year old man. "At once. Thank you, Healer."

As Melus skitters out—not so much like an adult after all—Korinna explains, "My mother refused to stay in the castle. She doesn't care for the king."

I liked Kassandra when I met her in Avydos. Someday—not today, but someday—I'd like to ask her about Sibyl. Who would have known her better than her own sister?

As Korinna and I get up to move to the next cot, Renald says heavily, "Haven't we discussed this, Korinna? How will you feel if we encounter a severe injury when you've used up your strength Healing sniffles?"

Korinna sighs. "Yes, Renald."

Korinna crouches beside the cot of an older man. He looks around forty, but it's impossible to guess the age of Earthmakers once they're past about twenty. The man covers his mouth with his sleeve and coughs.

"I'm sorry," Korinna tells him. "It looks like you'll have to heal the old fashioned way."

"No matter," he replies in a scratchy voice.

Korinna has him sit up. She places her hands on his chest and back and asks him to take deep breaths. She looks into his eyes and mouth. I have a strange feeling as I watch her, a feeling that crept up on me with Horik as well. I like her. I think we could be friends. Maybe we already are?

From the corner of my eye, I see someone large lean into the tent. I bolt to my feet. "What's wrong?"

Horik's lips are compressed, his eyes filled with worry. He motions me toward him, and I stride to the open flap and duck through.

"I think you should come back to the castle."

My heart knocks against my ribs. "Is it Logan?"

"I was on my way to see Heborian when I heard those Ancorites in the air. I followed them, and they went straight to the Arcon's room, where Logan was in a meeting with him."

I think of the damage to our bedroom when Logan chased them out. It could have been much worse than broken furniture.

"Was anyone hurt?"

"No, and I lost track of Logan because I couldn't see him from the Drift. I looked all over. I thought he'd gone into the city, and I started to head that way. Then I found him."

"*And?*"

"I wasn't trying to spy. I just wanted to make sure he was all right. He's in your rooms. I think you should go. He was...well, you'll see."

CHAPTER 28

I race through the Drift, skimming through the ragged, ruined barrier that sags around the castle. I speed toward our rooms, but none of my fear prepares me for what I find. At first, I can't make sense of it. Then horrified understanding fills me.

I slide from the Drift in the sitting room. My heart pounds hard enough to dizzy me. I inch toward the bathing chamber, flinching at the snap of leather. My hands are shaking by the time I reach the door.

I can't find my voice to announce myself. I turn the handle and ease the door open.

Logan doesn't look up. He's sitting on a stool, leaned forward, forearms on his thighs. With his head angled down, the messy waves of his hair hide his face. He's taken his shirt off. Over the curve of his shoulders, I see the upper edges of long red welts. His belt, wrapped tight around one fist, dangles to the floor.

I move toward him cautiously. He still doesn't look up. I'm not sure whether he knows I'm here, but I still can't find my voice.

I kneel before him, putting my hands on his forearms. He's trembling, and it makes his hair shiver. The moment seems to stretch on forever, then Logan shakes his head, denying something.

"I can't, Astarti. I can't, I can't, I can't."

The pain in his voice makes my heart clench, but I'm still too frozen with horror to respond.

"He said I wanted it, but I didn't. I *didn't want it.*"

Logan seems stuck, like these are the only words he can allow himself to say, but there's so much more festering beneath them.

I dredge up my voice, whispering, "What didn't you want?"

He shakes his head slowly, refusing the answer in himself more than he's refusing me.

"His control?"

Logan's trembling redoubles, like the words send a shockwave through him.

Lying, as I well know, works best when formed around a grain of truth. That is the only way to construct a lie that really hurts someone. If there's no truth, the lie can be dismissed. But if there is some underlying truth, no matter how small, that lie can twist a person up and make them believe that the lie is reality. It can *change* that person's reality.

What, then, is the grain of truth here? If I can't dig it out, if I can't use it to deconstruct Belos's lie, Logan will never believe it was a lie to begin with.

I whisper, "Just because you manage to force something on someone doesn't mean they wanted it."

"But they were weak enough that it happened."

"You don't believe that. Anyone can be overpowered. *Anyone*, Logan. Even the gods."

"But I—" He cuts himself off.

"You what?"

"I was—"

I wait. He's shaking so hard that his teeth rattle. I want to put my arms around him, to tell him he doesn't have to do this, but he does have to do this.

"I was—" He shakes his head again, refusing, but the truth tries to shake him apart from the inside, desperate to get out.

I whisper, "You were what?"

"*Relieved!*"

He tries to drag air into his lungs, but he can't. I slide my arms around his neck, cradling his head against me until the word has stopped choking him. Then, as though that word was the one thing holding it all in, the rest starts to pour out.

"I was tired. I was *so tired*. I didn't know how tired I was until then. I didn't have to—it wasn't my responsibility anymore. And I was *relieved*."

I know his weariness goes back much, much further than his time with Belos. My heart aches at the thought of the burden he's carried all his life, of how much he's had to control.

"I'm so tired," he breathes.

"I know, love, I know."

His tone changes abruptly, angry again. "And he knew it. He knew I wanted him to take over."

Here it is: the lie built around the grain of truth. And Belos has convinced him of it; he has made this twisted reality for Logan.

"No," I say, leaning back. "*No*. What have I told you about how lies work?"

"That they are really the truth underneath!"

"You know that's not what I said, and you know that lies are not truth."

"But this—"

"No. You were relieved"—he turns his face away, and I lay my hand on his cheek, not letting him escape—"and why shouldn't you be? Logan. *Logan.* Of course you don't want this burden—"

"But I do. I like the power. I like it, Astarti, I like it. Don't you see that's what's wrong?"

"No, that's not wrong. Of course you like your elemental power. You are supposed to. It's beautiful. It's you."

"It's horrible! You've seen—"

"It's dangerous, yes, I know."

"That's why I have to—that's why—"

His fist tightens on the belt. I lay my hand over his, but he twists it away. I move my hand to his wrist. He's not ready to give that up.

"You wanted that burden eased. That's why you felt relieved. That doesn't mean you wanted Belos to take control of your body and mind. There's a huge gap between those two things. Do you know what fills that gap? Lies. Manipulation. And *fear*, Logan. You are afraid that he's right, and that's why you've let yourself believe that he is. But he's not. He is *not*. Remember, please remember: this is how lies are made."

"But there's still truth under it."

"That's why the lie hurts so much. You were relieved." Again, he tries to draw away. I lay my hands on either side of his face. "You were relieved," I say it firmly, making him hear it. "That is all right. You can accept that. There's nothing wrong with it. And it *does not mean* you wanted Belos to control you."

Even though his face is still angled down, I can see that his forehead is wrinkled. I don't know if he believes me, if he's accepting my words, but at least he's thinking about them.

After a few moments, he lets out a shuddering breath. "There's…something more."

I sit back on my heels, returning my hands to his wrists. I let him take his time.

His breathing roughens as he tries to tell me. He makes a series of barely audible, inarticulate sounds. He starts to rock slightly. Fear crawls up my spine.

"He…" Logan keeps rocking.

Some deep instinct makes me connect this to Koricus's last words: *And that wasn't the only thing you liked, was it? Do you remember? Does it shame you?*

I have avoided those words in my memory, finding the others easier to reason with. But they're eating at Logan, poisoning him, and this is no time for me to be a coward.

I ask quietly, "Did he—?"

Logan growls. The sound is deep, rumbling up from his chest. He shakes his head sharply, and the hand clenching the belt jerks upward a little. But my hand is on his wrist. I don't shove him down, but I don't move. His hand lowers, forearm braced on his thigh again. He is steel under my hands. Low animal sounds roll through him.

I whisper, "Tell me what happened."

I still can't see much of his face, but the sounds he makes are of anger and hatred. But that hate, I fear, is for himself, and that's what makes it so horrible.

"I *thought* he was you."

I recall when Horik and I first found Logan in Belos's dungeon. He was confused. He didn't believe it was me. He acted like I'd been there before. I knew, even then, that Belos had worn my face to torment Logan, but I didn't let my thoughts run deeper than that.

"What did he do?"

Logan shakes his head sharply.

I wait.

"He came to me. As you. Like you were there to get me out. I should have hated his hands on me. I should have known from the first."

I ache for him, but he is wrong to blame himself, and I need him to see that. "Do not forget that Belos is a master deceiver. Or that he knows me well enough to make such a deception seem real. Besides, Logan, when Horik and I got to you, you were utterly exhausted. In that state, anyone would have been fooled, even me."

"But I was…" His mouth clamps shut. He breathes angrily through his nose.

There is another word here, another he hasn't been able to handle, but I think I can guess this one.

He tries again. "Just a light touch, nothing much. Nothing even happened. But that was all it took. That was all. He accomplished more with the lightest touch of his fingers than with the whip. He broke me then."

I close my eyes. Belos was getting nowhere with physical abuse, so he did what he does best. He lied. He found a way to make Logan doubt himself, hate himself. He destroyed Logan's reality, then he rearranged the broken pieces for his own use.

But this logic will not help Logan. He must get to the grain of truth, the reason this lie bothers him.

"Astarti, I was…" He grits his teeth, unable to say the word. "I…"

"You were—"

"Nothing happened!"

He doesn't want to hear the word any more than he wants to say it. But it must be said. It doesn't matter that nothing happened. What matters is Logan's view of himself. I have to make him look at this square on. Only then can he begin to deconstruct the lie that it is.

I whisper, "You were aroused."

He explodes up from the stool, tearing out of my hands. The stool clatters to the floor. Logan stalks to the far side of the bathing chamber. He braces his left hand against the wall, leaning hard on it, head hanging. His right arm is rigid at his side, his knuckles white around the belt. Now I can see his back fully. Angry red lines, some trickling blood, lie in stripes over his shoulders and down to the band of his pants. The sight makes my eyes prickle because he has done this to himself. He has repeated the wrongs that others have done to him and *that*, I do not understand. But this isn't about me and my horror.

I approach slowly. The air whistles through his throat. I lift my hand to his right arm. He is rigid and doesn't respond to the touch. I slowly walk my fingers around him, trying to turn him. He is far too strong for me to force him, and at first I think he won't yield. Then he gives in all at once.

He spins toward me, putting his back to the wall, and slides to the floor. He draws up his knees, forearms resting on them, that belt still in his white-knuckled grip. I sink slowly, kneeling between his feet.

"Lo-gan." I have to stop and steady my cracking voice. "Logan, this is nothing but another lie."

He says softly, wearily, "And what is the truth here?"

"That you wanted me. That you were happy to see me."

For the first time, he raises his eyes to mine. I bite my lip to keep from crying out. His eyes are red-rimmed and so, so sad. His irises are gray-green, defeated. I have never seen that before.

He can't take it. He looks away.

"But it wasn't you," he whispers. "It was him, and I…" His voice drops so low it's barely audible. "I'm so…" I can't help it; the tears are filling my eyes as he tries to dredge up this last word. "Astarti, I'm so ashamed."

He gasps, and I know it's coming at last. He starts shaking again, and his face twists. His eyes squeeze shut. He tries—he tries *so hard* to stop. He covers his face with his left hand, his right still gripping the belt. His stomach jerks; his throat works like he's choking. His lips are clamped tight, but a hiss, a huff, the first edge of a sob, works its way past them. He sucks in hard, trying to haul it back.

Shame is not something you can take from someone by telling them they shouldn't feel it. It doesn't work like that. I know. And nothing—*nothing*—kills you more inside. In this moment, I hate Belos more than I ever have.

I start to pull Logan toward me. He resists at first, then he spills into my arms. He still won't let out the sound, and he sobs silently into the crook of my neck, his whole body jerking with the force of it. My heart shatters. I press my cheek to his head, clench my hands in his hair. I hold him tight against me as the horror works through his body. I squeeze my own eyes shut, but the tears leak through.

Eventually, it's too much for him, and he can't stay silent. He gasps, choking, and I can feel his tears against my neck. His sobs come out broken, like he doesn't know how to cry. I have the terrible feeling that he never has before, at least not for himself. I let him learn to do it in my arms. I hold on, I hold on, I hold on.

At last, exhausted, he slides down my front, slumping silently into my lap. I stroke his hair. His arms are on either side of me, forearms on the floor. His left is curled around my foot, hanging on, but his right is still clenched on the belt. I try to work my fingers into his grip, to get him to let go, but his fist tightens in resistance.

I keep one hand resting lightly on his fist. With the other, I stroke through his hair and down his neck. I stop above the lash marks, which are raised, swollen flesh crisscrossing layers of similar scars. Seeing the overlay, I realize: this goes back to the beginning. I think of what he said that night I confronted him about fighting. He said that fighting helps him get control. At the time, that made no sense to me, but I think back further. The Ancorites were the first to whip him, the first to teach him the power of physical pain. They wanted him to release his magic so they could know what he was. They thought it would make him lash out, open up, expose himself.

I don't think that's the lesson he learned.

I close my eyes as the truth becomes obvious. How could I not have seen this? The truth is so simple. It's twisted; it's horrible. But it's clear.

I whisper because the silence is fragile. "When the Ancorites beat you, they wanted you to react. But you didn't, did you?"

He tenses at the question, but he's too tired to draw away from me. I keep my fingers moving through his hair.

"No," he says, his voice muffled against my legs. "Not for a long time."

"That's why you do this. It's how you first learned to bury everything inside."

He doesn't answer at first, then he says, "I need it."

"No, Logan. Not this." His fist tightens again on the belt. I don't try again to take it. I need him to give it to me. I stroke his hair. "I know that you don't want to hurt people—"

"I have *killed* people."

"I know. And that's a terrible weight to bear. But you cannot keep hurting yourself to prevent that."

"Yes, I can."

"No, Logan. It's not good for you."

He says wearily, "That doesn't matter."

"Yes, it does. You are going to have to find a way to balance what you are by nature with how you want to be. You keep trying to drive this wedge into yourself, to split off the part that scares you. But you can't. You will have to accept that part of yourself. *There is nothing wrong with it.*"

He starts to pull away, not believing me. When his head comes up, I catch his face in my hands. "The only thing wrong with you is that you keep shoving part of yourself away. You can neither bury it nor cut it out. It will always emerge, and it is worse for having been so brutally contained."

"But it's dangerous."

"Because you haven't learned to control it."

"That's what I'm trying to do!"

"Oh, love, that's not control. That is denial, and it's not at all the same thing."

He looks almost surprised, and for the first time, I see a hint of understanding in his eyes. For the first time today, I have hope.

But he challenges, his tone bitter, "And how am I supposed to learn control?"

I can't answer his question, and he knows it. All I can say is, "We will figure it out."

He pulls out of my hands.

"Logan, you are the bravest man I know. Have the courage for this. It won't be easy. There will be failures. But try, please, just *try*. Let us work on it together—"

"Don't you understand? You shouldn't have to do that. You think that's what I want for you? Why do you think I try to hide this?"

"I don't want you to hide it. It *kills* me when you do that. I want you to talk to me. I want you to trust me—"

"I *do* trust you."

"No, you don't. You don't trust me when I say that I want this. You don't trust me to see you fully and not turn away."

His eyes squeeze shut as I hit on the truth.

"I'm not turning away, Logan. Nothing about you scares me or disgusts me. I love you, all of you, and I need you to *stop hiding from me*."

He is still for a while, not sure what to do with this, then he turns toward me fractionally. It's hesitant, like he's still questioning me, giving me the chance to change my mind, to show some sign that I don't really mean it. I raise my arms. I silently beg him to come to me.

He shifts the rest of the way, lifting his arms in answer, and we pull each other in. I press my face into his neck. He presses his into mine. I slide my hand down his right arm to his fist, and it opens at my touch. The belt slides free, the buckle thumping to the floor. His right arm wraps around me, his hand pressing against my back, clinging to me instead.

Eventually, worn out, he begins to slump. I tug at him, urging him to his feet. We have to break apart a little to get up, but I don't take my hands from him. By silent agreement, we make our way to the bedroom.

Someone has cleared away the broken furniture and swept up the glass. Shutters are nailed over the window, making the room dim.

Beside the bed, I free my hands to unlace Logan's pants. I slide them off his hips. It arouses him a little, but I want him to sleep. He is physically and emotionally exhausted, and he doesn't put up a fight when I nudge him toward the bed. I strip off my own clothes and crawl in beside him. We snake our arms around one another. He is asleep almost at once.

He wakes maybe an hour later. His eyes slide open, and his arms tighten around me. His leg is between mine, his hip resting against me. The pressure from his arousal makes heat pool between my legs. When I trail my fingers down his side, he shivers. I slip my hand around his hip to touch his most sensitive, intimate places. He moans, head falling back.

He lets me explore his body, trusting me with it, accepting the pleasure I give him. But he wants to give back, and I let him.

He rises above me, his powerful body hovering over mine, and caresses me as I did him. He is in control of himself but not restrained. He slides a hand under my back. He rocks into me, beautiful in his pleasure, and that, more than anything, makes me fall apart.

CHAPTER 29

I wake late in the afternoon. For once, I don't jolt up to look for Logan; I feel him in my arms. He stirs when I do. The light that slips through the shutters lets me see his eyes. They are calm.

I'm not naïve. Logan is not healed. There is no magic to Heal the mind or the heart, and words can only accomplish so much at a time. But this is a beginning.

"I love you, Astarti."

That is the most beautiful thing I have ever woken up to, and it's difficult to get my mouth working to answer, "I love you, too."

He sighs against me, and we luxuriate in the warmth of each other.

I say, tucking my head under his chin, "The feast is tonight."

"Mm-hmm."

"I was thinking I might…"

"Might what?"

"Dress up. A bit."

I feel him trying to angle his face down to look at me. "Don't you have some kind of agreement that you have to?"

I could let it go at that. I could pretend I'm only fulfilling an obligation, but I want to be honest. And I want to know what he thinks. I admit, "I thought I might want to."

I bite my lip. Is this very stupid?

Logan brushes tangled hair back from my forehead and leans away to look at me. I meet his eyes and find them intent on my face. "I think you should do whatever you want."

"But won't I look fake and silly?"

Logan's thumb grazes my cheekbone to my ear. He doesn't pose an argument and doesn't get annoyed with my insecurity. He says simply and seriously, "No."

I let out a relieved breath. "All right."

I tighten my arms around him, snugging myself against his body. He returns the embrace, and soon we want more from each other. As he moves over top of me, I dig my fingers into the muscles of his back. When I feel the warm, swollen welts, I let go. But the loss of contact is terrible for both of us, and I press my hands to his back again. He sets a rhythm that takes over my consciousness. My mind expands until I am aware of all of myself and all of him. I feel the blending of the elements that make us what we are, the wildness that is Logan, and I give myself to him. For a moment, the boundary between our bodies vanishes. We are one, and we shatter together.

Lazy and content, I lie in his arms. My fingers trace the muscles of his back, skimming over the thin ridges of flesh that are his scars. I lurch up to see his back. The welts have vanished.

"Logan..."

He jolts like he's just now realized the pain is gone. "Astarti, you..."

219

"I *Healed* you." I look down at his face and find him staring up at me in wonder.

"I didn't know you could do that."

"I didn't think I could. Korinna tried to teach me, but I failed. I think…when we…" I blush, unable to say the words.

A line wedges between Logan's brows. "Don't be embarrassed by anything we've done."

"I'm not," I protest.

Logan pulls me down into his arms.

I insist, "I'm not embarrassed."

He says gently, "Sex is not a dirty word. I don't want you to be ashamed of it when we step away from our bed, as though it's something we hide away and don't talk about and pretend doesn't happen. I love you, and I love making love to you, and if I don't speak of it to others it's not because I think it's wrong or embarrassing. It's because it's only for us, and I won't share it."

His words make something click in my mind. I have been embarrassed. I've wanted this, have enjoyed it. But I've always tucked it away afterwards.

I don't want to do that again.

"You're right," I say. "I'm sorry."

He draws back to look at me. "You have nothing to apologize for," he says firmly, then, "What? Why are you smiling?"

I shake my head. "Just you."

He asks warily, "What did I do?"

"You just made me love you a little more, that's all."

His eyebrows jump. "Oh. Well, good. Then come here." He nips at my neck while one hand cups my breast.

I laugh. "Surely not!"

He growls, "What do you mean, 'surely not'?" and applies himself to his task with admirable determination.

I work my fingers under his chin and lift his head. His irises are solid gold, and it makes my breath hitch. Even so, I remind him, "I need time to get ready."

He sighs in resignation. When I make no move to leave the bed, he asks, "What is it?" Now his eyes are worried. He reads me so well.

"A while ago, your mother offered me herbs. Contraceptive herbs. I was wondering what you thought about that."

"I think what you do with your body is your decision. If you're worried, I can tell you you're not pregnant."

"How would you know?"

"I sense energies, Astarti. I've always been able to tell when a woman is pregnant because another life is growing. I sense you more strongly than anyone. I know that your body is not receptive to a child right now."

I bite my lip. "Right now? Or ever?"

Logan catches the end of my braid and combs his fingers through it. "I don't know. Do you want a child?"

"Not right now. But maybe someday. I'd like to know that I can."

"I'm sure most women feel that way. Most men as well, for that matter. I think there's no reason to worry that you can't. Your body is stressed now, and no wonder. But we should be more careful."

"Do you not want a child?"

"I want you, Astarti."

"But someday?"

"I don't know. I guess I never thought—"

When he doesn't go on, I prompt him, "What?"

He stares down into the tangled sheets. "What if it's like me?"

There it is. The pain that's not gone.

I brush hair away from his face. "Your child would be beautiful. And we would raise that child in kindness, and we'd never let him or her suffer as you did."

He's touched by that, and he has to clear his throat to answer me. His eyes still do not meet mine. "You really wouldn't mind...I mean, you would accept..."

"If I ever have a child, Logan, it will be yours."

Now he does look at me, and I see his hope. And his fear. He says seriously, "You don't have to make that kind of commitment, Astarti. I would never bind you."

My throat closes because he says that honestly and without any hidden, selfish purpose. He gives me the one thing I need above all: freedom to control myself, to make my own decisions. This is the very reason I cannot imagine leaving him. I wish I could put that into words for him, but I am too full of emotion, and all I can say is, "I know."

₧ ₨

When I slip through the doorway into the rooms that adjoin Logan's, I find that Clara has been busy. She peeks from the bedroom into the sitting room when I enter.

"Hot water in the tub," she says. "I'm just laying out some options."

My heart skitters at that, but I remind myself of Logan's words: *you should do whatever you want*. This is what I want. Not every day, certainly, and maybe never again. But today I feel like doing this.

The tub's blissfully warm water tempts me to soak, but the sound of Clara humming in the other rooms keeps me focused. I scrub and work the rose-scented soap into my hair. When I step out of the tub, I pull on a linen dressing gown and wrap my hair in a thick towel.

A fire burns in the sitting room hearth, and Clara motions me toward a padded footstool positioned before it. As I sit, I notice a small table arranged with combs, towels, bottles, and a steaming cup of something that smells sweet and a little spicy.

"What's all this?" I ask.

Clara says, seeming to brace herself for my refusal, "Your hair is very long and will take a little while to comb and oil and dry, so I thought you might enjoy a cup of hot chocolate."

"Hot chocolate?"

"Milk, chocolate, honey, spices. You've never had it?"

I tasted chocolate once in Avydos, but it's rare because imported. Clara presses the warm cup into my hands, and I take a cautious sip.

Oh. My.

Oh my, yes.

"You like it?" she asks, sounding a bit worried.

"Clara, this is the most incredible thing I've tasted in my life."

Her face splits into a broad smile. She picks up a small bottle of oil and looks a question at me, waiting for my permission. I unwrap the towel from my hair, and Clara shakes a few drops of oil into her palm. She rubs her hands together and starts to smooth the oil through my hair. She adds more oil, working from scalp to tips as I sip the sweet, warm drink.

When she starts to comb my hair, she shows more patience with the tangles than I normally do. She teases them out from the bottom and works upward. It feels...good.

Clara hums softly as she works, and I sit in idle contentment, enjoying the hot chocolate and the fire and her gentle combing. In this quiet moment, I realize what I should have seen long ago. Clara is kind. I have thought her silly. If I am honest with myself, I have even thought her a little stupid. I have seen the worst, not even knowing if it was true. An ache forms in my chest as I think of how I've treated someone who has never been anything but kind to me. I think how I have missed another chance to call someone friend.

Clara sets her comb on the table and starts pressing water from my hair with one of the fresh towels.

"Clara?"

"Hmm?"

"Thank you."

She goes still, hands still gently pressing my hair, then she resumes her work. "I know some of what you've done to protect us. I cannot repay you. None of us can. This is all I am able to give, though it may seem frivolous. All the same, you are welcome."

But it doesn't seem frivolous because I finally recognize what this is. It's not Clara foisting her style upon me, not at its heart. It is her trying to take care of me in the only way she knows.

I nod, and she picks up her comb to tease out a few remaining tangles. Between the warmth of the day and the fire, my hair is soon semi-dry. Clara explains that the way she does my hair will depend on the dress I choose, and we are headed to the bedroom when someone knocks on the door.

Clara scowls and says irritably, "I made very clear that you were not to be disturbed before the seventh hour."

She marches toward the door, clearly ready to give whoever is there a verbal lashing, but when she pulls open the door she stumbles back. "Prince Rood," she says in shock, all the fire gone from her voice.

He nods to her, then his eyes find me across the room. His cheeks color as he takes in my dressing down and loose, damp hair.

"Apologies," he says. "I can come back another time."

"Stay," I call. "Come in."

He has never come to see me before, and I am too curious to let him slip away.

He enters the sitting room cautiously. I motion him toward the chairs before the fire.

"I'll wait outside," Clara says, ducking out and closing the door.

Rood sits on the edge of one of the chairs, and I take my seat on the footstool. I'm sure I look silly in my dressing gown, but I pretend not to notice.

Eyebrows drawn together, Rood stares into the fire. Maybe it's only his expression, but he looks older than I remember him looking before Belos took him.

"I didn't know," he says at last. "What it was like. Being Leashed."

I'm not sure how to comfort him, and I don't think that's why he's here, so I wait for the rest.

He goes on, "I've been envious of you, and it seems so foolish to me now. I had no idea what you had been through, or what Logan had been through. Feeling it for even a few hours, I wish"—he breaks off, seeming to fight with himself before he can conclude—"I wish I had been better to you."

For a moment, I am too stunned to reply. Rood has always seemed so arrogant, too sure of himself to apologize. Indeed, I can see that this was not easy for him to say. But he did say it.

I tell him, "I wish you had not learned what it feels like to be Leashed."

He looks at me in surprise. "I would think you would have wanted it."

That stings, and I say a little sharply, "I wouldn't want that for anybody, much less for you. Why would you think that?"

He shifts uncomfortably. "Because our father…"

Ah, I see. Because Heborian gave me away. Because he kept Rood.

"None of that was your doing."

He looks into the fire. "He loved your mother, you know. In a way that he did not love mine. Everyone says so."

There is nothing I can say to that, and it's a pain I don't understand, though I see clearly that it *is* pain.

He says, echoing my words, "I suppose that was not your doing."

"No."

He sighs, sounding a little relieved, as though he is letting go of a resentment he didn't really want.

He stands abruptly. "I'll let you finish dressing."

"Rood," I call as he turns to leave. When he stops, I find I have nothing to say.

He inclines his chin, seeming to understand, then strides to the door, his boots ringing on the stone floor in the spaces between rugs.

I'm peering through the doorway into the bedroom when Clara, skirts swishing, hustles to catch me.

"I have to explain them!"

That makes my eyebrows climb. Clothes need an explanation? I humor her, standing back so she can precede me into the room. I do, however, look over her shoulder. The room is a rainbow of color, a forest of texture. Dresses hang from the wardrobe front and before the window. They spill over the backs of chairs and spread across the bed. Some are full and frothy, others sleek.

She says, "You're probably thinking it's a bit much"—I give her a wry lift of an eyebrow to confirm that—"but I wanted you to see the possibilities."

"I just need a nice dress. Any would do."

She puts a hand to her chest and closes her eyes, shaking her head slightly. "No," she mutters. "No, no."

"I just want to look nice for Logan," I insist, trying to train my eyes away from the streams of color.

"No," she says again, firmly. "You must never dress for another, not even for him. Never. The point of this is to decide how you want to present yourself *to yourself.*"

"Present myself to myself?"

She holds up a finger, asking for my patience, as she swishes toward the wardrobe. "How will you see yourself tonight?" She pinches the hem of a full and decorative green skirt, pulling it out to display the gown. "Regal and bold?" She lets that one drop and tugs at the next one, a slim red dress that looks clingy. "Smooth and sophisticated?"

When I frown down both of these options, Clara moves to the chairs and holds up a black dress heavy with black beading. "Mysterious and grand?" She lays this one back down and shows me the next, a frothy pale yellow dress. "Charming and sweet?"

As she sweeps to the bed, she explains, "When you put on a garment, it draws out those elements of yourself that it reflects. Do you see?"

I tilt my hand in a so-so gesture, but Clara is undaunted. She lifts a dark purple dress from the bed. The bodice and sleeves are fitted. The skirt sweeps out long and elegant, and a slit up one side reveals a black underskirt.

"Ooh," I say. "Maybe."

"Elegant but bold," Clara describes it. She lays it down and moves to the window.

Most of the dresses hung there, like the others, are too pretty and too grand. I don't think I like that. I interrupt Clara's litany to suggest we just go with the purple one.

"Wait," she says. "You must see the last one."

She hurries to the end of the arrangement and takes down a garment. She holds it out for my inspection. I approach slowly, taking in the unusual design. A full skirt of dark blue splits in the front, sweeping away to trail behind and exposing black breeches. The bodice looks like a separate piece, though it is constructed of the same dark blue material. It looks almost like a jacket, fitted through the waist but accented by a slight puff in the shoulders. Black embroidery swirls and eddies around it. The neck is high in the back and would almost reach my ears. It angles sharply in the front, plunging to a low point, though a black shirt of fine wool with a scalloped neckline would cover the chest.

"I thought so," Clara says with a smile. "Subtle, beautiful, dangerous. And the only one that can be worn with boots."

CHAPTER 30

"And done," Clara announces as she slides a final pin into my hair.

She motions me toward the full length mirror that stands in the corner and tweaks its angle until she's satisfied. I step forward cautiously, part of me expecting to find myself looking terribly silly.

"Well?" Clara inquires, twisting her hands together as I stare at my reflection.

"Oh, Clara."

"You like it?"

"I never would have thought—yes, I like it."

I don't look silly at all. At least, I don't feel it, looking at this reflection.

Clara hands me a small mirror so I can look at the back. She has done my hair in a series of braids, all of them swept up and gathered high on the back of my head. The standing collar mostly covers the Griever's Mark, though the upper edges show a little.

Clara notices me looking. "I can adjust your hair if you want."

"No. I don't mind it." I'm surprised that the statement feels honest. When did this change for me? I didn't even notice it happening.

Clara says, "You wait here while I see if Logan is ready."

She bustles away. I hear the front door open and close, then the distant rapping of her knuckles on the door to the other rooms. Over the last hour, I've heard a bit of movement in there and even a few different voices. One of them, I'm sure, was Heborian. Clara was working on my hair at the time, and when I made a move to get up, she said warningly, "Don't even think about it." Heborian did not stay long, and though I listened intently for raised voices, I never heard them.

I hear them now. Well, one at least. Though I can't make out Clara's words, her chastening tone comes muffled through the wall. Logan's deep rumble answers her. After a brief exchange, the doors open and close, and Clara comes marching back to me.

"You would think," she mutters, "that the son of the Prima would know not to wear *leather pants* on a formal occasion." She takes a calming breath. "At least the colors are right. He did accept my message on that."

I grin. "I don't know. I like how he looks in leather. I think I'd be disappointed if I didn't get to see that fine—"

"Well, yes," Clara interrupts, blushing. "There is that. It's just not *formal*. But, come. He'll be here any moment."

We're halfway across the sitting room when a knock sounds at the door. My heart skips a beat. Ridiculous, of course. I just saw him a few hours ago.

Clara motions me to halt as she proceeds to the door, opening it with a little flourish. She stands aside, smiling, as Logan stares across the room.

I stare right back. He's wearing a dark blue velvet doublet buttoned down the front, the top revealing the edge of his white shirt. He's not as transformed as I, perhaps, but the cut of the jacket, the way his hair is combed back—all of it is perfect, even the leather pants. He walks slowly into the room, breath held.

I can't keep up the grand silence. "Well?" I prompt as he reaches me.

He leans down and kisses my forehead. "Gorgeous. And very much *you.*"

I laugh, and some of the nervousness rings through my voice, "Really?"

"Oh, yes. Really."

"Clara deserves all the credit. She even modified this dress for me. So it could be worn with boots."

Logan glances down at the soft leather boots that reach to my knees. A big grin spreads across his face.

I grin back. But it slips from my face when Logan draws a silver bracelet from inside his doublet. I recognize the piece of jewelry at once, and now I know what Heborian was doing at Logan's door. Heborian tried to give that to me once before.

"That was my mother's," I whisper.

"Yes," Logan answers softly. "You don't want to wear it?"

"No."

"Will you tell me why?"

"It was my mother's."

It's answer enough for me, but it doesn't seem to be enough for Logan. He looks confused, but he slides the bracelet back into the hidden pocket.

"I'm sorry," he says. "I didn't know it would upset you."

"It's not your fault. Heborian is full of tricks."

Logan's jaw clenches briefly, and a thread of green curls through his irises.

I say, "It doesn't matter, not tonight. Tonight, we should just enjoy ourselves."

Logan nods and lifts his elbow for me to take.

"I'm not a lady," I remind him.

"Yes, you are. Boots and all."

I take a steadying breath and hook my hand in the crook of his arm. It's not how it's supposed to be done, but it feels right. A smile tugs at the corner of Logan's mouth.

"It works?" I ask.

"It works."

೫ ೪

The evidence of damage has been cleared from the dining hall. Notably, the crystal chandelier is gone, having shattered, Clara told me, when it fell. People are filtering in, so we're allowed to enter without particular notice. That is, until we come within hailing distance of the raised platform where Heborian sits. He beckons us.

We could refuse, but there's no reason. Besides, everyone I know sits up there. Horik and the remaining Drifters, Rood, Aron, Bran, and Gaiana, the Polemarc and several Counselors. A few seats are unoccupied but not open. Blue Drift-light floats where people would have sat. I count one light for each Drifter that died. One of those lights floats beside Rood, where Wulfstan once sat. I have thought little about Heborian's losses. Wulfstan was his uncle and advisor, perhaps even his friend. It is so easy to forget that Heborian is not simply king but also a man.

He watches us approach the dais, turning in his seat as we climb the steps at the back. I take the chair at Heborian's left, and Logan sits on my other side. Heborian doesn't comment on my clothes, but he nods approval. Then his eyes flick to my empty wrist and away.

Serving staff move up and down the long tables, both ours and those lining the floor below. I drink some wine and munch on the cheese and crackers. Logan drinks sparingly. I wish I didn't notice, but I do, and I am relieved. I watch the people. I don't recognize many, though the presence of the Earthmakers is noticeable, given that they wear their traditional robes. Aron and Bran are dressed in such as well. Some of Heborian's soldiers—the officers, I would imagine—occupy one table. The other tables are crowded with richly dressed people, though many plainer clothes can be seen toward the back. I've spent a few evenings in here, and it looks much as I remember.

When the tables are settled, the serving staff wheels out carts bearing huge tureens of soup. I accept only a small amount. Experience has taught me to pace myself. While I might consider soup a meal, I know that here it's only the first course.

When we get to the main dishes, it's harder to exercise restraint. Succulent pork and tender beef call to me from the platters. Because I can't choose, I take a bit of each and grudgingly make room for the onions and carrots. I do like vegetables, but with these cruel choices before me, I have to prioritize.

Logan, I'm surprised to find, does know how to eat at an event like this, and I self-consciously try to copy him. His manners do, however, look a bit rusty. He keeps frowning at his fork and adjusting his grip. When he notices me studying his methods, he puts his knife down and uses the side of his fork to cut the tender meat. He stabs a piece and brings it to his mouth with a who-cares shrug. Now *that*, I'm only too happy to imitate.

As the meal winds down, Heborian speaks quietly to one of the serving staff. The man nods and hurries off. Heborian stands from his chair, and a hush slowly spreads through the hall.

"Friends of Kelda," he calls out, his voice carrying through the room and banishing the last of the whispers. "We've faced some dark days together. Destruction and death have haunted us. But there are two things I would ask you to remember. One is that we prevailed because so many were willing to give their lives for this great city and our country. All hail the dead!"

Heborian raises his wine cup, and the gesture is echoed through the hall. Gooseflesh rises on my arms to see the communal acknowledgement of our losses.

"But," Heborian continues, "this is not a day of mourning. This is a day of celebration and certainty, and that brings me to the second point I would like you to remember. This land is my first priority. You may be certain I will always do what is needed to protect it. I would give my life for it. I would give my soul." He lets that fall heavily before offering a wry smile. "Of course," he adds, "we have made sure the Deceiver no longer offers such temptation to our people. We have vanquished our enemy!"

A cheer explodes into the air. Even up and down this raised table, everyone shouts approval.

I, however, am uneasy.

Why did Heborian say, *I would give my soul*, and not *I would have given it*?

Something tells me once again: this is not over.

I put these dark thoughts aside when the serving staff wheels out a broad cart that holds a towering cake. I count five layers and suspect that the bottom one is as big around as an oak tree. No wonder Horik got yelled at for stepping too close.

The cake takes a long time to serve. Our table is served first. Initially this seems like good fortune, but my plate is empty and my belly aching from the sweetness by the time the cake is making its way to the back tables.

Just when I'm ready to tell Logan I've had enough finery for the night, the music starts. I trace the sound to the far end of the room and find that a group of sharply dressed musicians have taken their places atop a platform in the corner. The broad space between the platform and tables is open.

Heborian rises from his chair and walks along the dais to Gaiana. It's a political gesture, but I'm glad of it. This celebration marks a new beginning. Heborian is signaling that it will be a time of cooperation. Of course, that is because cooperation benefits him, but I try not to dwell on that.

Heborian and Gaiana sweep across the dance floor. Her filmy robes float like banners around them. Heborian, I must admit, cuts a dashing figure in his snug red doublet and white breeches. He dances well, if formally, and if he still looks a little tired, I can't blame him. Gaiana is smooth and graceful, matching him effortlessly.

As others filter onto the dancing floor, Logan offers his hand. I take it, feeling his tension at once.

"It was a statement, Logan, nothing more."

He inclines his chin, accepting that, but I can see in his eyes that he is unhappy to have watched his mother with Heborian. He cannot forgive my father for yielding me to Belos. Even if I can make sense of Heborian's decision, Logan cannot. Of course, Heborian's other decisions heap upon that first one. I cannot ask Logan to let any of that go; I'm not sure I even want to.

As Logan leads me to the open space, I whisper, "I hope you remember I'm a terrible dancer."

"'Highly dangerous,' I think we decided."

"No, I decided that. Should I be offended that you agree?"

He gives me that half-smile of his, then says seriously, "You dance beautifully with your spear. Surely you can dance with me?"

"Are you offering to let me lead?"

That draws a worried line across his forehead. "Is that what you want?"

"No," I say quickly. "That was a joke."

"Then just relax, and let me show you."

When we are halfway through a song, I realize I haven't stumbled once. Maybe it's because I trust Logan, because I allow myself to move with his body. Then I realize that my feet aren't on the ground. Logan and I are floating just an inch above the floor, high enough to make my steps easy but not high enough for anyone to notice.

"Isn't this cheating?"

"I don't think there are actual rules for this kind of thing."

"Maybe not rules, but conventions."

"Since when did you worry about conventions?"

"Since never."

"Good."

Logan sweeps me around, and my skirt swirls, wrapping around us briefly before streaming outward. At the edges of my vision, the other dancers move in streams of color. Normally, I would avoid something like this, but it's different being here with Logan. I'm not lost in the crowd, not oppressed by it. I am centered; the rest flows around me.

As the music fades, Logan lets us touch the ground. A tall figure approaches. I grin at Horik in his fine shirt and vest.

"Where's your doublet?" I ask, teasing him.

"Too hot," he grumbles. He glances at Logan. "May I?"

Logan steps back, retreating to the edge of the dancing floor. As another song begins, I hold my hands up for Horik.

"You look beautiful," Horik says.

"And you trimmed your beard."

"That's your return compliment?"

"Just an observation."

"It looked funny with my hair so short. Besides, now you can see my tattoos better. I'm told they're sexy."

"You do look quite dangerous."

"Of course," he agrees. "I am the Man of Many Secrets."

I snort.

I do a better job of staying out of Horik's way than I did the last time we danced. I step on his toes once or twice, but he pretends not to notice.

When the song slows, Horik asks quietly, "Everything is all right? With…"

I recall that the last time I saw Horik was when he came to get me this morning in the refugee camp. The last he saw of Logan was…not good.

"It will be all right," I assure him. "It's better."

"I hope so, Astarti. You deserve good things."

"I have good things, Horik."

He looks doubtful, but he says, "All right."

That is when things go wrong.

The hair rises on the back of my neck, and a chill races down my spine.

Find them, bind them. Bind, bind, bind.

The Ancorites' ghostly fingers scrape through my energies, seeking, probing, testing. I spin as they sweep over me and away. I shove through the crowd, where people are shifting uncertainly. The music has stopped.

The wind stirs, beginning as a low whoosh and rising to a keening wail. Now people are scattering, clearing space around my destination.

But Logan cuts himself off before I get there. He is already walking away, the wind swirling at his back. The Ancorites whisper and flow around him. Tablecloths flutter and goblets topple as Logan and his pursuers sweep past the tables.

"Desist!" comes Heborian's shout from behind. "Norimosis! Harilos! Furiklesis! Desist!"

The Ancorites lift into the air, hovering above Logan, then they are gone. I glance back to see Heborian standing at the edge of the dancing floor, his face set with determination, his body language a silent challenge.

He knows their names.

They obeyed him.

I need to know why, but I cannot confront him and go after Logan at the same time. I jog to catch up with Logan as he storms from the dining hall.

I find him with his hands braced on the wall, leaning into it like a winded runner. Air swirls around him, making the flames of the sconces dance and gutter. Logan drops one hand to unbutton his doublet. He hauls at the neck of his shirt. When I touch his arm, he starts.

I say, "Look at me."

"I want to *kill* them!"

"I know. Look at me."

He raises furious eyes. The firelight flickers over the surging green, blue, and amber of his irises.

This, I realize, is our first test.

I ask softly but firmly, "What do you need?"

Emotion plays over his face, uncertainty sweeping through the anger. "I don't know."

"Please." I hold out my arms. "Come here."

After a moment of fighting within himself, he pushes away from the wall. He moves toward me stiffly, but all I ask of him is that first step. I close the distance, slipping my arms around him. He is unyielding at first, then he molds his body to mine. He lets out a deep breath. His chin rests on top of my head.

"Thank you," I say against his chest.

"I didn't do anything."

But he did. He let me help—he didn't turn away—and that is everything right now.

Heborian's voice echoes from the dining hall. I edge back to the doorway. Heborian stands on the platform that the musicians have abandoned. The crowd stands silent and trusting before him.

"You have nothing to fear! They want what we want: the security of Kelda and all lands. I *will* keep this city safe. Do you trust in your king or not?"

A resounding "aye!" booms from the crowd.

Heborian's face angles toward me. The distance is too great for me to see his expression, but I don't need to. I know what I'd find: a decision long since made. An acceptance of one more evil in the name of good.

Chapter 31

I decide that snooping will yield more truth than a confrontation with Heborian, and so, late in the night, I find myself walking the castle's battlements, looking for clues. Logan is asleep. I didn't want to leave him. It feels like a breach of newly found trust, but I didn't see a good alternative. If my suspicions are correct, and if I set this mad plan into action, there will be no going back. I must be sure.

I slide into the Drift at the approach of the guards. I could make up an excuse for my presence, but I don't want it reported to Heborian. I move farther down the wall and continue my search.

I know the weapons themselves aren't here because I would have seen them from the Drift. But I keep expecting the walls to show modifications to accommodate them. I find nothing, but I don't let that ease my mind. I slide into the Drift and skim toward the brilliant white glow of the harpoons.

When Kronos tore through here, he frayed even the protective barrier around Heborian's tower workroom. I duck around the broken, listless threads and slide out of the Drift. Half of the roof is missing, and starlight makes the floor glow dimly. The rubble has been pushed aside but not cleared. Heborian must not want anyone up here even to clean. Instinctively, I keep my footsteps silent. I shape a Drift-light and let it hover overhead.

The blue light catches on the long, smooth shapes of the bone harpoons. Half a dozen lean against the wall, the cruel barbs gleaming. The chains lie coiled like rope. The design, however, has been modified. The end of each chain is fitted with a long stake. When the hair lifts on the back of my neck, it takes me a moment to realize it's not just the sight of the harpoons that unsettles me.

Bind, bind, bind.

I shape my spear, not caring that it's useless against them.

Bind, they whisper. *Bind.*

Heborian appears from the Drift limned by a soft blue glow. The Ancorites swirl around him and fade at his back, but they are still there. I can feel them.

"What have you done?" I whisper.

His face is impassive, as always, though new weariness hangs on him. "I've been clear that I will do what is needful."

"You have an arrangement with the Ancorites. Don't deny it."

"I will ensure security."

"Speak plainly!"

"They want what I want, Astarti. What I need."

"But they want to bind the Old Ones. Would you turn on your gods that way?"

"Do you take me for a zealot and a fool? Do I strike you as a man who sets tradition above progress? I left much of Rune behind when I came here to start a new life and a new way. I will not have that crumble into the sea as so much of this castle did a few days ago."

"And Logan?"

"If he does not join them, he is not my concern."

"They may not return. They've not been seen since Kronos was freed."

"They will return. In a month, a year, in ten years. Maybe not for another fifty or hundred. But they will return." His face is stone where he says, "They are too dangerous to be allowed to live."

"Could that not be said of you? Or of me or any Drifter? What if humans banded together and hunted us?" I add, to hurt him, "Do you think the Keldans love you?"

But it doesn't pierce his armor. Nothing flickers in his tired eyes. "Of course they don't love me. But they are glad to have a strong king at a time such as this."

"And at another time? What if they turn on you?"

"You think they never have? I conquered this place. You think they liked that? But I have held it, and I will keep my hold of it."

I am getting nowhere with this, so I return to more practical matters. "You don't need to bind the Old Ones to do that."

"You don't know whether that is true. That is your guess, and it is based in compassion, not reason."

"Perhaps, but I think it entirely *reasonable* to learn more about them before seeking to destroy them."

"And how should we do that, Astarti?" He inflects his voice like it's a question, but he doesn't really mean it as one. He means that it's not possible to learn about them. Because they are too dangerous. Because they are too different.

I answer him anyway. "With courage, Heborian. By trying."

It doesn't move him. He says with finality, "You must think your way. I must think mine. It is a good thing, perhaps, that we are not as alike as it sometimes seems."

I feel distance grow between us. If I ever thought we might become more to one another, I was wrong. It is surprisingly painful to realize. I say, hardening my voice, "No, we are not so alike after all."

"I wish I could trust you to abide by my decision," Heborian says. The Ancorites whisper over his shoulder, sliding toward the harpoons. I lurch after them, but it's far too late. I know it even as I swing my spear. The blade cuts through the insubstantial forms of the Ancorites and the harpoons as they shimmer and fade and are gone.

"But," Heborian concludes as I wheel on him angrily, "I can only trust you to follow your own conscience. Perhaps it will all lead to the same place in the end."

With that, he vanishes into the Drift.

℘ ℛ

I slide from the Drift into the sitting room, where Logan is waiting for me. A candle flame dances in a glass-faced lantern beside him. The light plays over his elbow planted on the chair arm and the fist propping up his tight jaw. His expression is distant, holding me away. Even when he speaks, he doesn't look up.

"You say I don't trust you, but I think that you do not trust me."

That makes my heart gallop. "Why do you say that?"

"You had a suspicion, and you went to investigate it. Why did you not tell me?"

He has caught me; he knows me that well. "I wanted to confirm it before I said anything."

"Why? Why could you not have told me your suspicion, whatever it was?"

I don't want to answer because the truth is hurtful, but I also don't want to lie to him.

He looks up, his eyes wary, and says quietly, "Please tell me, Astarti."

I let out a slow breath. "Because it had to do with Heborian, and I did not think you would be level-headed about it."

He takes that in. "You are probably right, but I still wish you would have told me."

And I should have. What if he could have seized and destroyed those harpoons before the Ancorites took them? We would not be in this mess. I was cautious, as I always am, seeking information before deciding on my actions. I knew Logan would not be that way, and so I left him behind. But my cautious, thoughtful method has left me with a mess. A big one.

"I wish I had told you," I admit. "I'm sorry that I didn't. And I have a problem now. Will you help me fix it?" I hold my breath, unsure how angry he is with me.

He drops his fist, and all the distance that was in his expression vanishes. He is with me again. His eyes tell me that even before he says, "Always."

I pace before the empty fireplace and tell him what I learned tonight. By the end, he is on his feet, arms crossed and face scowling.

He bites out, "He said he didn't bring them here."

"Well, he didn't. But he's certainly making use of their presence."

Logan makes a cutting gesture with his hand. "That's still a lie."

I don't argue the point. We have bigger concerns.

He says, "So what do we do? Wait for a chance to get a hold of the Ancorites and destroy the harpoons?"

"That's one possibility, though we have to consider that Heborian could seek out more bones and make more weapons. He used you to find these bones because it was expedient. That doesn't mean that, given time, he can't find more on his own."

Logan's expression hardens, and I know what he wants to say. He tilts his face down, trying to repress it.

"Just say it," I tell him. "Get it out."

He shakes his head.

"It won't hurt me to hear you say it."

"But it would hurt you if I did it?"

"I don't know. Maybe."

"I won't do it, Astarti."

"I know."

"But I want to," he says. "I want to kill him."

"I know."

His arms loosen a little now that he's gotten to say it. Sometimes, that is all we need.

He shakes his head. "I don't see what we can do other than wait for our chance at the Ancorites."

I take a deep breath. "There is one more option."

CHAPTER 32

LOGAN

I let Astarti take me through the Drift to reach Belos's prison cell. Even for the brief moments we are in the Drift, everything in me rebels against the exposure. Astarti pretends not to notice how my energies surge, but she does hurry us past the dozing guard and straight to Belos. When we reach him, I am briefly calmed. He sits listlessly on his bench, arms chained above him. His energies are ragged and dim, marked by dark holes like they've been burned through. It's hard to believe this ruined man ever held so much power over me.

But when Astarti pulls me from the Drift—when Belos lifts his head and smiles that cold smile I remember so well—rage churns in my gut again. He may be diminished, but it's still him, and I am sickened by the memory of what I was under his power. He looks at me in a way that says he, too, can still picture it.

I cannot go through with this plan.

To give him what he wants? No. It's wrong on every level.

Worst of all, I will have to touch him. My hands start shaking at the thought. Nausea boils up, and I have to close my eyes for a moment. I open them to find him watching me, so pleased with himself.

He turns his sly smile on Astarti, taking in the leather pack slung over her shoulder. "And to think you doubted me. Will you never learn?"

I growl, "And how do we know you're not lying?"

He smirks. "The application of reason, of course. Astarti, I think, has it figured out. One thing, above all, makes it clear." He gives her the chance to answer, as though she is a pupil anxious to please her tutor. When she refuses to play his game, he continues without missing a beat, "Heborian kept me alive. Surely, Logan, you didn't believe that whole 'his death doesn't belong to you alone' speech? Heborian is far more practical than that. Tell me: did he ever announce a date of execution?"

I try to keep the surprise from showing on my face, but Belos's satisfied smile tells me I've failed. Heborian did not announce a date. And the execution would have made most sense before the feast. My mind has been such a mess that I didn't even notice.

Astarti did. At least, she's put it together with the other clues. "He's kept you alive to attract Kronos. He thinks Kronos will be drawn back to you."

Belos doesn't answer, but he looks disgustingly pleased.

"There will be a few rules," Astarti says.

Belos straightens as though to pay careful attention. "Oh, do tell."

"You will not lie about Kronos's location. If you mislead us, we have no use for you, and we will kill you."

"All right. Next?"

"You will tell no one who you are. We don't need that kind of attention. If you give yourself away, we will kill you."

"Anything else?"

"If you try to escape, we will kill you."

"I'm noticing a pattern here."

"I should hope so."

I cut in, "You're quite glib for a man in your position."

Belos opens his mouth to reply, but Astarti cuts him off. "What direction?"

"North."

"Can you be more precise?"

"No. I can't track him through the Drift, and the sense of direction is vague at this distance."

"And what distance is that? How far are we talking?"

"I haven't the foggiest idea."

Astarti studies him, unsure if he's lying. As far as I'm concerned, he's always lying.

Astarti concedes, "We'll have to take it a bit at a time. Logan?"

I set my jaw. I just have to not think about it. This will take me to my father, and that is all I can allow to enter my thoughts. We have to warn him not to come back here. We have to know what he wants. Belos is a tool, a means to that end. Nothing more.

But the second I put my hand on his wiry arm, revulsion swallows me from the inside. My lungs seize up. I jerk my hand back.

I spin away, pacing to the edge of the cell as he says, "Oh, come now, Logan. It's not like we haven't danced before."

"Shut up!" Astarti hisses.

Her hand touches my hip. She waits until I get my breath back then says, "You know we can't take him though the Drift without using the Shackle, not now that he's lost his Drift-power."

"I know," I grit out. "I'll do it."

We can't let him near the Shackle, not yet.

She whispers, "He has no power over you."

I let out a breath that shakes my whole body. How can she be so strong? Surely he must give her the same sick feeling he gives me? Surely it is worse for her, given that she spent so many years with him, *Leashed* to him? She says it was not the same because she was not possessed, but it was the same. He controlled her life, set her boundaries. Yet she can move on, move forward. Why am I so stuck?

It is the thought of Astarti and not of my father that makes me turn again to Belos.

Astarti adjusts her grip on the pack and takes my right hand. I lay my left on Belos's arm. Shudders work their way up my arm and through my body. Astarti squeezes my hand. I close my eyes so I don't see Belos's sickening face. I let myself dissolve. Astarti fades quickly. I know her energies, and they respond like an extension of my own.

Belos, however, flickers then solidifies. I tell myself it should feel good to have such power over his body, but reaching into him to alter his composition is far too intimate. I pull back—how that must delight him. Astarti's essence brushes close to mine, soothing and steady, certain I can do this. I let my mind focus on her. I force Belos to the edge of my awareness, where I touch his energies with little thought. His chains thump against the wall.

I draw us out of the cell, past the oblivious guard, and up the stairs. I slip us through the nearest window.

CHAPTER 33

LOGAN

The sun is rising when I shape us from the wind on a hilltop some thirty miles north of Tornelaine. This is about where Astarti and I got to the day I tried to follow Kronos.

Belos stretches, cracking his back. Suddenly his hands snap together behind him, bound by faintly glowing Drift-energy.

He raises a pale eyebrow. "Child, unless one of you wants to hold it for me, I'm going to need my hands."

I growl, but Astarti doesn't seem fazed. She releases the bond and informs him, "You may turn away, but you're not to leave my sight."

"Is there any need for this paranoia? I wouldn't get a hundred yards before you caught up to me from the Drift."

"Call it a jailor's prerogative."

Belos makes an appreciative grunt and turns away. There is something far too personal about the sight and sound of him unlacing his pants, even if I can only see his back. I look away, but I can't block out the sound of him relieving himself or of his contented sigh.

He laces his pants back up, and I return my eyes to him. He smirks.

"Since we're all rather bound together at the moment, it might be best if we get a bit more comfortable with one another."

"This isn't about you being comfortable," Astarti retorts. "This is about you doing as we say to extend your miserable existence a little longer."

He observes casually, "You never would have spoken to me like that in the old days."

Something snaps inside me. I don't even feel myself move. All I feel is a lash of fury and suddenly I am pinning him to the ground, driving my fist into his face. The crack of contact, the slickness of blood against my knuckles lets something unclench inside me.

He doesn't fight back. After a few punches, that makes me aware of myself and my actions. I pull him up by his shirt and yell, "Fight me!" but his head lolls back. Blood streams from his nose and split cheek. I drop him roughly and shove to my feet. I stalk several paces across the hilltop, away from both him and Astarti.

I stare out across the hilly green landscape, not really seeing it. I try to catch my breath, but something is too tight in my chest. I sit and draw up my knees, resting my forearms on them. I drop my head and force the air into my lungs, once, twice, three times. When I raise my head, I find Astarti seated beside me.

She says, "We don't want to kill him yet."

"I know that."

The truth is that even had we already gotten what we need from him, I wouldn't want to kill him that way. I have killed many men, but I've never beaten one to death. Belos has already polluted me enough; I can't let him leave that last mark on me. I won't let him make me into that.

Astarti asks, "Are you all right?"

"Yes."

"Are you being honest?"

"I don't know."

"He is going to taunt us the whole way to Kronos. That is the only power he has left, and he will make use of it."

The truth of that makes me feel foolish. "And I'm giving him just what he wants."

"Well, I'm not sure he wanted his nose broken," she says wryly, "but he did want to rile you."

Her humor breaks the hold that shame has on me, and I can look up now.

I study her, as I love to do. Her hair is still braided from the feast, bound high on the back of her head. It brings the shape of her face into focus. She is so beautiful, though it's not the fine lines of her jaw and forehead that make her so to me. It is the calm strength, the gentleness that can flow into deadliness like a river can pour itself into a roaring waterfall and flow on again with grace.

"How do you do it, Astarti? Why are you so much stronger than I am?"

"I'm not."

"Yes, you are."

Her face scrunches in thought as she works through an answer. She won't dismiss my words, but she won't accept them either. When she speaks, she looks out across the hills, not at me. "My struggles are different from yours. And I expect different things from myself and from the world than you do."

"What does that mean?"

She thinks a little longer, then says, "I expect evil, and I slide around it. I even work with it sometimes because I don't believe it's possible to eradicate it. When I find things that are good, I try to recognize them. I don't always succeed, but I try."

"Is it as simple as that?"

"It's not simple at all, but it's the way I am."

"I don't know if I can do that."

"You don't need to, Logan. You and I are not the same. You tolerate fewer evils, both in yourself and in others. You recognize good more quickly than I because you're not as distracted by the details. I worry about them. I sort through them constantly, but for you they are irrelevant. Even when you met me, knowing what I was, you cut through the details to the heart of me. That is something I was never able to do for myself, a clarity I could never achieve. Without you, I don't think I would ever have seen it at all. You find the essence of things, and the rest doesn't matter to you. I love that about you—truly I do, though it's not the way I am."

I take in the sight of her, everything in me starving for it. I need her; it terrifies me how much I need her. And it awes me how much I love and respect her. How can she be so wise? She is young, younger than I, far too young to have eyes that look so old. She can be playful, youthful, wonderfully silly—but she is no child. She is wise and strong and able to look at things that most cannot.

Because she can handle it, and because I'm afraid of what's happening to me, I tell her quietly, "I keep…snapping. I don't know how to stop."

"You're getting better, Logan."

Even though she doesn't say it dismissively or as a false reassurance, I still don't believe her. "But I'm not."

She hesitates to answer, as though unsure how I will take it, then she says, "You're starting to calm yourself down. More importantly, you're starting to accept a little help. Believe me, Logan, you're getting better. But we're not in a rush. You have to give yourself time; you have to be patient with yourself."

Her words make me uncomfortable, though I'm not sure why. I don't have a response.

Astarti doesn't expect one. She lets me think on this for a moment, then she pushes to her feet, silently telling me to let it go for now.

I follow her to Belos, who is lying in the grass with his head tilted back, trying to get his nose to stop bleeding. It's definitely broken. He struggles into a sitting position at our approach. I notice for the first time that his chest is also bleeding. That, I didn't do. That is from an old wound Astarti dealt him. Now that he doesn't have the energy of others to patch it up, it seeps blood.

He squints up at me. "It feels good, doesn't it, Logan?"

I'm not detached enough to let that roll off me, but I let it roll through. It did feel good, but it felt awful, too.

Astarti snags the pack from the ground and slings it over her shoulder. "The direction?"

"North."

She takes my hand, and I lean down to grip Belos's shoulder. This time, I am braced for it, ready for the sick churning in my gut. This time, it's easier to endure.

₮ ℞

We stop periodically to confirm direction. I make occasional adjustments to our course, but Belos is guiding us in a general northerly direction. We are near the border between Kelda and Heradyn when he collapses.

Astarti crouches beside him and lays a hand on his sweaty forehead. "I could try to Heal him."

254

Bile slides up my throat at the thought. "Please don't."

Her eyebrows draw together as she stares down at him, undecided.

I argue, "He doesn't deserve your energy."

"It's not about deserving. We need him."

She tugs his vest aside to reveal the half-healed wound in his chest. She takes a steadying breath then presses her hands to the wound and closes her eyes. It is agony to watch her give anything of herself to him.

She is still for a long time before she pops up suddenly. She shudders, shaking out her hands. "I can't," she says, wiping her bloody hands in the grass. "I just can't."

Belos's eyes open. He sits up, pulling his vest aside to stare down at the wound. "I didn't know you could do that," he comments, voice distorted by his broken nose.

The wound is still there, but it's closed somewhat, and much of Belos's color has returned. Even so, he's too weak to get to his feet on his own, and Astarti helps him up before I can protest or spare her by doing it myself. Honestly, I don't know if I could have.

She says, "It's late afternoon. We should find food and a place to stay for the night. We'll start again in the morning."

Somehow, I imagined this as a one-day venture. I hadn't thought ahead to spending a night in the same room as Belos. I close off the thought, shutting it into a dark corner of myself. If Astarti can do it, so can I.

By early evening, I find a town with enough traffic to support an inn. I shape our bodies from the wind well beyond the town, and we approach along the packed-dirt road. Carts and tents are gathered at the edge of the town, indicating some kind of event.

We have some coin Astarti pilfered from Heborian's treasury before we left. "Soldiers' pay," she called it. When we enter the inn, which is busily serving dinner, the innkeeper declares us "very lucky" because he has only one room left. Apparently, the local market is tomorrow. Of course, this means he charges us double what the room is worth.

The room is clean but simple. It has no windows, which I don't like, but it does have two beds. Belos thumps down on one.

A chambermaid in a white apron brings towels and hot water for washing. She arranges these on the washstand and crouches to start a fire in the hearth. It's surprisingly chilly for the time of year, and the promise of a fire is welcome.

Astarti unbuckles the pack and digs through for toiletries, tossing a cake of soap onto the empty bed. I lean against the wall, wishing I had something to do. I put my weight on my right leg, letting my aching left knee rest. Belos is watching me, so I stare back at him.

His gaze travels to my resting leg, and he comments, "I couldn't help but notice the way you walk, and a deaf man could have heard your knee clicking when we climbed the stairs. It didn't heal very well."

It delights him that he did permanent damage to my body. He weakened me and gave me pain that will remind me of him every day for the rest of my life. And he loves to see that understanding in my eyes.

Belos may be cowardly, but he's not stupid. I can't lay into him with the girl here. I'm not coolheaded enough to return a clever response, so I have to keep silent. My teeth are clenched so hard my jaw starts to ache. Though I may not say anything, the air thickens with tension. The chambermaid rushes through the rest of her tasks, wincing when the fire poker scrapes noisily on the hearthstones. When the fire is crackling, she hustles to the door, lurching to a stop when she realizes she hasn't asked us about food.

Her eyes never go to Belos, and I would like to think she can sense the wrongness in him. Her eyes do skim over me, but she doesn't raise her gaze above my chest. She looks shyly to Astarti. "Will you come down for dinner, or would you like food sent up?"

"Sent up, please," Astarti replies, her tone smooth as though to say that nothing is wrong here. Of course, the effect is somewhat ruined when she asks for clean bandages and more hot water. Not that anyone could have failed to notice Belos's blood-crusted face.

The girl shifts uncomfortably but offers a polite, "Yes, miss."

"Kicked by a horse," Astarti explains, as she did to the innkeeper.

Whether the girl believes her, I don't know, but she dips a shallow curtsy and leaves.

The extra water and bandages arrive first. Though Astarti makes Belos wash himself up, she does wrap a bandage tightly around his chest. The bleeding has mostly stopped, but he's gone white in the face again. Between that and his swollen, bruised nose, he looks pathetic; he really does. I don't know why he's still getting to me.

When dinner arrives, we eat our stew and bread in silence. The only sounds are of chewing and the scraping of our spoons against the bowls. As before, these small, personal sounds creep under my skin. I cannot believe I am eating dinner with him. It is the most unnatural thing I have ever done.

As soon as Belos has laid down his spoon, Astarti binds his hands with Drift-energy and anchors him to his bed. A faint thread of energy flows from his bindings to her hand.

"Isn't that a clever trick," Belos says appreciatively.

I pretend not to hear him: his casualness, his comfortableness with this situation as though he is still the one in control. I *pretend* not to hear it, but I do. I've felt mildly nauseated all day, and the food churns in my gut at his tone.

It's a good thing I'm so tired; otherwise I would never be able to sleep tonight. Maybe I won't anyway. But I do long to lie down. The day's tension, the effort of taking us all through the wind, and the sleepless night—or nights?—before have me yawning. Astarti and I kick off our boots, but we don't remove our clothes.

Belos, watching us, says suggestively, "Don't let me stop you."

My blood surges through my veins. He will *not* degrade that. I stalk over to his bed, peripherally aware of the wind swirling in my wake. Belos gazes up at me, unconcerned.

I remind him, "You don't need your tongue to point out a direction. If you'd like to keep it, I suggest you silence it."

"You always were touchy about matters of sex."

Air whips around me. I cannot listen to him anymore. I *have* to shut him up.

I rip the air from his lungs. He chokes, unable even to gasp. His face purples and his eyes bulge, and I revel in the sight. I *do* have power over him. And he has none over me.

Then I realize what I'm doing.

And I realize that I'm wrong: he does have power over me. He is controlling the way I feel. At every turn, he is controlling me.

I let go.

Belos gasps and falls like a ragdoll to the mattress. I didn't even know I had lifted him up.

I spin away from the bed, trying to get my own lungs working, but they are tight, like a fist is closed around them. Astarti approaches me slowly. I meet her worried eyes. I still can't breathe. I still can't think. I silently beg her to help me.

She looks…relieved. She takes my hand and leads me into the hallway. Air starts slipping through the fist around my lungs, but it comes whistling, unwilling.

I want to hit something. I want to be hit. I need it to focus. I need to get everything back under control so I breathe again, so I can be myself again.

Astarti lays her hands over my clenched fists. When my fists start to loosen and my lungs start to work, she slides her hands up my arms, over my shoulders and up my neck until she's cupping my jaw. It's like she sweeps all the anger out of me, leaving calm in its wake. I don't know how she does that. I wonder if it's some magic that I don't understand, but I think it's just her.

I meet her eyes, which shine in the light of the bracketed sconce. I want to tell her that I'm frightened. I think I have been all my life.

I don't know if this is what she sees in my eyes, but she says softly, "I know. I know."

She lets me be weak for a moment, and that is all I need to be strong again.

CHAPTER 34

I know I should sleep. We can't guess what tomorrow will bring. At the least, it will be another long, tense day of travel. Logan is asleep only because he's utterly exhausted, but I can't escape the feeling that someone should keep watch. Belos lies quietly, eyes closed, but I don't know if he's sleeping. I sit on my pillow and lean against the wall. I keep the pack under my knees. If I do doze off, I can't risk Belos prying into it. I've bound him to his bed, but it's not enough peace of mind for me. He's fooled me too many times.

This has been the strangest day of my life. I know what's getting to Logan. It's not just Belos's comments. It's the normal, everyday things we are being forced to do together. I don't like it either. It's not that I haven't done such things with Belos before. I've eaten hundreds, thousands, of meals with him. I've seen him wash his face. I've even heard him urinating before. But this is different. Before, I would turn half my mind away from those sights and sounds, as Heborian's servants do because he is king and ranked so far above them. Today, Belos is below me, and this bizarre inversion, which should feel good, only feels strange.

His personality, too, puts me ill at ease. He's less erratic than before, not given to the fits of temper that I remember. His cruelty now is petty and small. I can't help but wonder if this is because he is now only himself when before he was an amalgamation of all those he had Taken. Is this the real Belos?

Several times today, I've caught him looking dejected, listless, beaten. His sneering smile slides over it as soon as he feels my eyes on him, but he's not as quick as he used to be. I wish Logan could see how broken Belos really is. Maybe he does see it. Maybe it haunts him that someone who is now so weak once held such power over him.

I feel Logan twitch in his sleep, and I lay a hand against his chest. I knew he would dream tonight. That is another reason I am awake. Logan wouldn't like it if he knew I'm keeping watch over him, but I will follow my own will in this.

Logan quiets at my touch, relaxing into sleep again. I study his face in the low, warm light from the hearth. My mind paints memory over the sight, and I see again the fear in his eyes when he stood with me in the hallway. When I met him, I never saw fear in his eyes. Since then, I have seen it on occasion, slipping through the cracks, but this is the first time he has trusted me to see it fully. My throat tightens at the memory. I don't know if I'm right to be breaking down these walls he's built around himself. I don't think such walls are good, and I don't think they really protect him. They just let him keep suffering out of the sight of the rest of us. But as I pull his walls down a little at a time, I expose him. I am forcing him to face his pain and his fear. I worry: will he crumble when these walls are gone? What if they are the only thing holding him together?

No, I tell myself. He's stronger than that—I know he is.

261

But it's hard on him to do this, to let me help, to admit to himself that he needs help. He sees, now, how Belos manipulated him into believing warped truths. It is another way Belos has wielded power over him. However, recognizing Belos's lies doesn't mean Logan is past them. He needs what we do not have: time and peace to sort through all this, to heal. Instead, he must fight this battle within himself even while he faces other, equally difficult conflicts.

And what about me? What do I need?

It's a strange question to ask myself in the middle of the night in this room with my lover and my pseudo-father-turned-enemy. I know what I want, at least in a vague sense. I want time with Logan. I want time to figure out what I want, I suppose. At the same time, that terrifies me because I have no idea what I want beyond Logan. Without the constant pressure of things that must be done, fights that must be fought, what will I do with myself? I have never imagined a life not shaped by necessity. How would I shape my life by choice?

Frankly, I doubt there will be a chance to find out. I have betrayed Heborian. Perhaps I have betrayed everyone. Part of me believes there will be no coming back from this.

Logan makes a low sound. I stroke his hair, hoping he'll settle. Sweat breaks out on his face, and a line wedges between his brows. His body tightens, muscles etching with strain as his limbs start to twitch. I hate this. I dream, too, but it's not like this. He needs rest, *real* rest, but his mind will not give it to him.

I shake his shoulder to wake him before it gets worse. He gasps awake. I keep my hand on him, though I expect him to tear away from me.

He doesn't. He rolls onto his side, pressing his face against my hip. One arm is trapped beneath his body, but his other comes across my legs. His fingers dig into my thigh like he's holding on for his life. I press my hand to his head, clasping him to me, hoping he stays.

Slowly, his body relaxes, and he falls asleep again. Relief washes through me. And hope. He has never turned to me like this, not without me practically forcing him. He has never fallen asleep again so quickly. I stroke his hair, more for my own sake than his, struggling to keep my fingers light so I don't wake him.

I feel eyes on me.

I turn my head to find Belos watching. The Drift-light from his bonds shines on his open eyes. He doesn't say anything, doesn't smirk or sneer. He doesn't look like he feels anything at all.

I hate him for witnessing this. I hate that he gets to taint my joy in this small improvement. I hate that he gets to see Logan's suffering, much of which he caused.

I close my eyes, forcing my awareness away from Belos and into the feeling of Logan lying against me. I will make that my reality. I have him. He has me. The rest of the world can just go away.

CHAPTER 35

Even before the sun rises, merchants and farmers are setting up their stalls in the town square. With Logan and Belos behind me, I follow the scent of meat pies to one of the carts.

"They're not hot yet," explains the ruddy-faced baker. "Half an hour."

I have no interest in lingering. "I'll take them as they are. Six, if you please." From the corner of my eye, I assure myself that Belos cannot look over my shoulder before I dig some coins from the pack.

"Suit yourself." The baker shrugs and plucks half a dozen pies from the baking stone set over a low fire.

Belos inquires, "What are you so protective of in that pack?"

"My privacy."

"You may be a good liar, Astarti, but your lover is not. He bristled like a cat at the question."

I don't allow myself to look at either of them. Protesting will only give Belos the chance to read both of us for clues.

When the baker hands me the first two pies, I shove them at Belos. Tempting as it may be to let him starve, that wouldn't serve our purpose. Besides, I do *not* want to have to Heal him again. I pass the next two pies to Logan and keep the others for myself.

We sit on the steps of the inn to eat. Though the meat is cooked, the pies are cold in the middle. Logan watches me from the corner of his eye, as he has been doing all morning. When I stifle a yawn, he frowns. Ah. So that's what this is about. I probably do look tired.

Belos picks up on the tension, though one would think his swollen nose hurts too much for him to think about anything but that. He's tougher than I've given him credit for.

He says, "I hope you can stay awake today, Astarti. After that long night."

I give him a humorless smile. "You know I am well used to sleepless nights."

Logan demands, "What does he mean, 'long night'?"

Before I can answer, Belos says with mock surprise, "You didn't realize she was keeping watch over you?"

Logan turns a thunderous look on me. "Is that true?"

I try to silently communicate that we shouldn't argue in front of Belos. It's what he wants to see. Either Logan reads this in my face, or he comes to the same conclusion on his own. He turns to Belos.

"Your tongue, remember? An unnecessary detail."

Belos clamps his lips shut with mocking emphasis, his eyes dancing with delight the whole time. Logan looks resolutely away from him.

I can't eat all of my second pie, so I give it to Logan. He inhales it so quickly that I offer, "I'll get you another if you're still hungry."

"No. I'd rather get moving."

We make our way to the edge of town. I take Logan's hand. Belos holds out his own, laughing silently when Logan scowls. Logan grabs him by the arm and takes us into the wind.

ℬ ℭ

Logan doesn't stop until we've crossed over the narrow strip of Heradyn and the broad channel of ocean that lies between it and Rune. I settle into my body on a rocky bluff that looks down to a strip of beach. Dozens of people move up and down the muddy beach, many wading out in the surf. They seem to be looking for something.

I wonder aloud, "What's going on down there?"

Logan squints down at the moving figures. "Clamming?" he guesses, then shakes his head. "No, the tide's wrong."

I rub my arms for warmth. "It's so cold. Even for Rune."

Logan mutters, "Something's not right." He casts a suspicious look at Belos, who shrugs.

I admit, "Something did feel different. In the wind."

Logan nods.

I narrow my eyes at the beach below. A man washes something off in the ocean then holds it up. It's about the size of a fist and gleams red-orange in the sunlight.

Logan says, "I'll go look. Stay here."

He vanishes, and the rush of air pulls my hair after him.

Not one to miss an opportunity, Belos sidles closer to me. "What is it about him? Is it because he's handsome? Or is it his pain you like?"

I wheel on him. "Do not speak to me."

Once, I would have felt too much awe to treat him with such scorn. Perhaps as much has changed in me as in him. I can't pinpoint a moment, but I'm not afraid anymore. I'm not even angry, not for myself at least. Strange. I feel like I should be. But

Belos seems so…small to me now. He's like a child casting stones.

He looks away. Is he jealous of Logan?

Suddenly, I have to know something, and I have only a moment while Logan is gone. I pin Belos with a stare. "Why did you pretend to be me? When you had Logan."

"He told you about that?" Belos sounds genuinely surprised.

"Why did you do it?"

"Because I knew it would hurt him. I knew it would make him more ashamed than anything else I could do to him. *That* is power, Astarti. The ability to make others ashamed. It breaks them."

A shiver works through me because he's right: that is power. Cruel, selfish, without purpose. But it is power.

Belos wraps his arms around himself against the chill. "Why do you think I harass him so much? He gives in to it. It hurts him. How can you love someone so weak?"

"That's not weakness."

He raises a sardonic eyebrow. "He's vulnerable. That is weakness."

I know I shouldn't play this game with Belos, but I can't help arguing, "He could kill you, you know. I'm a little surprised he hasn't yet."

Belos makes a dismissive gesture. "That doesn't make him strong."

"It does. That he's able to resist? That takes strength. You would see that if you understood what his life has been."

"But I do. I've *lived* in his mind. Do you know what makes him weak? He will not embrace what he could be. He restrains himself out of fear—"

"I would call it compassion and decency."

"I don't care what you call it. To restrain oneself is weakness, a weakness born of fear. You can only be strong by seizing everything you can in yourself and from others."

"If you call that strength, I will gladly accept weakness, both in myself and others."

"You always were soft."

That doesn't hurt me, but my next question might. I want it to expose Belos, but it could expose me as well. I take a resolving breath. "Why did you ever love me?" He stiffens, and I insist, "You did. You can deny it if you like, but I know the truth."

He looks at me, suspicion in his eyes. "Why do you ask that?"

"I'm curious."

"Liar."

I try again, honestly this time. If I accept the truth, it cannot hurt me, no matter what Belos makes of it. "It felt good that you loved me, in your own way. But looking back, I don't understand it. My life could have been worse—I realize that. Why wasn't it?"

Belos looks away. For the first time ever, I have made him uncomfortable.

"You've lost everything. Your Seven, your power. At this point, what does it cost you to tell me?"

He says in a strained voice, "It costs me the only thing I have left."

"Why? Because you're ashamed that you ever cared for someone?"

He says nothing. I'm not sure I've hit on the truth until he turns away. I've been guessing, gambling, pretending to be certain where I was not. For once, I have beaten him. For once, something in him is laid bare. He did love me. It was a selfish love—a terrible thing, really—but it makes me see him, just for this moment, as a person. A cruel, selfish, weak, unforgivable one, but a person nonetheless. It is a strange sensation. The world resettles itself around this idea.

The breeze swirls around me, and Logan shapes himself from the wind. He frowns at Belos, who is still looking away and gives me a questioning look. I make a face that I hope says, *It's complicated.*

Logan nods down to the beach. "Amber. It seems to have washed up on shore recently. Too much at once to be natural."

"The Old Ones?" I venture.

"I would assume. They're nearby. I can feel their energy. It's in the air, in the earth, in the water."

"Can you sense Kronos yet?"

His jaw tightens. "No. But let me guess: north?"

Belos has recovered his smirk. "Of course."

Chapter 36

LOGAN

The air grows colder the farther north I take us. While that in itself is not surprising, it shouldn't be *this* cold. Frost blankets the ground, even though it's summer. As we travel inland, away from the moderating force of the ocean, snow swirls through the air. As we reach the more remote settlements, crops stand frozen in the fields, and the rivers are ribbons of ice.

I no longer need to confirm direction. I only need to follow the cold. Had we brought Belos only as a guide, we could kill him now.

A lone mountain, white with snow, stabs the sky in the distance.

As we near the mountain, they start to come, flitting around me. They are playful, curious. They tug at me like children asking me to join a game.

They are not the only strangeness in the air. Time plays tricks on me. For a moment, I forget why I'm here. I drift, suspended. I am looking for someone. One of the Old Ones skims around me, laughing. I start toward her before I remember who she is. She tried to sink the whaling ship. Reality reasserts itself. She is not my friend. I don't know her. Astarti drifts into my awareness, dispelling the strangeness. I speed along again, my thoughts fixed on the mountain.

When we reach the rocky base of it, I shape us from the wind. We sink in snow to our knees, shivering in our thin summer tunics.

"Why did we stop?" Belos asks through chattering teeth. "He's up there."

"I know."

I crunch through the snow, needing to get away from him. Astarti follows.

I ask her quietly, "Did you feel them?"

"Yes."

"They do something to me. I don't like it."

Astarti, arms wrapped tightly around herself, stares into the rocky hills dotted with fir trees weighted by snow. "Every time I'm near them, it's like time…shifts. Like I'm caught in some dream."

I turn to her in surprise. "Yes. Exactly."

Belos crunches through the snow. "Neither of you have any idea what he can do. You have no idea what he really is."

Astarti turns to look at him. "You came with us willingly. You could have taken your chances with Heborian, but you chose this. Why?"

"Finally, you think to ask."

"Heborian wanted you to draw them to Tornelaine, and that didn't frighten you. You still want something from them."

"You think Heborian wanted to draw them to Tornelaine?" His tone is condescending. "More destruction in his own city?"

"But you said…" Astarti trails off. "You never said that. I said that, and you said nothing."

Belos's lips twitch. "Perhaps you've been spending too much time around honest people."

Astarti demands, "But if he didn't want to draw them back to Tornelaine, why did he keep you alive? Your only use is your connection to Kronos."

"Hmm," says Belos. "Interesting."

Astarti frowns. "But…"

A wind whips around us. Astarti looks questioningly at me, but I'm not doing this.

Snow swirls into the air and gathers itself into a face. The Old One brushes icy fingers across my cheek before floating near Astarti.

She says, in the ancient language of the Earthmakers, "Pretty girl."

I've never heard any of them speak before, and all I can do is stare. When I find my voice, I ask, in the same ancient speech, "What do you want?"

The Old One floats back to me. "Make new. All things new." Her expression hardens. "But this one." She darts to Belos, who watches her warily. "No."

"We will take him to Kronos. Kronos will choose his fate."

The Old One hovers, undecided, then she starts to dissolve, whispering, "He waits."

∞ ∞

I take us up the craggy side of the mountain. Snow lies thick between the blades and boulders of stone, and it whips into the air with our passing.

I sense Kronos within, a deep and ponderous weight in the heart of the mountain. I'm not confident I can draw the others through stone without harming them, so I hunt for an entrance.

Near the top, I find a crevice that seeps the cold air of the mountain's belly and take us through. The sunlight is at just the right angle to flood the passageway, and it catches on the rough faces of raw gemstones embedded in the rock. The light falls like a blade on the rough floor of a cavern, flashing against the red, green, blue, and pure white stones. It is like a stained glass window has shattered. No. It's like a window yet to be made. My imagination expands as I skim over the stone. So many things could be made. So many possibilities.

Kronos sits on a rocky chair of sorts, facing the sun. He is stone and jewel, like the chair. They are melded together; or perhaps they were formed together. Light plays over his gleaming emerald eyes, making them catch fire as the old Runish tales tell. His ruby lips glisten like fresh blood. A cloak of sapphires hangs from his shoulders, and a crown of diamonds rings his head.

As I shape us from the wind, settling to the cold floor, Kronos rises from his chair. Stone cracks and crumbles as he breaks free. The gems glitter and flash with his movements. The image trips and slides. Stone softens into skin, and the gems settle into subtler, more human shades. The crown of diamonds becomes a crown of light, like the pinpoints of distant stars. Yet, the other image overlays this one. He is the man before us, and also the mountain with all its rough riches.

I hold myself still as he approaches. With each step, his feet meld with the floor, turning briefly to stone before they pull free. He stops before me. He is the same height as I—perhaps he has made himself so. His bright eyes gaze into mine.

"I know you," he says in the modern tongue of my people but with a heavy accent of ancient days.

He does not try to embrace me, and I'm glad. This is no tearful reunion—it's not a reunion at all. It's a meeting, and I think we are both more curious than anything. I have wanted this, yes, but I'm not looking for affection. I don't need him to declare me his son. I want to understand him. I want to understand myself.

He asks, "Will you travel with us?"

"Travel?"

His eyes flick to the cavern roof, but I know he is looking beyond, much as he did in my vision of him in the Dry Land when he gazed across the sky.

"The possibilities stretch infinitely, even here." His voice hardens when he adds, "But we have learned too much anger in this place, and it hampers our makings. We would find a new beginning."

Loss cracks open within me, like a fissure in rock. "You're leaving."

His eyes glitter with possibility. "You could come with us and begin to make. You also have learned much anger here."

Here it is. The offer. To leave with them, to cut all the ties on my power and find out what it is to use it, to *really* use it, without restraint, without fear. I would not have to close it inside myself. I would not have to hate it.

But.

I would have to choose that one thing and give up all others. Not only would I lose Astarti—which is unthinkable—I would lose everything I have made of myself. It would make my whole life to this point false and wasted, a series of mistakes.

He is presenting me with the same decision I have been presenting to myself: be one or the other. To go with Kronos would set me free in one sense, but it would bind me in another. It would bind me to that one aspect of myself, as though the rest is not real and valid. It would mean closing something *else* inside myself instead—everything in me that is human.

An inversion, not a solution.

My mind skips back to the hallway at the inn, then to the bathing chamber in Tornelaine. Moments when I have been weakest, yet I found peace at the end of them because Astarti made me look at them, accept them, live them. She didn't let me run away or bury part of myself.

To go with Kronos would be to continue burying myself, continue turning away, and I am beginning to see that such a thing can never bring me peace. Once, I did not think peace was a possibility. Now, though I've felt it only in small moments, I know that it is. Astarti has given me what no one else ever has—what Kronos cannot give me—hope that I will find a balance between these parts of myself. I would rather try to find that than keep running.

And, of course, the answer is simple when I think of Astarti herself. I would let her go, if she asked it, because I would never bind her. But I would never choose a life without her.

She is stiff behind me, expecting me to leave her, as she has expected before. It hurts a little that she thinks I would, though I know it's my own fault. I've turned away from her too often for her to have faith in me.

Kronos reads my energy, the way it flows toward Astarti. He nods. I don't know if he's disappointed, but he doesn't look surprised. A small breath goes out of Astarti behind me. I want to tell her I'm sorry. I want to touch her. But I won't share that with Belos, who hangs at the edge of my awareness.

I say only, "When do you leave?"

"Soon," Kronos answers. "But I would cleanse myself first, for I will take no more of this world with me than I must."

Astarti presses forward. "We've brought the Shackle, if you would like to take him into the Drift and cast him out."

Kronos's face darkens like a sky ready to storm, but he turns none of his attention on Belos. "Let me see it," he rumbles.

Astarti unbuckles the pack and pulls the gleaming white Shackle from it. She offers it to Kronos, but he doesn't take it.

"Do you know what this is?"

"I do," she says carefully. "I am sorry."

Kronos reaches out a single finger and runs it along the chain that drapes between Astarti's lifted hands. "She chose to travel that bend in the river, and she left an echo of herself in this world. I do not mourn her; I only mourn this reshaping of her memory."

She. Someone specific. "Who was she? Was she the only one that died?"

"No, but she was the only one who loved this world enough to give so much of herself to it. Her name was Gaia."

That startles me. "Like my mother."

Kronos gazes again into my face. "Your mother is a distant, distant echo of her, but, yes. Perhaps that is what drew me to your mother in the first place."

He doesn't love my mother, even though she still yearns for him. I suppose I should not expect him to love her. Perhaps he does not know love; perhaps anger is all he has learned.

Astarti asks, "Why is the land dead in the place where she died?"

"We abandoned it. She was our mother, and she was gone, and there was nothing more for us there. We wanted something new."

"You didn't destroy it?"

"We drew all the energy from it and took it with us to reshape."

A dark thought creeps upon me. "Will you do that again? Take all the energy from this place?"

"We almost did once. But our children were like crops planted in a field. They did not want to travel with us, nor would they have us take back what we had given."

276

Astarti asks, "Is that why they made war on you? Because you were going to strip their lands of energy?"

"We never had the chance to decide," he says bitterly. "They bound us here with chains forged from our very own essence. We had taught them too much, and they had their own ideas of how to use that knowledge."

I press the point: "Would you have destroyed them?"

"I do not know. We had not yet learned what it is to suffer."

"And now?"

He lets out a deep breath, and wind swirls from him through the cavern. He still has not decided. He doesn't know what he will do.

With his power no longer bound by the limited imagination of another, no longer cut off from the other energies of this world, it is expanding. I *feel* its growth, the way it blends into the world around us—the way they feed each other. Indeed, the world's energy—its life, on which we are dependent—is his to command. To give or to take.

For the first time, I understand Heborian a little. This world has only two hopes: that Kronos has learned compassion as well as anger, or that Heborian succeeds in binding him once more.

Kronos's hand closes on the chain, and he pulls the Shackle away from Astarti. "Poor Gaia. How she would have grieved to know that her body was carved into weapons and chains. She did not even know what those were. We never imagined such things." He slips one Shackle cuff onto his wrist, muttering, "Gaia would understand."

Belos steps forward.

Willingly, with anticipation in his eyes.

For one foolish moment I allow myself to believe that he only wants his energy back from Kronos, that he wants to be whole.

But when has Belos ever wanted only what belongs to him?

CHAPTER 37

When Belos steps forward so eagerly, I realize that this is the opportunity he has waited for. I've kept him in the corner of my eye, expecting something. I still don't know his aim, but I can read him well enough to see he has a plan. In the moment before Kronos pulls him into the Drift, I latch onto him. With the same thought, so does Logan.

We are wrenched into the Drift.

The rush of energy along the glowing Shackle chain almost rips me away from Belos. His energy flares as the part of him lodged in Kronos surges back. Even with the return of his energy, Belos surely cannot hope to challenge Kronos. Kronos's wild power thrums around us, more terrible than the Hounding, more shattering than a bursting mountain.

My mind splinters.

As before when I have been in the Drift near Kronos, time bends and folds. I am layers of myself: a child, delighted by the Drift; a young woman, Leashed and ashamed; my own present self, clinging to this man who has made me all these things. There is nothing I can do but hang on.

Threads of energy twist and tangle through Belos and spool away from him into the Drift. Vaguely, I sense a similar unraveling of my own energy. I desperately will myself to focus on Belos. I brought him here, to this opportunity; I cannot let him get away.

Golden light and raging wind surround us. They blend and swirl in a confusion of substance. Suddenly, the light flares like the sun. It fills me, blinding me, burning everything else out of me. Whatever I thought I could do here, I was a fool.

I am light.

I am nothing.

I think, *I am dying.*

Pressure engulfs me; darkness consumes me.

Suddenly, I am released, and the physical world settles awkwardly around me. Or *I* settle awkwardly, like a sailor on land after months at sea. My body feels strange and heavy.

My cheek is pressed to cold stone. At first, I think I am back in the cavern, but there is too much light beyond my closed eyelids, and the scent of mountain pine is too strong.

Someone groans, and I peel open my eyes to see Logan flop onto his back. His face is white, and his eyes are squeezed shut. I drag my hand out from where it is trapped under my chest and touch him. He is solid, real. We are alive. He opens his eyes and rolls toward me. I run my hand down his body as he runs his down mine. My hand finds only the familiar contours of muscle and bone. I rest my forehead against his, too relieved to think.

I sit up slowly, and Logan does the same. We are on a rocky outcropping on a mountainside, surrounded my scrubby trees and scraggly brush. In the far distance lie wooded foothills that roll and drop, rising to occasional bare hilltops.

"Twenty minutes, at best guess," hisses a sly voice somewhere below.

I freeze. I know that voice, but it cannot be. He is dead.

A slight scuffing sound jerks my attention to the scrub-covered boulders at my right. Belos! He is creeping away, weaving between the rocks with the Shackle in hand.

I lurch in his direction, but Logan grabs my arm and presses a finger to his lips, then he points down. Slowly, we creep to the edge of our rocky outcropping.

Below stand a dozen black-cloaked figures. No. Impossible.

But it's not impossible.

Kronos has brought us here—or perhaps Belos compelled him to? Though it's not a *place*, exactly, but a time.

Straton points to the east. "Arathos will most likely bring his Wardens there. If we bring the Leashed from there"—he points south—"the Wardens will have little warning."

"See to it," Belos says.

Belos.

This is not the Belos I know, but a younger version of him than the one which disappeared among the rocks. This younger Belos stares out across the foothills, excitement in every line of his body. There is an air of possibility about him. He is less worn, more hopeful. Yes, that is hope. He sees great things ahead, and that is what tells me this is before his war. He doesn't know he is about to lose and be driven into the Dry Land.

He sends the others about their duties. There are at least a dozen of them, many I don't know. I watch Theron, young and not yet weighted down by his crimes, vanish into the Drift.

Fearing our discovery, I shape my spear. But we remain unnoticed. Perhaps we are not fully here.

Just beyond the younger Belos's sight, our Belos creeps around the boulders. I draw back slightly. Surely not.

He is sneaking up on himself.

With the Shackle.

I dart a shocked look at Logan. His grim expression tells me he sees it too.

Perhaps because I am warier of the Belos I know—the one hardened by decades of loss and planning and Taking—than the one I don't, I draw breath to shout. Fingers of air settle over my mouth.

Wait, Kronos whispers and takes his hand away.

I bite my lip and decide to trust him, if only because he has no reason to aid Belos.

The younger Belos yells when our Belos leaps on him from behind. The younger whirls around, but his older, cannier self knows just what to expect. He dodges a blast of energy, which cracks into the rocks behind. When the younger shapes his sword, our Belos ducks under it and slips the Shackle on his younger self's other wrist.

The energy humming from the Shackle makes the ground shake beneath me.

The Shackle glows bright white then blue then, with a flash, it bursts.

Both of them stagger back, stunned. Our Belos freezes. I have never seen him freeze before. For once, he is out of options. For once, he has reached the end of his plan, and it has failed, and there can be no escape.

He sees it, at last, his folly, and he knows what is coming because he knows himself quite well. He closes his eyes.

The younger Belos yells with rage at having been surprised, and he plunges his Drift-sword into the heart of his older self. When he wrenches his sword free, our Belos falls at his feet.

The younger crouches down, panting, scowling with anger. He nudges our Belos with his foot, rolling him onto his back. The younger gasps and takes a step away. He shakes his head, denying what he sees as he gets his first clear look at the man he killed. He takes another step back, and another, still shaking his head. He vanishes into the Drift.

We wait for a while, expecting younger Belos or the others to return. I stare down at the limp body, scarcely daring to believe. When the others don't come back, I rise silently to my feet and creep along the path that Belos took. Logan creeps along behind me, and a breeze wafts over us.

Belos is dead by the time I reach him; maybe he was dead when he fell. His eyes stare blindly into the sky above.

Logan says, still stunned by the perversity of Belos's actions, "He tried to Take his own soul."

I crouch beside Belos's thin, worn body. Blood covers his chest from the old wound I dealt him, and I wonder if it would have killed him in time. His face is a bruised and swollen mess from the blows Logan dealt him. He has been in a long process of defeat.

I say, "It wouldn't just have been his own soul but also the energy he had already harvested from others at this point in his life."

"Madness," Logan mutters, unable to comprehend this level of depravity and greed and desperation. "Why wouldn't he try to take it from someone else instead?"

Kronos shapes himself from the breeze and stands beside us with all the weight and solidity of the surrounding boulders. "This was his river. He could travel no other."

His words tease something in my memory. "I read a story about your people. They were walking a river backwards. One stumbled over a stone and was surprised because the stone had not been there before. It was time, wasn't it? They were traveling time."

Kronos says, "I do not know the story, but time is much like a river—constantly changing, with a thousand million possible courses it could take."

"But you knew this would happen. That's why you brought him here."

"I allowed him to bring himself here. I knew this was a possibility, but it wasn't the only one."

"So you would have let anything happen?"

"Gaia gave me a gift, for she loved me best and, perhaps, trusted me most. All time and all possibility flow through me. I touch infinity. I see potential. Belos was closing off other possibilities. Whatever he chose at this point would have led to his destruction. He was choosing death, whether he knew it or not, turning toward it because he lacked the imagination for other possibilities."

I glance down at Belos once, stunned he is dead. Somehow, despite his brokenness, this doesn't seem possible.

I look at Logan, who is also staring at Belos. Emotion chases over his face. At first, he looks angry, like he's been robbed of a fight he longed for. Then he raises his eyes to mine, and the anger eases from his face. The color swirling though his irises slows, like a breeze settling. He pushes to his feet, ready to be gone from here.

I rise and turn away from Belos. I, too, am ready to be gone. When Kronos extends his hand, I take it.

CHAPTER 38

When Kronos draws me into the Drift, time and light press around me once more. I lose track of Logan and even of Kronos. I am wrapped in myself, caught in the strange layering of time. After what happened with Belos, I pay more attention, and I find the threads of my life weaving around one another, all the moments that I've lived tangling into a mess. If it is not a mess, it is a pattern far too intricate for me to follow. I flow back and forth and around in this weaving, catching brief sensations of times long past. If I could follow the threads correctly, maybe they would take me forward, but I find myself moving back.

I catch on a moment, a sweet and clean moment that I cannot place. I seize it, press myself into it, desperate to know what beautiful thing I have forgotten.

Light engulfs me, then darkness.

I am compressed into nothing, and again it feels like I must be dying.

Then I fall to my hands and knees and know at once that I am in the physical world. My body weighs me down. Air moves around me. But I know, even before I open my eyes, that I am in a room.

My hands are sunk in something soft, and I open my eyes to find a thick sheepskin rug beneath me. Heat washes my legs, and I jump at a crackle of fire.

"Are you all right?"

I jump again at the voice. I look up to find I'm in a large, wood-paneled room hung with tapestries and with an open wall, a kind of balustrade, that looks out to the distant sea. A slim blonde woman looks at me with concern.

"Are you hurt?" she asks. She wears light, filmy robes like an Earthmaker, but a fine woolen shawl drapes her shoulders. A delicate silver bracelet encircles one wrist.

"No."

"The fire is going strong now. Thank you."

I glance back at the hearth, where fire licks at fresh logs. There is something familiar about this hearth. In fact, this whole room is familiar, though the open wall overlooking the sea is different. But I know the pattern of this wood floor, the dimensions of this room, the feel of the air here. I know where I am, but I can't quite believe it. I certainly can't believe this woman is...

A thin cry comes from the edge of the sheepskin rug, and the woman rushes past me to reach an ornately carved cradle. The woman's silken robes flow behind her, and a long blonde braid hangs messily down her back. She reaches into the cradle and picks up a dark-haired infant.

"Hush now, love," she croons. "Hush, hush."

Humming softly, she rocks the infant in her arms. She wanders to the open wall and sits on the edge, leaning her back against a smooth stone column.

She calls to me, "Could you bring her blanket?"

I lurch into motion. I bang into a chair, making it screech against the hardwood floor.

"Sorry," I mutter, but the woman waves it away, her eyes never leaving the baby.

I cautiously approach the cradle and peer into its plush depths. I snag the white knitted blanket from the cradle and start toward the woman. I approach slowly, weighted down by the strangeness and terrified of the yearning I feel. Afraid, too, of letting her really see me.

When I hand her the blanket, she smiles kindly. I expect her to stare at me, to realize she doesn't know me, to demand why I am here.

She wraps the infant in the thick blanket and motions me to sit. I lean against the balustrade, tense and ready to flee.

Sibyl—for it can only be her—looks out to the distant sea, where the sun hangs on the horizon, near to setting. She says, "This is my favorite time of day. The world quiets down, and tomorrow's possibilities lie unspoiled ahead of us."

She is less fierce than I have imagined her, but maybe it is only that she holds her child in her arms. Heborian once said that when I was born, she had little thought for anything else.

My eyes twitch to the infant and away. I cannot assimilate that just yet.

The door opens, and Heborian—as though conjured by my thoughts—walks into the room.

Sibyl calls to him, "Come see your daughter and perhaps you won't look so grim."

He stalks across the room, a younger man than I know. He has all the lithe grace of a wolf and an expression just as dangerous. Sibyl passes the bundled infant to him. He takes her in his arms, cradling her close to his body. He rocks her gently, but his face loses none of it grimness. If anything, he grows more somber.

Of course, I know why. His deal with Belos was made before I was born, and at this time I have already been promised away. The only one here who doesn't know that is Sibyl. I want to tell her, but the words stick in my throat. When he is gone, I will tell her.

"My Astarti," Heborian murmurs. I start, but his eyes are on the infant in his arms. "Sibyl, love, go get yourself some supper. Let me have a little time with our child."

She pushes away from the balustrade reluctantly and says, "Of course."

I want to follow her, but I seem frozen in place. Heborian has not noticed me, and I don't want him to.

When Sibyl is gone, he cradles the infant closer to his face and presses a tender kiss to her small, delicate head. I cannot equate that fragile child with myself.

Despite his affection, I recognize the look of intent about him. He is planning something, and the wisp of regret in his eyes will not hold him back from it.

He says to the infant, "I would spare you this if there were another way. But there isn't. There wasn't. There cannot be. And I am a ruthless man, my little Astarti, so ruthless."

He gently shifts the infant until she is upright and leaning against his chest. He tugs down the plush blanket to expose her neck. She wraps a small fist in his hair, grabbing one of the Runish braids. She makes a "Gah!" sound and tugs. Heborian does not seem to notice.

A blue glows blooms around his fist. It tightens and intensifies until it clings only to his finger, extending from it like a pointed fingernail.

I know what he is about to do. I don't know why I don't try to stop him.

When he bleeds the first branch of the Griever's Mark into her skin, she wails. He bounces her gently, murmuring, "Hush, hush," much as Sibyl did. The back of my own neck prickles, as though the Mark is being freshly cut into my skin.

He mutters in Runish as he raises his finger again to make the other branches. When he is done, he holds her to him, rocking her gently as she cries. Tears stream down his own cheeks to catch in his bread. He buries his face against her swaddled body, rocking and bouncing to quiet her.

"It doesn't hurt so very much," he says. "Hush, now, hush. It is the only thing I can give you that he cannot take away."

As the infant cries in his arms, slowly quieting, I keep a hand pressed over my Mark. It is not how I have imagined this moment. Finally, she falls asleep.

When Sibyl returns, she knows at once that something is wrong.

She closes the door behind her, and all the fierceness I've been told she possessed appears in her face. "What is it? What's happened?"

"Nothing," Heborian says.

"Don't you lie to me." She holds out her arms for the infant, and Heborian passes the bundled child to her.

"She's sleeping," Heborian protests as Sibyl begins tugging the blanket aside to inspect the infant.

When she finds the Mark, she exclaims, "What is this?" and the baby wakes, crying.

"Protection," Heborian says gruffly, and I can see the distance growing in his eyes. Distance from Sibyl, and from the baby. The Mark may be protection, but it is also what I have always known it to be: a way of letting go.

"Protection?" Sibyl says doubtfully. "From what?"

"The world is dangerous and cruel. You know that better than most."

"She's a baby!"

"Even children are not safe," he says heavily. "You know that."

"If you're referring to that boy they sent to the Ancorites, let me assure you that no such thing will happen to my daughter."

Heborian turns a hard expression on her. "Parents cannot protect their children from everything."

"Perhaps not. But it should be their first priority."

Heborian doesn't answer, but I know his mind. I was not his first priority, nor was Sibyl. The kingdom, always the kingdom.

He turns away and leaves without another word.

When the door closes once more, Sibyl rocks the baby back to sleep, but her ease never returns.

The sun vanishes below the horizon, and the room glows pink and orange. But it fades, and soon the room is dim, lit only by the fire in the hearth.

When Sibyl lays the baby in her cradle and covers her, she looks at me. "You will wake me if she's restless?"

"Yes," I croak.

"Then goodnight."

I watch her disappear into the bedroom. After a while, I sit on the sheepskin. I don't look at the baby, but she is always at the edge of my awareness.

I stare into the fire, torn.

I am on the edge of sleep, curled on my side, when a face shapes itself from the flames. "Why are you here?" Kronos asks.

"I want to save her."

"The baby?"

"Sibyl."

Kronos gazes at me for a long while, saying nothing.

"Is it possible?" I ask. "Can I change things?"

"Do you really want to?"

"Of course. Is it possible?"

"There are many possibilities. You will have to decide."

"On what?"

"On what you are willing to sacrifice."

The word hangs in my mind as I drift into sleep. Surely saving a life is not a sacrifice?

                          ℘ ℂ

I pick my way through a battlefield littered with corpses. I am looking for someone, but I don't know whom. I nudge one stiff body then another. The faces are bloated, the features distorted by death. What if I don't recognize him?

Him?

Suddenly, I am running, desperate to get to him.

I see someone in the distance, picking through the corpses as I have been doing.

"Logan!"

He looks up. His clothes are torn, his face streaked with the blood and grime of battle. When he sees me, his face breaks into a wide grin, and he is racing toward me. The sun sparkles in his eyes like they are precious gems. I throw my arms wide to meet him.

Something snags my foot.

I am falling.

Falling and falling.

And falling.

                          ℘ ℂ

I wake with a jerk on the sheepskin rug. For a moment, I think I am in the hut where I once stayed with Logan, but the sheepskin is too clean, and the room is too big. I stare at the cradle beside me, utterly bewildered.

Then I remember.

I rise to my knees and peer into the cradle. The firelight plays over the sleeping infant, making a dancing blend of light and shadow.

Her skin is pale and fine, contrasting sharply with the thick dark hair. I don't know enough about infants to judge her age. Less than a year, certainly, or Belos would have her by now.

Looking at her, so unaware, makes my eyes sting. I know what she will face. For the first time, I can see that she is me, and I grieve for her. For the first time, I have sympathy because I can recognize that this is not her fault.

I trace the Mark on the back of my neck.

Why did I not stop him?

℘ ℭ

Throughout the next day, I follow Sibyl like a half-acknowledged ghost. No one seems to notice me but her. I don't want anyone else to notice.

We walk along the beach for hours. Sibyl carries the baby in a sling wrapped around both their bodies. She doesn't ask me to share the burden, and I don't offer. It's partly that I would feel too strange holding my infant self, but it's more that I love to see Sibyl holding her.

Sibyl picks up an oyster shell and shows the baby the flood of color inside the dull exterior. The baby grabs for the shell, exclaiming with infant delight.

"No," Sibyl says gently. "Sharp."

She tosses the shell back into the surf, and the baby laughs. It's a sweet sound, one I did not expect.

At one point, Sibyl stops and gazes out to sea, a lonely expression on her face. I follow her eyes but see nothing. The Floating Lands are out of sight today, but I suppose they are never far from her thoughts. Then the baby laughs at a seagull, and Sibyl smiles and walks on again.

I am deeply touched to see Sibyl so happy with me. I am glad that I was a comfort to her after she was cast away from her people. Will Logan be cast away? The question is still unanswered.

Logan.

I have never felt so far away from him, not even when he was a captive of Belos. Where is he? Why am I alone here?

"What is it, love?" Sibyl asks. At first, I think she is talking to the baby. Then I find her eyes on me.

"I was thinking about someone," I tell her as I hurry to catch up.

"A man?"

"Yes."

She gives me a teasing smile, and her cheeks dimple. She takes my hand and squeezes it. "I like you," she says.

"You don't know me. I do not think you would like me if you knew me."

"That's a terrible thing to say."

I look away. "But it's true."

"That's not fair. You must give me a chance."

"We don't have a chance," I tell her. I want to tell her why. I want to tell her what is coming. But, again, it sticks in my throat.

"Let's get back," she says. "The tide is turning."

€ ͒

I curl up again on the sheepskin rug, thinking. Maybe she would not be ashamed of me. I want to tell her what I've done. I want to know for sure.

I stare into the fire, looking for Kronos, hoping he can answer me. But the fire crackles and pops, oblivious to my questions.

ᔪ ᔭ

The next day, we walk the beach again. Sibyl loves the shoreline. Either that, or she is looking for the Floating Lands. I would like to think that she simply enjoys being here with her daughter.

We sit in the sand while the sun is high. Sibyl spreads her skirt and turns the baby loose in the confines of her legs. Sibyl's eyes are on the back on the baby's neck, where the fresh blue tattoo is edged with red.

"She'll be all right," I assure Sibyl.

Sibyl looks up. "She will be strong. I'm sure all mothers say that, but I know it in my heart."

"She'll be all right," I say again, and this time, I know it is true. She will be. Because I am.

When Sibyl gets up and wraps the baby again in the sling, snugging her to her body, I stay where I am.

I say once more, stuck on this, "She'll be all right."

Sibyl says, "If she is kind, I will be happy."

Sibyl turns and walks away, but I do not follow.

My eyes fill with tears as I watch her retreat.

Am I kind?

My mind sticks in my past, catching on every moment when I was not kind. Or strong. I push ahead to more recent things, since I broke from Belos and started to act for myself. I begin to find what I am looking for. In moments. In pieces.

Does it add up to a kind and strong woman, as my mother hoped I would be?

Logan would say it does, for he has always seen the best in me. When he looks at me, I feel like I am that woman my mother would be proud of. Someday, perhaps, I will see that when I look at myself.

"Are you ready?" Kronos is sitting beside me, his feet made of sand.

"Can I not change it? Sibyl's fate?"

"Perhaps. But what would you change it into? You cannot guess. You cannot know. You can go on with the life you have, or you can throw it away to see what you might get instead."

"But Logan…"

He lets that drift away on the breeze.

I say, "I would be someone else, if I had not lived the life that I've lived."

"Yes."

I look down the beach, but Sibyl is long gone. I say, "Take me back."

CHAPTER 39

I stagger in the cool dimness of the cavern after the sudden release from Kronos's wild energy.

"Astarti!"

Logan's voice seems to come from everywhere at once, and I wheel, disoriented. He grabs me into his arms and swings me around. The world swoops and spins, but I don't care. I am centered.

He sets me down but doesn't let go. Neither do I. My ear is pressed to his chest, and his heart thunders against me. He is trembling.

"Are you all right?" I ask.

"I am now. You were gone so long I was afraid you wouldn't come back. Kronos wouldn't let me go with you."

"You didn't get stuck in your past?" So many things he would surely like to change, so much pain he might have spared himself.

"No," he says firmly. "I didn't go into mine. I've spent too much time there already. I want to move forward."

I tighten my arms around him, reveling in the warmth of his body and its familiar contours. "So do I."

Kronos settles into form beside us. "He is coming."

For one bizarre moment, I think he means Belos, then I remember that Belos is dead. "Who?" I ask, grasping for my bearings after all that has happened.

"Your father."

"But how?"

Even as I ask, I find the answer myself.

It all fits together in a pattern I should have seen before we ever took Belos from his prison. What is Heborian if not a pragmatist and an excellent judge of character? What use did he have for Belos except to find this place? And why else would it have been so easy for us to get Belos out?

I say weakly, "He must have lodged part of himself in Belos. Belos may be dead, but his trail led straight here."

It's too horrible to believe, too obvious to deny.

Logan's jaw tightens. He has no trouble believing it of Heborian.

"He knew we would take Belos—that's why he did it. He knew just what to expect. But that he would pervert himself that way…" I shake my head, unable to finish.

I am still reeling from this new knowledge when someone appears from the Drift. I shape my spear automatically and slide away from the others to make space.

"Peace, Astarti," rumbles Horik deep voice. He steps into the gray curtain of light that falls through the crack overhead. It must be early evening, though I don't know of what day.

"Is that what Heborian brings?" I challenge Horik. "Peace?"

"He doesn't want you hurt. Nor do I. Please leave this place."

"You realize what he must have done to track us here?"

Horik's grim silence is answer enough.

"And you would serve him still? A man who would tie himself to Belos, who would accept that taint willingly?"

Horik does not try to justify Heborian's actions. I already know the justification, and I'm glad Horik leaves it unspoken. Anything can be justified from the right perspective. But this is a line he should not have crossed, for if he is willing to do that, then he is capable of anything and cannot be trusted.

Horik says, "I am sworn to him, Astarti. Please do not ask me to break my oath. I will, if you force it, but I beg you not to."

Kronos moves forward, his footsteps cracking like stone on stone. "We leave this place. There is no need for further death."

Logan asks, "And how will you leave it?"

Kronos looks long at Logan then long at me before he says, "Intact."

Horik tells him, "He does not believe you will stay away."

Anger sparks in Kronos's eyes. "We will *not* be bound again. You may tell him that. Go."

Horik looks, if anything, disappointed. And torn. Hefting his axe, he looks hopefully to Kronos, but Kronos makes no move.

My chest aches to see him looking for death here, hoping for it. I tell him firmly, "We will not kill you, Horik."

He says, "Better death than the other courses open to me. I must either break my oath or betray my friends."

"I am sorry, Horik—I am. But I will not yield."

Kronos insists, "We are leaving. There is no need for this."

"You cannot leave," Horik says grimly. "He has already caught one of you."

"*WHAT?*" The word booms through the cavern, shaking the ground beneath and making dust fall from the ceiling.

Kronos explodes into the air, shooting through the crevice. The wind that swirls in his wake rips me off my feet, but I don't wait to fall. I leap into the Drift.

The dark bulk of the mountain is dim and dreamlike from within the Drift. The lighted forms of several hundred Earthmakers and human soldiers gathered at its base are the reality. I spot Heborian's bright form near the front.

My attention catches on the glowing white harpoons that stand around Heborian, ready to be fired. One, anchored to the ground, stretches into the sky, chain straining, its hook embedded in the body of a frantic Old One, whose energy flickers and flashes as she strains to get free. Another form, shifting through degrees of substantiality, surges around her. Kronos. And he's right where Heborian wants him.

I slide out of the Drift near Kronos and have to shift myself into the wind to not be flung to the deadly stones below.

I try to shout, but my voice is nothing but air. He doesn't notice me, so frantic is he to free the one trapped. I catch a glimpse of Logan as he moves in and out of the wind. I do not know if he's trying to help free the Old One or if he's trying to drive Kronos away to safety.

The setting sun blazes against the snow, making it look like fire burns along the ground where the force of men is battered by the other Old Ones. Their forms shift as they sweep through the gathered men. They are deadly wind flinging shards of ice. They are the stones of the earth rising to trap and crush. Heborian ignores it all, focused on his purpose. Bluish Drift-energy builds around him as he prepares to fire another harpoon, and the faint, ghostly shapes of the Ancorites whisper around him.

I follow his aim to Kronos, still furiously tearing at the harpoon lodged in the captured Old One.

I have to choose. I must sacrifice one of them, for I am not fast enough to reach Heborian before he fires.

I am not fast enough.

My spear, however, is.

I am half wind, half myself as I call my spear, glowing with the blue radiance of the Drift.

I aim it at my father—and throw it as hard as I can.

CHAPTER 40

Time seems to slow, though perhaps that is only because I am keenly aware of the importance of this moment, and my mind traps every detail.

The spear flies straight and true toward Heborian, but it is not the only thing streaking that way.

Logan—a blend of wind and himself—flies in the spear's wake. At first, I think he is turning on Heborian with the same realization I have had. Then I see: he is trying to catch my spear.

He might be fast enough to do it.

But he is not only moving after the spear—he is flying into a wall of harpoons and swords.

I explode after him in a gust of wind, screaming like a shrieking gale, but I cannot possibly catch him.

The spear is no more than a foot from Heborian when Logan grabs it, jerking it aside and turning his body so that his shoulder—instead of my spear—slams into Heborian's chest. The harpoon fires but flies off course. Logan, grappling with the spear, goes sailing over Heborian's toppled form and barrels into the line of men bristling with blades.

I put on another burst of speed, but I arrive only in time to watch the soldiers and Wardens being flung away from Logan as he rises in a torrent of wind and stone. He extends his hand toward the earth, and his sword flows into his grip.

Heborian is staggering to his feet, grabbing for another harpoon when Logan swings a fist and knocks him to the ground. Logan's sword point comes to rest on Heborian's exposed throat, and everyone around them goes still.

I settle into my body a few paces away. Logan's chest heaves, and blood runs from his forehead, over one eye, and down his cheek. Heborian, I can see now that I am close, is gray-faced and weakened by illness.

The gaze he fixes on Logan, however, has all his usual sharpness. "Do you intend to kill me?"

"I might," Logan hisses.

"Then why did you save my life?"

"So that if you die today it is not by Astarti's hand. You have already weighed her down with enough burdens; I won't let your actions demand this of her as well. Make no mistake, I will kill you myself if I must. But better she hate me than herself."

"Logan," I call softly.

"Astarti, please. Let me handle this."

The Ancorites, who fled the fight, come whispering back. They flow around Logan, trailing their fingers over him. He shudders, and his shoulders hitch with tension. He cannot deal with them and Heborian at the same time, and he is clearly choosing Heborian.

Bind, bind, bind.

It is the sight of them, cruel and thoughtless, tormenting him when he can do nothing about it, that sets my blood on fire. I lash at them with everything in me, and it is Drift-energy and wind and water, earth and fire. I hook claws of energy into their insubstantial bodies and rip them away from him. They flicker in and out of shape, more ghostly and strange than anything I have ever seen. Their faces, as they take brief shape, are skeletal and worn beyond what life should allow. It is long past time they were dead. But as I reach into their energies, as I touch their emptiness and loneliness, as I feel the long, wretched stretching of their existence, my anger cools. I do not forgive them for what they've done to the Old Ones or to Logan, but pity stirs in my heart.

Where I meant to destroy them, I find something else flowing from me—the warm energy, the empathy—of Healing. There is only one way they can be Healed, and though it comes to the same as destroying them, it feels different in my heart. I meld their elemental energy with that of the earth, letting them dissolve, helping them let go. The last thing I feel from them, as they turn to dust, is relief.

Wind howls down the mountainside behind us, and I spin to watch a storm of wind and snow streak our way.

Movement snags the edges of my vision, and I jerk my head toward Logan and Heborian. Heborian has used the distraction of Kronos's thunderous approach to roll away from Logan's sword. Heborian leaps for the nearest harpoon. Logan swings his sword at Heborian's back. From the line of soldiers, someone lunges forward, a blade slashing for Logan. I shape my spear and thrust, only at the last moment seeing it is Rood I am attacking. In a flash of blue, an axe flies into my line of sight, and Horik's huge form appears from the Drift.

Suddenly, everything freezes, even the scream in my mouth.

Though my mind is free, my limbs are frozen mid-strike, sheened and smooth with ice. Everyone around me is the same, the clear coating making watery paintings of the forms within.

We are toy figures, posed mid-fight, all of us about to destroy ourselves as we destroy each other.

The whole world has turned crystalline, gleaming with the pink and orange of sunset. Oddly beautiful, but so still and so deadly.

Snow gathers into Kronos's form. It hardens to ice until he is a moving sculpture. He does not try to put us at ease with a body like our own. He is the ice, the storm, the unrelenting cold.

He gazes at the imminent destruction. His eyes come to rest on me, and he treads silently through the snow to reach me. The sunset paints his smooth, clear face with all its fiery colors.

He lifts a hand of ice to my cheek, though I cannot feel the touch. He draws his hand back and examines his finger, where a tear clings like a raindrop, like a diamond, sparkling with color in the light of the setting sun.

He closes his hand, trapping my tear within it. He walks to Heborian.

He says, in a voice like the wind, "Death may make life, but this destruction is not creation, and I cannot abide it."

He tilts Logan's sword away so that is will swing clear of Heborian. He nudges Rood's sword off its mark, where it was about to lodge in Logan's back. He pushes my spear away from Rood's neck. Horik's axe, aimed at someone behind me, he tilts downward. He walks to my back where I cannot see and shifts yet another weapon, and only then do I realize I was about to die.

Kronos comes back into my line of sight and sweeps a hand across the sky. In the east, where the blue has deepened most, the stars begin to emerge, glittering as though in response to his gesture.

"We will walk the stars, as we intended to do long ago. But I cannot leave Gaia like this." He gathers the harpoons in a swirling cloud of wind and snow. One flies to him from where it fell at the base of the mountain. He must have removed it from the Old One Heborian had caught. She is nowhere to be seen, and I can only hope that she is not dead.

The harpoons spin faster and faster until they are a blur of white. When the whirlwind slows and settles, there is nothing but snow.

Kronos walks to Logan, still frozen mid-lunge. I cannot read the expression on Kronos's icy face, but his voice, when he speaks, is soft and full of farewell. "Remember, my son: the raging wind is also a sweet breeze, the torrent of water can be a trickling stream, fire may burn low and comfortingly, and what the earth grows best is grass."

Kronos moves away from us, and the other Old Ones drift to him in an intricate jumble of form and substance. Together they rise up, beginning to glow. Each glow shrinks and brightens until they are points of light, like stars, then they shoot into the sky and are gone.

$\mathcal{SO}$ $\mathcal{CR}$

The ice binding us slowly dissolves, and we fall, an inch at a time, to the melting snow.

CHAPTER 41

When I collapse into the slush, I don't look to see who almost killed me. We almost killed ourselves, and the blame lies so thickly over us all that trying to shift it is both pointless and cowardly. We all reacted, linking ourselves together in a chain of death.

Stiff with cold and shivering in my wet clothes, I push to my hands and knees. I cannot yet raise my head. Someone falls beside me. I can see only the scuffed leather at his knees, but I know every inch of him, and I gasp Logan's name as he pulls me into his arms. I wrap my own stiff arms around him, and they slowly warm. I hold on as tightly as my strength allows, and his arms encircle me almost painfully. But it is a good pain, such a very good pain.

As my numbness fades, I feel every detail of him: his stubbled jaw pressed to my cheek, his hair curling into my eye, his tunic clinging wetly to his hard, lean body, the belt pressing coldly to my stomach. Most of all, his thundering heartbeat, which booms through his whole body in time with my own.

The rest of the world starts to intrude. Men groan, weapons slide into sheaths, chainmail clinks, and boots crunch and slide through the melting snow.

Logan and I unwind enough to stand, but he doesn't take his hands away from me. He is wary, unsure whether the fight is over.

Aron and the Polemarc emerge from the shifting line of men. So. They were part of this. Aron's eyes stick at Logan's chest, not rising to his face, but Clitus looks him in the eye.

Clitus opens his mouth to speak, but Logan cuts him off. "There is no need to speak of it." Logan's tone is weary rather than angry, and he's right. There is nothing to say.

The Polemarc's jaw tightens, but he nods. "The Wardens will take Heborian's troops through the Current back to Tornelaine. Someone will need to stand in Heborian's place until he is recovered or until..."

As he trails off, the sight that has been catching the corner of my eye grows to a prickling awareness. I follow the Polemarc's eyes to where Heborian lies in the melting snow. Horik, Rood, Lief, and Jarl crouch around him. I break my contact with Logan to join them, though Logan stays close to my back.

I kneel, the slushy snow soaking my knees anew. Heborian lies half-sunken in the snow, his skin wan, his eyes dull.

"Did the Old Ones do this?" Rood directs the question at me with some anger.

None of us will soon forget what happened this day. Rood may never forgive me; he may never believe that I acted without thinking, that I didn't want to kill him. It is a faint excuse anyway. I did almost kill him. Suddenly, I am weary, so very weary.

I tell Rood, "The Old Ones didn't do this. This, he did to himself."

Rood's jaw clenches, but he doesn't argue.

Heborian makes no response. I'm not sure if he is unable to speak or simply unwilling.

Logan says tightly, "We need to get him out of the snow."

Horik works his hands under Heborian's prone form. "Lief and Jarl should return to Tornelaine with the others. I will take the king to Sunhild. Rood, you come with me. Astarti? What of you?"

℅ ℆

We step from the Drift outside Sunhild's hall, within the light of the guards' torches but far enough back that they don't immediately attack. They spring from the door to the steps, Drift-weapons at the ready and cries of alarm on their lips. Logan, Rood, and I raise our hands in surrender.

Horik, with Heborian slung over his shoulder, addresses them in Runish. I catch Heborian's name in the exchange, and the guards wave us forward.

When the heavy doors swing open and we step into the light and warmth of the hall, Sunhild rises from her seat at the central hearth. Her harp notes fade into the air. Color drains from her face at the sight of us, and she strides across the hall. Her heavy gray braid swings with her long stride, and her amber necklace flashes in the light of the braziers.

Sunhild goes straight to Horik and Heborian, and her fierce Runish words make Horik stiffen.

He answers her in Keldan, "He has been cutting away his soul, Sunhild, and this is what is left."

She lays her gnarled hands on her son's hanging head and closes her eyes. "What have you done?"

She beckons Horik to follow her, and the rest of us trail uncertainly behind until she snaps, "Stay here."

Logan, Rood, and I hover by the hearth, letting the heat chase off a little of the chill.

Rood darts a look around, taking in the stark wood paneling of the walls and the raised platforms running the length of the long, narrow hall. Sunhild's retainers—her huskarls—hover around us, fierce with their Runish tattoos and the weapons held so casually. *Just cleaning them*, their body language says. *But we are ready for you.* Their eyes linger mostly on Logan. The last they saw of him, he was possessed by Belos, and he tore a hole in the roof. My eyes drift to the ceiling, where beams of bright new wood and a section of fresh thatching mark the repair. Logan frowns up at it, his expression slightly confused. I doubt he remembers that very well.

Rood shakes his head. "He wasn't so ill this morning."

I tell him, "Belos was not dead this morning and the portion of energy Heborian lodged in him was not yet gone."

Rood's eyebrows draw together, and he scowls into the fire. He rubs his hands together. He doesn't say anything, but his expression speaks loudly enough. He is troubled by what his father did. Relief eases my chest.

"Did you know?" I ask him, keeping my voice carefully neutral so that he doesn't mistake the question for an accusation.

"Not until he called the men together. He tried to leave me behind. Again. I snuck in with the Wardens. The Current was…incredible, like a golden river flowing between the trees." He shakes his head. "I've never seen anything like it."

"He told you, though?" I am curious, and it makes me push him. Heborian is so stingy with information that I find it surprising he would tell Rood.

"I accused him of it. There was no other way he could have known where you had taken Belos. He guessed, Astarti, everything you would do."

"I know. Apparently, I am more predictable than I like to think."

A smile teases the corner of his mouth, and a breath I did not know I was holding eases out of me.

"I'm sorry," I whisper. "I did not know it was you." I want him to know this, not to erase my guilt but because I can't bear the thought of him believing I would willingly kill him.

He mutters, darting a look at Logan, whom he almost killed, "I'm sorry, too. I did not know how quickly everything could go wrong."

Logan says gruffly, "We all have much to be sorry for, enough, perhaps, that we can let it go."

Rood's mouth tightens briefly, then he sighs. "Yes. I think that's best."

80 CZ

After dinner with Sunhild—which mostly amounts to an interrogation—Logan and I are taken to the same private room we shared last time we were here. Logan and I share a look of mutual relief to be free of company as the chambermaid leaves us with a half-barrel of steaming water and some spare clothes. I don't know what became of my pack. Probably still in the mountain cavern.

Logan ushers me toward the barrel. He unties the laces of my semi-dry tunic. I raise my arms as he lifts it over my head. He tugs my breast-band free. His fingers brush gently over my cold-pebbled skin and tightened nipples. The touch is sensual, wonderful, arousing. He kisses my cheek, my jaw, my ear. My hands start scrabbling at him, tugging at his clothes, but he sets my hands gently aside. He tugs my pants loose and pushes them off my hips, trailing kisses down my hips and thighs as he kneels to pull my socks and pants off my feet.

Still kneeling, he wraps his arms around my legs. His face is pressed to my belly. Though it has me panting and clutching at him, wrapping my hands in his hair, he only holds on.

"I love you, Astarti," he says against my flesh. Though the words are simple, I hear everything in them: how much those words mean to him; how afraid he was to lose me—either to death or to time; how he will never leave me or turn away.

I slide down, and his face turns upward. The sight of him clasping my naked body, letting me pass through his arms, fills all the cold, empty places that have formed inside me through this long day.

I kneel with him, bringing my face to his. "I love you, too."

I kiss the corner of his eye, where a tear clings to his lashes. I feel him smile against my jaw.

He eases me toward the tub, which is only large enough for me to kneel in. The water, though, is blissfully hot. Logan dips the washing cloth in the water and gently scrubs the grime, the cold, and the sorrow from my body.

When I stand from the water, he wraps me in a linen towel. He tries to usher me toward the bed, but I plant my feet.

"That's not how this works."

He starts to look stubborn, then he sighs. He plucks off his tunic and kicks off his pants as I tighten the towel around myself and kneel by the tub. I trail my fingers through the water. It's no longer hot, but it's warm enough. He crouches in the tub because his legs are too long for him to kneel. He relaxes as I clean the signs of the fight from his body, gently wiping away the lingering traces of blood from his face. The gash near his hairline has stopped bleeding, but it's red and painful-looking. He flinches when I press my lips to it, then his body eases as I let my energy flow into him. I trace a finger over the Healed flesh.

"You're getting good at that," he says.

"I like it," I tell him. "It's what I want to do."

He looks at me like I am utterly beautiful. "Then you will."

When he stands from the tub, his bad knee cracks loudly. The damaged joint is stiff from the cramped position, and I steady him as he steps from the water.

"I wish I could Heal that."

"Not everything can be erased or cast off. But I can carry this with me."

"I'll help you, when it gets too heavy."

He pauses as my words sink in, as he considers all I am trying to say. He pulls me to him, the water that slicks his body seeping through my towel. "I know. I will do the same for you."

Our hands meet at the edge of the towel, pulling it free by unspoken agreement. He presses hard against me. I touch him in all the ways I've learned he enjoys, and he shows me he's been just as good a student.

When he lays me down, he is gentle but firm, his body commanding mine, mine commanding his. He slides himself into me, our bodies completing each other, just like our souls.

CHAPTER 42

I stand next to Rood at Heborian's bedside. Morning light streams through the window onto Heborian's still figure. Horik hovers behind us, uncertain of his place.

Resting through the night has brought some color back to Heborian's face, and he fixes his eyes on me. He finds the strength—or maybe the will—to speak. "Just you."

Rood casts me a nervous glance as he leaves with Horik. At first I think he is worried for his father, but when he gives me a slight nod I realize he's worried about me.

I am not worried. Nothing Heborian might say could hurt me. For the first time, I am sure of myself with him. We have both learned where we draw our lines. Though I am grateful that Logan caught my spear, to spare me the memory of having killed my father, that doesn't mean I wouldn't throw the spear again.

Heborian's thoughts must be on the same moment, for he says weakly, "So. We are more alike after all."

"In some ways," I admit, sinking onto the edge of the mattress. To deny that would be absurd, but that doesn't make me his reflection.

"I was proud of you," he says. "That you had the steel in yourself to kill me for what you thought right. You should be queen, Astarti."

"No," I say firmly. "You know better than that, or you would not have held Rood away from all these things."

"That was weakness."

"That was your soul telling you when you were wrong."

He closes his eyes wearily.

I ask, because I want to know for certain what is killing him, "You've been doing it for years, haven't you? Carving away at your soul. The barriers. Belos. Even the bone weapons." The last is a guess, but his silence confirms it. "That is what gives them such power. And that is why you are dying now. You've cut away too much of yourself."

"Rood," he says. "Will you help him?"

"When he needs me. But I will not live in Tornelaine. I will have a life of my own choosing."

A slow breath goes out of him. "You deserve that."

I had planned to tell him that I saw my mother, but I find that it doesn't matter now. Logan is right: we need to move forward.

I lean down and press my lips to his forehead, which is clammy with sweat. "I forgive you," I murmur, even though he has never asked my forgiveness. As I draw back, his fingers lift from the blanket to catch my hand. He squeezes weakly. I smile down at him, telling him I understand what he is saying, that I've known it for a while. Yes, in his way, he loves me.

I stand from the bed. "I'll send in your son."

"Your brother," he corrects.

"I'll send in my brother."

In the hallway, I find Rood and Horik waiting anxiously. Rood is so young for all that is about to fall on him. By the end of the day, he will be king.

I don't know if he will welcome the gesture, but I decide to risk his reproof when I step to him and offer my arms. He haltingly leans into them. Though the embrace is awkward, I feel in it the promise that someday it will not be.

"He wants you," I tell him.

He breaks away from me, nodding, and disappears into the room.

℘ ℆

I find Logan sitting on the porch steps with Sunhild. The snow is quickly melting in the fields, revealing patches and swaths of green.

I ask, "Will the crops survive?"

"Many of them," Sunhild answers.

"And the people? Will they survive the loss of their crops?"

She says wryly, "Many of them." She pushes to her feet. "Rune has been through worse." As she turns to leave me with Logan, she adds, "He is much better. You have done something."

I shrug. "I love him."

Sunhild cracks a smile. "Ah. The best magic of all." At first, I think she is laughing at me, but her expression grows wistful and she says, leaving us, "I miss my husband. Do not waste a moment."

I don't intend to.

I take my place beside Logan to watch the melting icicles drip in the sunlight. When my legs grow cold from the stone, Logan pulls me into his lap. He presses his face into my hair and breathes deeply. After a while, he reaches inside his jacket. He pulls out a glittering silver bracelet, letting it catch the light.

"I will keep it for you until you want it."

"I want it."

I hold out my wrist and let him hook the bracelet around it. It lies comfortably, warm with Logan's body heat, against my skin. It is not a reminder of my failures, as I once thought; it is a reminder of a woman who loved me and who did not get the chance to live. I settle back against Logan's chest. His arms tighten around me.

When heavy footsteps sound behind us, I stay where I am. I am not embarrassed to sit like this with Logan. Besides, it's only Horik.

He starts to turn away, thinking we prefer to be alone. I call to him. He sits beside us, letting his long legs dangle down the steps. He says in obvious relief, "He is not angry with me."

"I didn't think he would be."

"He could have stripped me of my position. I moved to save you when I should have moved to save him. I broke my oath."

I don't want to dismiss what Horik has said, for it means too much to him. I ask carefully, "If you had to do it again, would you choose differently?" That is what matters most: whether his guilt is over his actions or over the oath.

He looks at me in surprise. "Heborian asked the same thing."

"And what did you say?"

"I said I would do the same again."

It's no small thing. He chose me. I whisper, "Thank you, Horik."

He claps a large hand on my shoulder. I kiss his knuckles, which makes him chuckle. The sound is such a relief to hear. I can scarcely bear to see Horik so grim.

He says, "Rood and I will stay here until the end, then I will guide him back to Tornelaine. What of you?"

"I have said my goodbye. I'm ready to leave."

Logan stirs beneath me. He, too, is ready. He has only been waiting for me.

Horik asks, "What will you do? Go back to the city?"

Logan shifts to look down at me. I look up, speaking to him more than to Horik. "There's only once place I ever loved, but I don't know if it's still standing."

Logan grins and pushes me to my feet. "We'll find out."

Horik rises with us, and I throw my arms around his thick waist. He hugs me back. I say into his shirt, "You're a good friend, Horik."

"Don't say that like I'll never see you again," he chides.

I draw away from him to rejoin Logan, who is already stirring the wind around us. I promise, "I will see you again."

As Logan shapes us into the wind and we rise from the steps, Horik calls after me, "You better! You still owe me money!"

EPILOGUE

LOGAN

Bran hands me a newly whittled peg, which I pound into the tabletop to connect another leg. Tools and wood shavings lie scattered across the paving stones I laid over the summer. Now, with fall coming on, I have to seize these last warm days to work outside.

Bran, sitting on the low wall I built to keep the sand out of the patio, works on another peg. He gazes over the hut, though I'm not sure it can be called that anymore. The walls are stone, and the whole thing is much bigger. The roof is shingled with clay tiles, and the windows have sturdy shutters. There's a garden started in back, and I can hear the goats jumping on the wooden boxes I put in their pen. "The great mountain range," Astarti calls it.

Bran asks, "You do all this by hand?"

"I might have cheated a little," I admit.

He nods sagely. "Thought so."

In truth, I cheated a lot. I would have liked building it all by hand, but there wasn't time. The roof of the former hut had collapsed, though that could have been from age as easily as from the wildness of the Old Ones. Actually, this remote island escaped largely untouched. Most of its trees survived because this was too far away from the city to be of any concern to Belos. Many seedlings have been taken from the woods here to the main island to begin restoring life there. It will be a long process. Though earthmagic may speed things up, trees can only be rushed so much. Besides, not everyone has returned to the islands to help, and that slows things as well.

Rood, in rebuilding Tornelaine, has tempted some of our best craftsmen to stay. I can't complain. The more our people mix with the others, the better.

When Astarti steps from the Drift into the courtyard, Bran jumps and drops his peg.

"Sorry," she says, setting down her pack.

Bran retrieves the peg and goes back to whittling. "How does that not startle you?"

I shrug. "I feel her approach."

Bran tosses the finished peg at me, and it bounces off my shoulder. "Didn't feel that approaching, did you?"

Astarti snorts. "Why, Bran, was that a joke? Is that allowed in the Earthmaker rulebook?"

He fights back a smile. "I guess I've been spending too much time with you."

"If that's how you feel, you don't have to eat with us." Astarti crouches to open the leather pack, peering inside with great drama and raising an eyebrow.

Bran hops down from the wall. "No need to take it like that, Astarti."

She grins and pulls cloth-wrapped bundles from the bag. We sit among the tools and wood shavings, arranging the food on the overturned table.

"It'll be finished tomorrow," I promise.

"That's what you said yesterday," she reminds me.

I sniff, which is all the answer I think her comment deserves.

The bread is slightly smashed, and the glaze on the ham has run everywhere, even onto the apples and honey cakes, but no one complains. While we eat, Astarti tells us about her day in Tornelaine. Though my mother and Feluvas returned to Avydos to serve as Healers, Korinna chose to stay in the city, and Astarti has been working with her to learn more of Healing. Korinna's decision surprised me, and I only stared at Astarti blankly when she said, "Horik is there." I said, "Of course he is," to which Astarti, shaking her head, muttered, "Oblivious."

After Bran leaves, Astarti helps me gather up the tools and move the half-finished table inside. I feel rain coming.

I crouch in front of the hearth, where the coals from yesterday are banked. I brush the ash aside and arrange kindling over the coals. I breathe deeply and try to still my mind. I sense the heat and spark of the coals, feel their potential to grow, to consume, to set a whole forest on fire. But they don't need to be so wild. Fire, my father said, may burn low and comfortingly. And that is neither waste nor confinement.

I draw the heat from the coals into the kindling, teasing the sparks to life. It goes well at first, but as the flames burst to life, they eat greedily through the kindling, consuming it too quickly. I toss a few logs onto the fire before it burns itself out.

This was Astarti's idea, that I use my earthmagic for these small things. There were a few disasters in the beginning. There will be more, I'm sure. But it's getting better. It helps to let out a little at a time. The fist I once kept clenched so tightly inside myself has eased. It's still there, but I'm learning to relax it a little.

Astarti settles onto the sheepskin rug beside me, commenting, "At least you didn't singe your eyebrows this time."

"We'll call it an improvement then."

"When you finish that table, what do you think about working on a bed for us?"

"I thought you liked sleeping by the fire."

"I do, but this rug is always full of sand, and it gets everywhere when—" She cuts off when I lean into her and bite along her jaw in that way she loves.

"When what?" I prompt, easing her to the rug.

"Oh, never mind," she mutters and tugs me down.

ABOUT THE AUTHOR

Katherine Buel grew up in Kansas with two passions: stories and horses. She's taken both of those with her through much of the upper Midwest, then out to Maine and back again.

She also loves mountain biking and kayaking—and too many other things that there's never enough time for.

Printed in Great Britain
by Amazon

67432300R00196